Lairds of the Isles

Should duty come before love?

The windswept islands of the Outer Hebrides
are a close-knit community, where the local laird
lives to serve his people, and outsiders aren't
always welcome. But as the MacDonald family
moves between London and the isles,
all that could be about to change...

Book 1
A Laird for the Governess

The Laird of Ardmore has sworn never to remarry...
until he meets his feisty new governess!

Book 2
A Laird in London

When the Laird of Broch Clachan travels to London,
he doesn't expect to find himself a wife!

Available now

And look for book 3 coming soon!

Author Note

I do hope you enjoyed *A Laird for the Governess*, the first in my Lairds of the Isles trilogy, set between London and the Outer Hebrides. This second book focuses on Angus, Laird of Broch Clachan, who travels to London with his sister to try to persuade an English lord to sell back some lands to the islanders.

Keep an eye out for book three, *A Laird for the Highland Lady*, in which the spotlight rests on Eilidh Ruadh and her reluctant attraction to Maximilian Wood!

CATHERINE TINLEY

—

A Laird in London

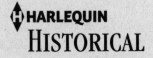
HARLEQUIN

HISTORICAL

Recycling programs
for this product may
not exist in your area.

ISBN-13: 978-1-335-72360-4

A Laird in London

Copyright © 2022 by Catherine Tinley

For questions and comments about the quality of this book,
please contact us at CustomerService@Harlequin.com.

Harlequin Enterprises ULC
22 Adelaide St. West, 41st Floor
Toronto, Ontario M5H 4E3, Canada
www.Harlequin.com

Printed in U.S.A.

Catherine Tinley has loved reading and writing since childhood, and has a particular fondness for love, romance and happy endings. She lives in Ireland with her husband, children, dog and kitten, and can be reached at catherinetinley.com, as well as through Facebook and on Twitter, @catherinetinley.

Books by Catherine Tinley

Harlequin Historical

Christmas Cinderellas
"A Midnight Mistletoe Kiss"
A Waltz with the Outspoken Governess

Lairds of the Isles

A Laird for the Governess
A Laird in London

The Ladies of Ledbury House

The Earl's Runaway Governess
Rags-to-Riches Wife
Captivating the Cynical Earl

The Chadcombe Marriages

Waltzing with the Earl
The Captain's Disgraced Lady
The Makings of a Lady

Visit the Author Profile page
at Harlequin.com.

For my sister Donna,
who shows us every day what courage is.

Chapter One

Burtenshaw House, Sussex—March 1811

Miss Isabella Jane Margaret Wood, sister to the Viscount Burtenshaw, did not, at first glance, appear to be the typical society maiden so beloved of drawing-room duennas. While her glossy brown curls might have been condemned as commonplace by some, her deep-brown eyes framed by dark thick lashes lent an arresting beauty to her delicate face and, properly presented, she might turn many a head at Almack's.

Today, however, she would have earned nothing but condemnation from the censorious critics of the *ton*. Her gown they would consider abhorrent, her activity shocking. Not only was she working as part of the yacht's crew, she was currently engaged in an easy conversation with a *servant*, no less.

'I do not know how I can stand it, Cooper,' she murmured to the older man currently working with her to tidy some lines. 'I should much prefer to stay here all the time, with you and Max.' She glanced at her older brother, currently grinning with delight at some comment made by one of the sailors. 'What a pity Max did not inherit the title! My life—and his—would have been so much better if Max had been the eldest, not Freddy.'

'Now then, Isabella,' Cooper replied with all the ease of a man who had known Miss Isabella since birth, 'you know it does no good to dwell on such things. We all know that you and Max take a different approach to matters than the Viscount, but as the eldest he was raised to it and we know not what burdens he must bear.'

Cooper's soft Scottish accent—as familiar to Isabella as her own—hinted at a warning and Isabella sighed, acknowledging it. 'You know as well as I do that Max is unhappy. And soon we shall be forced to travel to London, to leave behind the small amount of freedom we have.'

Gesturing at the yacht, the open sky, the glistening sea, she added, her voice tight with frustration, '*This* is where I am happy, Cooper. Here, with you. To think I must once again be stifled in ballrooms and drawing rooms—it is insupportable!'

Cooper's brow furrowed. 'Aye, I know, lass. But you will manage, for all that. You have your mother's steel within you.'

Isabella smiled. 'Thank you, Cooper. I shall try to remember that when I am faced with dull people and cheerless conversation. Mama disliked London society as much as I do, I know. I remember her speaking of it.'

They exchanged a glance of shared memory and understanding, and Isabella felt a fleeting sense that Mama would never be truly gone as long as people remembered her with fondness.

Three years since you died, Mama, and I miss you still.

It did not occur to her that her papa, who had died a

to return the lands he holds. Lands that rightly belong to the people here.'

She raised an eyebrow. 'Man to man? When he ignores your letters and seems to have no intention of selling to you?' Her tone softened. 'You must know that planning this is impossible and the whole thing may take more ingenuity than you are used to. Our parents sent me to school in Edinburgh so I could learn how to be a fine lady. I never liked it and I never thought it would come in useful, but if this Lord Burtenshaw will be in London for the Season, then it is *I*, not you, who might have more chance of persuading him.' She fluttered her eyelashes. 'Oh, Lord Burtenshaw,' she simpered. 'I am my wits' end.'

He could not help it: he had to laugh at her playacting. What she said made a strange sort of sense, but all his instincts were screaming at him that he should not take his fiery sister into the heart of the *ton*.

No. It would not do. He shook his head. 'Eilidh, I shall not be moved on this. You are *not* coming to London and that is my final word on the matter!'

Burtenshaw House, Sussex

Frederick Wood, the Viscount Burtenshaw, was displeased. There were a number of niggling contributors to his discontent, not least the fact that such a noble house and title as Burtenshaw should be cursed with a family name as commonplace as Wood. *Wood!* Why, any lowly servant or mere tavern man might have such an everyday name! It surely was beneath his dignity to be addressed by all and sundry as Wood.

Plank, they had dubbed him in boarding school,

using the soubriquet mercilessly—particularly once they understood his aversion to it. They with their ancient and lofty surnames—the Fancots, Darcys, Talbots and Audleys. Even the plain Smiths had renamed themselves Smythe or Headington-Smythe at some point in the past.

Would that he could do the same. On marrying the uninspiring but well-dowried Prudence Price, he had fleetingly tried the sound of a twin surname in his mouth. *Price-Wood. Wood-Price.* He shuddered. Not only was the result doubly abhorrent, he could not in all conscience promote the Price family to any station higher than they deserved.

He sighed. No, there was little he could do. At least his title disguised his commonplace appellation. *Viscount Burtenshaw.* With a flourish, he added his signature to the document before him, then raised his head as the door to his library opened.

'You wished to see me, Brother?'

He set down his pen, eyeing his younger sister with disfavour. She had bounced in without knocking, her brown curls all disordered and her dress—

'What on *earth* are you wearing, Isabella?' He eyed the dull brown gown with horror. It was plain, ill-fitting and had clearly been preserved with camphor, for the repulsive aroma was now reaching his delicate nostrils.

'This? I found it in Mama's old trunks. It was perfect for our sailing trip today. You would not wish for me to get one of my fashionable silk or muslin gowns all filthy and perhaps even torn after a day on the boats, now would you, Freddy?'

'Frederick,' he corrected her reflexively. 'Who accompanied you?'

'You need not be concerned,' she replied airily. 'Max was there and Cooper, of course.'

'I do not like you spending so much time with Cooper.'

She laughed. 'But he has been a friend to the family since before we were born! Why—'

'I am aware,' he replied shortly. 'That does not mean you should be spending every day in his company. He is not of our class. Indeed, he is not even English! Besides, he is a servant.'

'Stuff! That is not fair on Cooper. He has been a good friend to us all of our lives.'

'A friend to you and Max, perhaps. Not to me!'

She considered this. 'I believe you are right! How curious! Now, I wonder why?' Frowning, she thought about it. 'I believe Cooper came here after you were born. Perhaps at that time he was not in a position to befriend you and look after you the way he did me and Max.'

Freddy drew himself up. 'I would have thought it rather more likely that Papa protected me, as his heir, from any such associations.'

'True! Papa never gave a care for me or Max. You were the only one he bothered with. But why should you take against Cooper?'

'To me he is, and always will be, a long-established servant. I pay his wages, and so there can never be easiness between us.' Not liking the martial look in her eye, he made haste to take the conversation elsewhere. 'Regardless, you should not be spending so much time with him.'

'But Max and I have been unable to sail all winter! Today we had fine weather and light winds, and had our first foray out since last autumn.' She tilted her head to one side. 'You should come with us, Freddy. How you can bear being shut up in this old library day after day quite confounds me.'

He shook his head, unwilling to admit that, even now, he felt unsettled on the water.

Give me the safety of solid ground at all times.

'As the eldest, I carry responsibilities that you and Max do not. Since Papa died I have been head of this family. That is why I wished to speak to you.' He drew himself up, anticipating the battle to come. 'You are twenty now, Isabella.'

She took a quick breath. 'And? What of it?'

He persisted. 'Twenty and *unmarried*. It is unseemly.'

She snorted. 'Fustian! Why, you were not married until four and twenty and Max is twenty-five and remains unwed!'

'Your brother may do as he wishes; it is all the same to me. But ladies must marry at a younger age and your spinsterhood reflects badly on the family name.'

'You mean to suggest, I suppose, that it reflects badly on *you*!' Her tone was bitter.

He inclined his head regally. 'As the current Viscount, I am the embodiment of the Burtenshaw lineage, tradition and name, so, yes, it does.' He took a breath. 'And I insist that you marry by summer, or I shall choose your husband myself!'

She gasped. 'You would not dare do such a thing!'

'Dare? Of course I would dare!' They glared at each other, near-identical expressions in their dark eyes. All three siblings had inherited their mother's brown eyes, but in character Freddy was every inch their father's son.

'Indeed,' he continued pompously, 'as your guardian

it would be my duty to do so. I have been more than indulgent, Isabella. Most maidens are married by eighteen yet here you are, almost on the shelf. You will travel with my wife to the London town house next week and this Season you must choose a husband from among your admirers.'

'You know I detest the Season and would much rather be here all year round. I am more comfortable on a boat than in a ballroom and with plain honest folk rather than the fakery of the *ton*.'

'Fakery! How dare you denigrate the highest echelons of society!'

She tossed her head. 'I will allow there are a few good people among them. But I should prefer not to take part in the Season this year, Brother. And there is no point to it, for I do not intend to marry any time soon.'

His tone was implacable. 'And I have decided. As head of this family and your legal guardian, as is my right. You *will* go to London and you *will* be married this Season, whether you wish to or not! And *that*, dear Sister, is my final word on the matter!'

London—three weeks later

'Eilidh! Eilidh, wake up! We have arrived.' Angus gently shook his sister's shoulder. Like himself, she was exhausted after more than two weeks of travel—first, by ship to the Clyde, then by rumbling coach through Scotland and England. Despite his earlier conviction that Eilidh should not accompany him, he was now rather glad that she had persuaded him, for despite his status at home, travelling to the heart of English society was an entirely different prospect.

The notion of 'London' had almost been lost in the eternity of being jostled hour after hour in an uncomfortable coach, of endless nights in a series of roadside inns, and of the tedium of long days trapped in a carriage, when they were both used to busyness and being useful and purposeful.

Seeing that Eilidh was stirring, he turned his attention outwards. It was difficult to see in the fading light of evening, but the house Searlas had hired in Mayfair looked reasonably appropriate. Lydia, their cousin's English wife, had advised Searlas on the best locations for a visiting laird and his sister. The choice of Mayfair would apparently announce to the *ton* that Angus, Laird of Broch Clachan in the Outer Hebrides, meant to take his place in society.

The coachman had lowered the step and Angus followed his sister out into the balmy London evening. Behind their coach, the second carriage was just arriving. It contained Searlas, Mary, who was Eilidh's personal maid, and the rest of the baggage. Angus took an appraising look at the building. Number Eleven Chesterfield Street was a three-bay town house, five storeys tall, with a fanlight above the door and elegant sash windows. As he paused in the street, surveying the building that was to be their home for however long it took to achieve their purpose, the front door opened and a footman emerged, clad in full livery.

'Lord!' Eilidh's voice was soft. 'And so it begins, Angus.' Servants at home were simply friends and colleagues with different responsibilities and in the Islands people were judged by their actions rather than by their roles. The very notion of livery to denote the hierarchies of London society seemed demeaning to those who cooked, cleaned and assisted others.

Glancing over his shoulder, Angus noted that both Mary and Searlas had descended from their carriage and were moving to take their places behind himself and Eilidh. Yes, behind them, but only because, as Laird, Angus was expected to lead. He valued Searlas's counsel just as much as any person's.

The people here, though, would expect him to respect the restrictions placed on them by English society—to break the rules of the *ton* might affect Angus's chances of succeeding in his aim to buy back the lands taken from the islanders more than sixty years before.

With a deep breath and acknowledging that the ridiculous inward conflicts he was experiencing were due to meeting his *own servants*, Angus stepped forward and led his sister inside.

The hallway was spacious, well appointed and elegant, with delicate plasterwork and an Adam fireplace. It also contained more than a dozen servants, lined up and ready to meet their new master and his sister. Butler, housekeeper, footmen and serving maids were all introduced—the men bowing and the women curtsying. Angus introduced himself, Eilidh and their attendants, and said something about his confidence that they would no doubt be skilled and reliable at their work. The butler, Ayling, then began directing footmen to start bringing in the luggage, while the housekeeper, Mrs Ellis, showed him and Eilidh to their rooms on the second floor. The fine carpets and wall hangings, along with the delicate furniture, were a far cry from the simple, well-crafted furniture at home in the Broch and the steady hum and clatter from the street outside was dis-

turbing. Looking out of the window in the gathering
dusk, Angus saw a man emerge from the house opposite. He was elegantly clad in evening breeches, a pale
waistcoat and a plain black jacket, and he exuded an air
of confidence that Angus found decidedly intimidating.

I am a long way from Scotland.

Squaring his shoulders, he followed the butler to the
drawing room. Everything seemed alien—the elegant
furniture, elaborate chandeliers… Even the damned
staircase seemed overly ostentatious to a man more used
to unadorned stone walls and solid carpentry. Somehow, his sense of dislocation in the house reflected his
anxiety about this entire trip to London. Never had he
felt so out of place, so unsure. It was not a feeling he
liked. It was vital that he regained the lost lands. But
right now, his inner voice was whispering that he had
little anticipation of success.

'Are you done yet, Sally?'

'Just a minute more, Miss.' The maid was pinning
up Isabella's hair—a process that Isabella always found
tedious. 'There! You look delightful.'

'Thank you.' Isabella's reply was mechanical. As
ever, she placed little value in such things as hairstyles
and gowns, although Freddy would no doubt have something to say about it if she was not dressed in her finery.
And she certainly did not wish to attract suitors, no matter what Freddy said. Stifling a sigh, she slipped lightly
down the stairs to where her sister-in-law was waiting.

'Finally!' Prudence looked displeased. But then, 'displeased' was Prudence's resting state. Although in her
early thirties, she might have easily passed for forty.
Having done her duty by presenting her lord with two

sons in the first three years of her marriage, Prudence now enjoyed a little more freedom. At eight and six, the boys were now old enough to be left in Sussex with their nurses and so Prudence had allowed herself to be persuaded to travel to London for the Season.

'I know my duty,' she had said to Isabella, somewhat grimly. 'Lord Burtenshaw requires me to find you a husband and that is precisely what I shall do.'

Her habit of referring to her spouse by his title still disconcerted Isabella at times. In almost ten years of her marriage to Freddy, Isabella had not once heard her brother's wife use his given name. She wondered if Prudence called him 'Lord Burtenshaw' during their private, intimate moments, then shuddered at the very notion.

'Let me peruse you, Isabella,' she said now, pursing her lips. Isabella pressed her lips together as Prudence eyed her slowly from head to toe. 'I still say you are rather scrawny—' neither of them glanced at Prudence's ample bosom, though Isabella knew that Prudence was unaccountably proud of her plumpness '—but the dress is acceptable and Sally has not done too badly with your hair.'

'Can we go?' Gritting her teeth, Isabella allowed Sally to place an elegant cloak around her shoulders. Hanging her fan on her arm and accepting her reticule from Sally, Isabella fell into step behind her sister-in-law. Tonight, if she could hazard a guess, would be crushing.

Angus could not sleep. Though exhausted from seemingly endless travel, now that they had arrived in London the enormity of his task had finally hit him, like a punch to the gut. His letters to Lord Burtenshaw via his agent—a man called Inglis—had been polite, then increasingly persistent. He had had no reply to any of them.

Sliding out of bed, he crossed to the window and opened a shutter. The room was uncomfortably warm, so he slid the window up, hoping for a breeze to blow away the tangled thoughts preventing him from resting.

It makes no sense.

Why was Lord Burtenshaw so determined to keep what for him must be an unimportant parcel of land that he would never visit, never value in any real way? Angus had offered a fair price for the property—a house, a number of farms and fisher cottages, and an expanse of untamed lochs and moorland. Apparently the current Viscount's grandfather had been awarded it after Culloden, presumably in gratitude for his support of Elector George. It had been confiscated from a branch of the MacDonald clan and the injustice of it still rankled in Benbecula.

The spoken history of the islanders had no recollection of a visit from any Burtenshaw, nor indeed from Mr Inglis whose name featured on the much-hated communications about increases in rent. Instead, the Viscount sent his factors—hired enforcers and rent-collectors. Every quarter day without fail they would arrive from Aberdeen, demanding money or goods from the farmers, fishermen, and estate workers who still remained on the land.

The manor house had begun to fall into disrepair after the current Viscount had instructed that no further funds were to be 'wasted' on maintaining it, near six years ago—a clear signal the family had no use for the place. The islanders still spoke sadly of An Taigh Buidhe—the elegant, yellow-painted house that had been one of the most beautiful dwellings on Benbecula sixty years ago. The manor house now stood empty, cold and failing, its yellow render faded and cracked—a symbol of the neglect from the arrogant absentee landlord.

A small clock on the mantel chimed four times. Soon it would be dawn. At this time of year in the Islands, there were barely a few hours of darkness. By midsummer there would still be light in the sky at midnight. Not so in London.

A carriage rumbled up the street, stopping outside the house opposite. Idly, Angus watched as the same elegant gentleman he had seen last night exited the carriage and went inside the house.

My, they keep late nights in London!

Whatever party or event the man had attended, it had clearly just finished. A soft hiss alerted him to the fact that it was now gently raining. Sticking a hand out of the window, he waited to feel the healing coolness on his skin. Nothing. Even the rain was warm.

Sighing, he withdrew his hand and padded silently back to the bed.

'How was last night, Miss?' Sally drew back the curtains in Isabella's chamber, allowing bright sunlight to stream in.

'Crushing, Sally—just as I knew it would be. Crushing, and trying, and humiliating. Prudence made sure to tell everyone I was determined to marry this year and so I found myself the centre of attention for every ageing widower and jaded roué eager to ascertain, I suppose, the size of my dowry.'

She shuddered. 'A stream of them stopped with Prudence where she sat with the other matrons and I have no doubt that I was the subject of their conversation. I was forced to dance and smile, and behave politely to gentlemen who have no more interest in me than they would a prize filly!'

'Ah, I am sorry, Miss.' Sally crossed the room to the small table, where she had set a tray when she came in. 'Here you are, Miss. Fresh bread, butter and honey— just as you like it.'

'You are a treasure, Sally. Thank you.' Sitting up, Isabella began slathering the bread with yellow butter, pausing only to pour herself some tea. As a breakfast, it was simple, restorative and delicious—and so much more satisfying than the elaborate dishes on offer at last night's soirée.

Sally crossed to the armoire. 'Now then, Miss. I suggest the blue silk for tonight and for a day dress this pretty printed muslin. What do you think?'

Isabella waved a dismissive hand. 'I care not, Sally, as you well know. As long as they are reasonably comfortable I shall be content.' She frowned. 'I cannot be cooped up in the house all day. I shall need you to accompany me to the park in an hour or so.'

'Very good, Miss. Fresh air always agrees with you.'

Isabella grinned. 'While being in the company of my brother and his wife makes me decidedly *dis*agreeable. Now, do not give me that look! I am quite happy to admit the fault is mine.'

Sally inclined her head, disapproval at Isabella's candour clear in the stiff line of her figure. 'You must know

I cannot comment on such matters, Miss. Now, would you like a bath before we go to the park?'

'Hmm? No, thank you. I need to get outside as soon as possible!'

St James's Park was awash with people. Angus, trying hard to maintain a semblance of confidence, sauntered through the leafy lanes with Eilidh, taking in the range of people. Everyone was there, it seemed. They must have seen nearly a hundred different people already and they had only been in the place for twenty minutes. Green Park had been the same, full of people all milling about randomly as if at a fair or gathering. Very few spoke to anyone outside their group.

'So many people,' Eilidh muttered. His opinionated sister was rarely this quiet.

'It is no different to a Gathering, Eilidh. Why, we saw this many people at the shinty game last summer!' His voice, thankfully, exuded a confidence he was far from feeling.

'Yes, but we *knew* them!' Eilidh turned to look at him. 'Whenever there is a Gathering, or a shinty game, or a wedding, we know most of the people there. This—' She gestured vaguely. 'All of these people are strangers to one another. How can we possibly find Lord—' she lowered her voice as two young men passed, eyeing her up and down '—Lord Burtenshaw in such a place as this? Perhaps we should instead simply attempt to visit him in his home.'

Angus took her arm, tucking her hand into the crook of his elbow. He did not like the way some of the men were eyeing his sister. Not at all. Laughing lightly, he tried to reassure her. 'Now, you know that that is not the done thing and is quite likely to set him against us. Lydia was very clear on that point. Now, recall that Edinburgh can be just as busy as this. Why, I have seen much bigger crowds in the Haymarket!'

'Aye, that may be true.' She frowned. 'When I went to school in Edinburgh the teachers took us to the Assemblies and to church, and occasionally to the Physick Garden, but we were never out in such crowds as this.'

'Besides,' Angus added, 'we clearly cannot expect to find the lord in question by chance. Searlas and Mary are making it their business today to befriend the London servants in order to ask questions—for, as we know, servants know everything. We need to know his habits, his acquaintances, the places he likes to frequent. And in the meantime we can familiarise ourselves with the fashionable places of London.'

Eilidh nodded, seemingly a little reassured at least. 'I am still glad I came. It is all so diverting!' Her laugh sounded false and he squeezed her hand.

'Look! Cattle!' He indicated the far side of the open sward, where a herd of cows was contentedly grazing.

'In the middle of the city? How curious!' By unspoken agreement, they changed direction towards the herd. While they were not the long-haired, fearsome-looking beasts common to the Islands, still there would be something comforting about the familiarity of being near a herd. As they approached, they realised it was a milk herd, with enterprising milkmaids selling fresh milk by the cup. Londoners of all class, creed and colour were buying the milk, drinking it straight away and seemingly enjoying it.

Angus bought two cups, handing one to Eilidh, but his eye was caught by two women awaiting their turn to buy. A high-born lady and her personal maid, he guessed, seeing that the younger was wearing a printed muslin embellished with lace, her dark hair arranged in an elaborate coiffure, while the other was dressed plainly in grey bombazine. His eye returned to the young lady. She was very pretty, with flashing dark eyes, a delicate face and a slim figure. Taking a coin from her reticule, she paid the milkmaid, who pocketed it in a leather purse strapped around her waist.

'Ah, delicious!' Angus barely heard Eilidh's exclamation, his eye still fixed on the lady just a few steps away. Even now she was taking a sip. Her lips were rose-pink and delectable and Angus allowed himself a moment's distraction. Perhaps being in London might yet offer certain diversions. Even though he was here on an important mission, that should not prevent him from admiring the scenery.

As if sensing his regard, the lady looked up. Never prone to shyness, Angus raised his glass to her and she lowered her head, seemingly lost in confusion. He stifled a grin. It had been a while since he had graced the Assembly Rooms of Edinburgh, but he had, it seemed, not lost the art of flirtation. And if there were many young ladies in London as pretty as this one, he would be content. He replied to Eilidh, then glanced back at the young lady. She was now studying him and Eilidh, her brow furrowed, and as soon as he caught her eye, she looked away.

If we were at home in Benbecula, I would simply go and speak to her.

While he had never engaged in a serious courtship of any lady and his heart had as yet never been in serious danger, he had enjoyed numerous light flirtations since his first fixation with a pretty seamstress at the age of eighteen, ten years ago.

Things were different here, he knew. One needed a formal introduction before speaking to anyone of note. Mild frustration ran through him. If all doors were closed to him, how was he to even *find* Viscount Burtenshaw, never mind influence him to sell the land in Benbecula? Oh, he had the man's address and that of his agent, for he had been writing to him, but he knew that one could not simply call on a peer of the realm unless there had been a formal introduction. Hopefully the servants could share some further wisdom on that score.

He eyed the lady again, his gaze sweeping down from her dark hair, past her delicate shoulders and down further, lingering appreciatively on her exquisite figure. The muslin dress she wore was very fine and he imagined it revealing the outline of her legs, should he manage to see her with the sun at the right angle.

'Who would have thought,' Eilidh was saying, 'that we could get fresh milk in the middle of a London park?', but he barely heard her, so lost was he in his appreciation of the young lady's beauty.

Isabella was enjoying a novel experience—a fleeting sense of interest in a gentleman. As she sipped her milk she could not resist glancing his way again. He was looking towards her and, as he caught her gaze, he lifted his glass to her in a silent greeting. Confused, she lowered her head, feeling her cheeks and neck fill with heat.

Well! So I am not completely immune to the charms of men, then.

Cautiously, she glanced his way again, her gaze sweeping swiftly over him. She liked what she saw. A handsome face, chestnut hair with bronze tints glinting briefly in the sunlight. A fine, strong figure that she was certain offered nothing to shoulder padding or any other tricks of tailoring.

His Highland clothing had drawn her eye initially, although something about it was…*different* or unusual in some way she had not yet identified. There were numerous kilted soldiers in town—all part of the Highland regiments—but they tended to travel in packs, rather than… Her eye strayed to the young lady accompanying the Highlander. She was pretty, with riotous auburn curls barely tamed into an acceptable coiffure. Her gown was rather outdated. Even Isabella, who was indifferent to fashion, knew that. There was no maid with her. Was she the man's courtesan? Or was she possibly his wife? Surprisingly, the thought sent a brief pang through her. Although she had no intention of obeying Freddy's outrageous orders, she would eventually, she supposed, marry. It seemed unfair that the first young man to have piqued her interest should already have another lady on his arm. She frowned. This business of choosing a husband was fraught indeed!

Eilidh was still talking about the milk. Angus refocused his attention. 'Hmmm? Yes, it is surprising indeed!'

'And they are so well organised, with tables and benches, and tin cups for all!'

Abruptly, Angus turned, senses alert. Three horsemen were approaching at speed from the far side of the field. As they thundered closer, whooping and shouting, he realised the riders were deliberately trying to frighten the cattle. *Damned fools!* Already, the herd was restless, tails flicking and heads raised. A moment later and they had begun to move. First, the cows with calves, their protective instincts firing, then fear spread like a wildfire through the entire herd. Angus's heart was suddenly pounding. The *amadans* on horseback clearly had no idea how dangerous a stampede could be.

Moving at speed, the cattle thundered away from the horsemen. One unfortunate gentleman got a kick in the gut from a frightened cow, as he had foolishly moved to stand directly behind the animal. As the milkmaids expostulated and the customers gasped and shrieked, the herd fled to Angus's left, swiftly followed by the three horsemen, who seemed to be enjoying themselves immensely. They were all young, Angus noted as they passed, and dressed like gentlemen.

Drunk, he guessed. *And it is barely midday.*

If they had done it in Benbecula they'd have been whipped. Not that anyone at home would dream of doing anything so reckless.

'Idiots!' Eilidh's pronouncement attracted the attention of the dark-haired lady, whose expression suggested she shared the sentiment. Her maid took a deep breath, then held forth in an animated way about the foolishness, heedlessness, and general selfishness of the horsemen, while also checking that the young lady was not too distressed. 'Such a thing to happen, Miss, and in the middle of St James's Park! Shocking, I tell you!'

Angus, while inwardly agreeing with the maid, could not help but notice she had addressed the young lady as 'Miss'.

She is unmarried, then?

He turned his eyes back to the herd. Frightened cattle were unpredictable and the fools chasing them had probably never been near a stampede in their useless existence.

'Oh, no!' The maid pointed shakily towards the herd. Just as Angus had feared, the cattle had wheeled around and were now running straight at them! In seconds they could all be trampled. Milkmaids and milk customers scattered in all directions as the frightened herd thundered towards them.

Both Eilidh and the lady's maid had bolted to the left—a sensible option, for there was a stand of trees nearby. For some reason, the lady herself had dashed to the right and, as the herd changed direction again, she realised she had accidentally put herself directly in their path. Belatedly she tried to turn back, but Angus, rapidly calculating, realised she was in serious danger.

The horsemen were behind and to one side of the animals, making it unlikely that the herd would veer off again before they mowed her down. As he dashed towards her, Angus could not help but see, in his mind's eye, the Beauty trampled and broken by solid hooves. The adult cows probably weighed as much as sixty stone each. She would have no chance.

He had never in his life moved so fast. Reaching the lady just before the herd did, he stepped in front of her, flailing his arms and shouting as loudly as he could. Already frightened, the cattle reacted to this new threat as he had hoped, the leaders swerving away a little—just a little, but hopefully enough. As the followers thundered behind, he kept shouting and waving his arms, praying that the cows to the back would see and hear him.

It almost worked. Right at the end a young heifer—clearly terrified at taking up the rear—saw him too late and careened into him, knocking him off his feet. It all happened in an instant. First, the shock of impact, then his body sailing through the air. Finally, he felt himself connect sickeningly with the woman behind him. There was nothing he could do. With a jolt, he hit the earth, the young lady half under him.

He could neither move nor breathe. His chest muscles were frozen, locked solid. He had been winded before, but could not recall ever having felt it so severely. He lay there, listening to the sound of thundering hooves recede and wondering how on earth he was not dead. Afterwards, he would recall the absurd beauty of the blue sky above him and a lone goshawk gliding far above. Then, the groans of the young lady.

Good. She is alive, then, too.

The lack of air in his lungs was becoming uncomfortable. Trying not to panic, he dragged in some air, his throat screaming with stridor. At the same time he managed to roll a little to his left, enough so that the lady could shuffle out from beneath him.

'Oh, Lord! Are you well, Sir?' He could sense her moving behind him, then he felt a gentle hand on his shoulder. Her face came into view, her brow furrowed with concern. The hand on his shoulder was trembling. His eyes met hers and, strangely, his panic subsided.

If this is the last sight I shall ever see, then I am content. Dark eyes, eyes a man could drown in...

He still could not breathe and the lack of air was too much. His lungs were too starved. His head swam and the world turned black.

Chapter Two

Isabella scrambled to her knees, her heart still pounding at the near-death experience. She had no doubt that, without the Highlander's intervention, she would have been killed, trampled to death. Glancing up, she saw the herd were almost at the far end of the field already. The idiotic gentlemen chasing them wheeled off to one side and disappeared into the trees, either tiring of their 'sport' or perturbed by the fact they had almost killed someone. *Two someones.* Her and the handsome stranger.

He had not responded to her query and she did not like the sound of his limited, laborious breathing. She put a hand on his shoulder, shuffling closer. His eyes were open, but he seemed unable to speak.

Lord! Is he badly hurt?

Strangely, Isabella's mind could not seem to work. She had no idea what to do for him. All she was capable of was to look at him helplessly, taking in how *beautiful* he was—how strong and healthy and handsome and perfect—and understand that he might be dying in front of her. His face was pale, his lips now tinged slightly blue from lack of air. His gaze met hers.

Please do not die!

His breathing still sounded noisily strange and she felt her own breath catch in sympathy. Her hand was still on his shoulder and she could feel his warmth through her thin glove. His eyes fluttered closed and she sent up a silent prayer.

Let him live!

Pounding footsteps alerted her to the approach of his companion, who dropped to her knees beside the Highlander, her expression one of great distress. 'Angus! Angus!' she cried, laying her hands on him. Isabella removed her own hand from the man's shoulder. The young woman spoke again to Angus, but in a foreign language—not a language Isabella recognised, although something about its cadence was familiar.

He seemed to respond to the lady's voice, moving his right arm and then—thankfully—opening his eyes again. They were pale blue with a hint of green, or possibly grey—the colour of the sea on a cloudless day. His lashes were dark and surprisingly long for such a masculine man. Isabella shook herself at her unexpectedly poetical response to him, even as relief flooded through her. *Angus.* It suited him. It was strong and uncomplicated and decidedly Scottish.

Oh, stop it! she told herself. *The knock must have addled your brain.*

The most important thing was that he yet lived. His breathing even sounded a little more natural now.

The red-haired lady was running her hands over him, seemingly checking for injuries. 'No bones broken,' she murmured in English, 'though I'd wager at least one cracked rib. You great big idiot, Angus!' Her voice choked with emotion.

He managed a half-smile at this and Isabella sat back on her heels, relief flooding through her.

'Miss! Miss!' It was Sally, hurrying towards them. 'Are you well? When I saw what happened I was sure you were a goner!' The maid seemed not to notice that tears were flowing down her face. She sank down beside Isabella, gripping her arms and searching her face. 'Tell me! Are you injured?'

Moved by Sally's concern for her, Isabella made haste to provide reassurance. 'A little shaken, that is all. This gentleman took the full force of the blow that was meant for me.'

'You are trembling, Miss! And little wonder!' She turned to the Highlander, who was still lying down on the grass. 'Sir, I cannot thank you enough! You have saved her life!' Remembering her station, she then clamped her lips shut.

Pushing himself up into a sitting position, Angus smiled. 'Ach, 'twas nothing. I was just a little winded for a moment.' His breathing still sounded a little laboured, but thankfully his colour was returning to normal.

'Nothing? *Nothing?*' His companion lapsed into the other language again and, from her tone, she seemed to be remonstrating with the man.

Unabashed, he continued to grin and Isabella felt her fears begin to subside. Perhaps, after all, no one would die today. She sat, simply looking at them both as they conversed, her own heart gradually settling into a more normal rhythm, although her pulse was still fluttering at the sight of the handsome Highlander.

'Now then, Eilidh,' he said in a matter-of-fact tone, 'it is all very well the four of us sitting on the grass as though we were eating a picnic, but we have not even introduced ourselves.' He twinkled at Isabella, whose heart did a stupid skip.

Eilidh blushed a little and turned to Isabella, impulsively taking both her hands. 'My brother is correct and I am being inexcusably rude. I do not know if you have brothers, but they can be the most maddening creatures!'

'I have two, both older than me!' Isabella could not help but smile. *They are brother and sister!* She could see it now—the similarity in their eyes, their hair, even their expressions.

'Then you will understand something of my frustration.' She smiled. 'I am Eilidh—that is, I am Miss MacDonald. This is my brother, Angus.'

Eilidh. Isabella tried it in her head. *Ay-lee. What a pretty name!*

He stuck out a hand and Isabella took it. 'Mr MacDonald,' she declared earnestly, 'it is a pleasure to meet you. Thank you so much for your intervention just now. I am indebted to you!' Her voice shook, which was a little surprising since she had thought the fright-induced trembling in her body had been subsiding. Clearly her mind was beginning to catch up with what had just occurred. It was nothing to do with those blue-green-grey eyes that were holding hers so steadily. Nothing at all.

'My pleasure, Miss—?'

'Oh! Wood!' She flushed, embarrassed by at her own rudeness. 'I am Isa—er—Miss Wood, that is. And this is my maid, Sally.'

What on earth ails me? I cannot even speak properly.

Telling herself not to be so foolish, she made to rise, feeling uncharacteristically weak. Instantly, Mr MacDonald rose smoothly to his feet, then offered a hand. 'Miss Wood?'

She took it, allowing him to help her stand. Instantly, the ground seemed to sway a little and she raised a hand to her head. 'Oh, dear. Forgive me, I am not normally so feeble.'

Sally hastened to her side, and she leaned gratefully on her maid. Somehow, Mr MacDonald still held her right hand. Gently, and with surprising reluctance, she withdrew it.

He was frowning. 'You are pale as milk, Miss Wood. Perhaps you should rest a little longer before attempting to walk.' Glancing around, he stepped away from them, returning almost instantly with a low stool belonging to the milkmaids. 'Here. Rest yourself for a moment.' He set the stool in front of her and Sally helped her sit on it. Although she protested weakly, in truth she was glad of it, for her legs still felt decidedly soft.

I might have died!

Pushing the thought away, she focused instead on breathing slowly and carefully, but she could not prevent being conscious of being under scrutiny. Sally was all solicitousness, patting her hand and speaking calmly to her, while Mr MacDonald and his sister were eyeing her with similarly concerned expressions. It was Mr Mac-Donald who had taken the full force of the blow and yet there he was, looking and sounding entirely uninjured while she, who had been protected from most of the impact, was the one who was behaving like a weakling. In this moment, Mama's steely courage seemed far away.

Glancing around, she now became aware that interested spectators were arriving to exclaim and stare. She dropped her gaze, unaccustomed to being gaped at in such a way.

'Well!' Eilidh—Miss MacDonald—sat down firmly

on the grass beside Isabella. 'What a lovely day it is! Blue skies and green grass, and a danger averted. All is well.'

'Indeed!' Isabella sent her a grateful smile. Now, instead of being a spectacle—a grown woman sat on a milking stool—they were now two ladies engaging in gentle conversation in the park. 'Sally, can you find my parasol please? I lost it in the midst of everything.'

'Of course, Miss!' Sally quickly found it, and was pleased to inform Isabella that it was undamaged. Opening the parasol, Isabella angled it to shield both herself and Miss MacDonald, adding to the air of insouciance that, she hoped, now surrounded them.

There followed quite the strangest conversation that Isabella had enjoyed in a long time. She and Eilidh discussed the weather and the poor, frightened cattle, and the joys and travails of having brothers, while Angus went to assist the milkmaids regather the cattle and Sally, along with a few other good citizens, gathered together the various objects that were strewn about the grass—hats, reticules, even a pocket watch that had been dropped in the panic. The gentleman who had been kicked in the gut had managed to walk away, though his face had been creased with pain.

'We are from Scotland, you know.' Eilidh offered, glancing up at Isabella.

'Yes, I had worked it out. I have a fondness for the Scots, although I have never been there. My…friend is from Scotland.' She pictured Cooper, heard in her mind the soft burr of his accent.

Eilidh, hearing the hesitation, sent her a saucy glance. 'A *particular* friend, Miss Wood?'

'Lord, no! Cooper is—my eldest brother calls him a servant, but he has worked for our family since before I was born. I consider him a friend. He speaks with great wistfulness about the Highlands.' She frowned. 'I am pondering now why he has never moved back there. I wonder why I never questioned that before.'

Eilidh nodded. 'Strange indeed. Most Scots cannot stay away from home for very long. My brother and I shall only remain in London while we must. I am missing my home already and I know Angus is, too.' She sent Isabella a piercing glance. 'It is not allowed, then, for servants to also be friends? We had been informed that was the case, but perhaps you can confirm it.'

Isabella shook her head. 'It is not allowed at all! My brother—my oldest brother, that is—abhors the relaxed friendship that Max and I have with Cooper.'

'Max?'

'My other brother. He is in the middle, while I am the youngest.' She smiled. 'Max and I share an easy relationship, much like you and your brother, I think?' Daringly, she looked across the sward towards the Highlander. He was succeeding in calming down the agitated beasts, who remained tightly bunched together, tails flicking wildly. Stragglers were joining the herd, though clearly they remained rather anxious.

My, he looks good in his Highland clothing.

'Angus?' Eilidh shrugged. 'He and I agree on most things, but when we disagree we do so spectacularly.' She leaned closer. 'He actually planned to come to London without me!' She smiled smugly. 'I knew I would bring him round though. He is here on—on a matter of business, which I hope I can assist him with. We arrived only yesterday and we are staying in Mayfair, which I understand is close to everything of importance. Besides—'

she twinkled '—I had a desire to visit London, just once in my life!'

Isabella grimaced. 'I should prefer to be anywhere *but* London, Miss MacDonald. I tried to persuade Freddy—my oldest brother—but he was adamant I must come.'

And adamant I must marry this Season, she added silently.

Eilidh sighed. 'Such trials are put before we women. Sometimes the men have their way, but, I think, we are victorious on many occasions, too.'

'You are right!' Isabella felt hope course through her. One way or another, she might thwart Freddy's plan to marry her off. 'When we are resourceful and determined—'

'And clever!' Eilidh interjected.

'Yes, cleverness, too, is there. I think they underestimate us sometimes, do they not?'

'Sometimes? Most of the time!'

They broke off to watch the cattle. Angus had finally succeeded in approaching a particular cow—a large dun creature with a bell tied around her neck. Slipping a leading rope around her neck, he seemed to be speaking softly to her the whole time and completely ignoring the others. Isabella could not help but feel anxious again. Why, at any second something might spook the agitated herd into another stampede.

As she watched, transfixed, he began leading the dun cow towards the corralled area near the trees to their left. To Isabella's amazement, the rest of the herd followed docilely behind them. One of the milkmaids swung open a section of the fence and the cattle all followed the dun cow inside.

'Good,' said Eilidh in a matter-of-fact tone. 'The dun cow must have been the herd leader.'

The milkmaids closed the fence, then spoke to Angus, clearly grateful for his assistance. His work done, he approached the ladies, chestnut hair glinting copper-bronze in the sunlight. 'Hopefully those poor cattle can settle themselves now. What those boys did was criminal!'

'Boys?' Isabella tilted her head to one side. 'From the brief glimpse I had of them, they were similar in age to yourself!' She estimated Mr MacDonald to be somewhere in his late twenties, while Eilidh seemed younger—perhaps a similar age to Isabella herself.

'Boys,' he repeated firmly. 'They do not deserve to be called men.' He peered closely at her. 'I am glad to see some colour in your cheeks, Miss Wood. Are you feeling better?'

'I am, thank you.' There was a brief silence, during which her mouth suddenly seemed strangely dry. She broke his gaze and rose, all busyness, and Miss Mac-Donald also got to her feet. 'Thank you again for saving me today. And thank you, Miss MacDonald, for sitting with me until I was recovered.'

'It was my pleasure.' Angus—Mr MacDonald—took her gloved hand and raised it to his lips. Even through the thin fabric, his kiss sent delightful tingles darting through her. She withdrew her hand and offered it to his sister. 'It was a delight to meet you, Miss MacDonald. I do hope we shall meet again.'

Eilidh smiled and said all that was proper. As she walked away, Sally by her side, Isabella had to fight hard not to turn back for one last look at them. Instead, she allowed Sally to chatter all the way home, expressing her shock and horror at the horsemen's actions, her terror, and her relief and gratitude towards the Scottish gentleman.

'Sally.' They were just about to go inside. 'Please do not speak of this to anyone.'

'Not speak of it? But you might have died!'

'Exactly.' Sally's brow was furrowed, so Isabella explained. 'If Freddy or Prudence hear of this, they are likely to order me to give up walking, or only go out in Prudence's company.' She shuddered. 'I do not know how I would manage, cooped up all the time. These walks are my only sanity in a world full of ballrooms and afternoon tea!'

'But if you walk out with your sister-in-law, it is still walking. I really think I ought to tell them, Miss.'

Isabella took both her hands, addressing her pleadingly. 'Walking with Prudence is like taking a turn about the drawing room. She goes no faster than a snail and cares only for propriety and being seen. When we walked together before, she told me to shorten my stride, lest I appear mannish. *Mannish!* Because of walking!'

Sally bit her lip.

'Sally, I am not asking you to lie to anyone. Just… you have no need to mention it. Do you?'

The maid nodded slowly. 'I suppose not. But if anyone asks me, I shall tell them the truth. I do not wish to lose my position, Miss.'

'I know. I appreciate this.' She did know. Both Freddy and Prudence were capricious employers and regularly turned staff off for perceived misdemeanours. Sally was one of the longer-serving servants, having been with the family for five or six years. Isabella felt a pang of sympathy for her. A single woman in her fifties, Sally would find it difficult to find other work without a reference. The tyranny of it all struck her anew. 'It is so unfair that power is held by just a few people and they can make us do what they will.'

Sally eyed her steadily, not allowing herself to signal agreement, but Isabella knew the maid understood how things stood. Squaring her shoulders, she went inside.

The second footman was waiting for her. 'Her Ladyship requires your presence, Miss. As soon as you return, she said.'

Isabella's heart sank. 'Thank you, James. Is Her Ladyship in the drawing room?'

He confirmed it and Isabella mounted the stairs, wondering what was in store. 'Good day, Prudence,' she declared airily, entering the grand room and trying to appear unconcerned. Prudence turned around from her writing desk, rose and walked toward her favourite armchair. There she sat, straightened her skirts and set some papers on her side table before turning her attention to Isabella.

'Finally you are returned. Where on earth were you, Isabella?' Disapproval was writ in her expression, in the set lines of her face.

It is even in her shoulders, Isabella noted.

She shrugged, determined not to accept Prudence's vexation. 'Walking in the park, as I do every day.'

'You are not normally gone for three hours!'

Isabella's jaw dropped. Had it really been so long? She glanced at the clock on the mantel. 'How did it get to be this time?' Grimacing, she turned to her sister-in-law. 'I am sorry, Prudence,' she declared frankly. 'No doubt you were worrying about me. I shall take shorter walks in future.'

'Indeed you will, or you will give them up entirely!'

She picked up the paper from the side table. 'Now then. I have been making a list of eligible gentlemen for you to consider.' She passed the paper across to Isabella, who took it, frowning. 'Those on the left live with female relatives—mothers, sisters, aunts—so we will call on them all in the coming days. The others do not and so we can only access them at balls, soirées and the like.' She rubbed her hands together briskly. 'I had begun this task through a sense of duty, but actually I believe there is enjoyment to be had here.'

'Enjoyment? For whom?'

Prudence sighed. 'I was given the choice of only three men, Isabella. Your list is a veritable feast of manhood!'

Three men, yet she chose Freddy? Lord, what must the other two have been like?

Isabella ran her eye over the list. 'A *feast*? Lord Embury, who must be sixty-five? The Honourable Geoffrey Barnstable, who is so licentious that the ladies call him the *Dis*honourable Geoffrey?'

'Nonsense! I have never heard anyone speak of Mr Barnstable in such a way!'

Yes, because you are invisible to him. He saves his despicable behaviour for attractive debutantes. She stabbed her finger at the paper. 'Sir Horace Lazenby? How could you even consider such a man?'

'Sir Horace is received everywhere and is fabulously wealthy!'

'Yes, wealthy on the backs of slaves! We all know about the plantations he owns.'

'My dear, you refine too much on such matters. As his wife, why should you care where his wealth comes from?'

'But I do care! I care very much!' She set the paper down. 'This is hopeless. I cannot marry any of these!'

'But you have never even met some of them! Lord Welford is lately returned from the Continent, while Mr Craven normally stays in his estate in Yorkshire.' She leaned forwards to add, in a conspiratorial tone, 'I have it on the best authority that he is seeking a wife and that he intends to take her to Yorkshire, away from the *ton*. You would like that, would you not? Never to have to endure another Season? For you have said so, many times.'

Isabella snorted. 'Not if I simply exchange one prison for another! This Mr Craven may be the worst of men, yet you and Freddy would happily see me sent to Yorkshire with him, where anything may happen!'

'Do not make such unladylike noises, Isabella. And for heaven's sake, sit up straight! Of course we would not wish you to marry someone truly heinous. Your brother is being perfectly reasonable in giving you the pick of all the gentlemen this Season. Now, are you going to engage in this, or are you going to continue to act like a spoilt child?'

Isabella felt a little uncomfortable. Perhaps she was being somewhat unreasonable, for it was true that some of the gentlemen named on the list were strangers to her. Indeed, only today she had encountered a man who had piqued her interest. Who could say that such a thing would never happen again?

'I suppose, if I was to marry someone reasonable, I would have a little more freedom than I do currently.'

Prudence smiled. 'That is the spirit and I am glad to hear you say it! A young lady has very little freedom, as you know. As a married woman—particularly after you have done your duty and provided an heir—you are at liberty to live your life free from certain…expectations.'

There could be no doubt as to her meaning. Isabella

flushed a little, reflecting that the marital act must be uncomfortable indeed for women if the production of heirs removed the expectation for wives to co-operate with something objectionable. For a moment, she allowed herself to wonder how Prudence saw her life.

'Prudence, are you happy?' The words had left her lips before she had time to consider them.

Her sister-in-law looked startled, then thoughtful. 'I would say that I am…contented.'

'Then—you are not *un*happy?'

'No. Not unhappy. Not happy. Contented.' She patted Isabella's hand. 'Your brother is a good man. I know you find him stuffy, but he has always treated me with decency and for that I am thankful.'

Isabella could only nod, dropping her gaze so that Prudence would not see the mix of pity and horror she was currently feeling. From Isabella's perspective, Freddy did *not* always treat Prudence with decency. He could be cold and harsh, and was often critical of his wife.

Like Papa used to be with Mama.

Yet Prudence had found a way to be contented. Isabella shuddered inwardly. How could this be the fate of women? Surely there must be a way to escape such a future?

Her thoughts returned to tonight's entertainments.

Perhaps the MacDonalds will be there.

Lifting her head, she gave a bright smile. 'Thank you, Prudence. Now, where are we bound this evening and who is likely to be present?'

Chapter Three

Isabella curtsied, thanking Mr Craven for the dance.

'Would you like some punch, Miss Wood? I would be happy to fetch you some. Or perhaps you might like to take some air on the terrace?'

'Oh! I—thank you, but no. I must return to my sister-in-law.' She was no green girl and had no intention of allowing any man to take her to the terrace for 'some air'.

'Very well.' His smile fading, he bowed curtly and left her.

Isabella sighed inwardly.

Men are such babies!

They could not take even the slightest hint of rejection and seemed to expect ladies to be delighted by their interest in them.

Prior to this, Mr Craven had not done too badly. He was neither ancient nor repulsive and had seemed reasonably polite and well spoken. However, given his petulance just now, Isabella was strongly tempted to cross him off her list.

She considered him further. He was not old, yet she could not call him young. Not ugly, but certainly not handsome either. She chuckled inwardly, conscious that, somehow, she had become ensnared in Prudence and Freddy's plans. Freddy's threats were outrageous, of course, but perhaps she might enjoy the relaxation of restrictions that marriage would bring. Recalling Prudence's stoicism, she suppressed a shudder and reminded herself that Prudence had found ways to feel content.

The problem is that contentment will not do for me. I want happiness and freedom, and joy!

Briefly, she imagined the thrill of sailing across the open sea. That was her one true happiness, her only freedom.

Since childhood, when she had begged Cooper and Max to let her accompany them on their boat trips, she had developed a love of the sea and boats, and sailing. Cooper had been an excellent teacher, instructing both her and Max with kind persistence, and Isabella was truly proud that she had mastered the art of sailing. It was physically challenging, plus all of the crew had to be alert to the very real risks to them all while out at sea. It felt…*purposeful* and exciting, and something to be proud of. Something truly hers, for she had worked hard to learn and improve herself, until the day Cooper had declared her a true sailor. Could someone like Mr Craven ever truly understand that?

As she made her way across to where Prudence sat with the other duennas, she scanned the room for what must be the hundredth time.

They are not here.

A stab of disappointment went through her. Apart from Max and Cooper, there were few people in this world she called friends, but she had been struck by the affinity she had felt with Miss MacDonald. Something about her no-nonsense friendliness and genuine concern for her brother had struck a deep chord in Isabella.

I should like to make a friend of her.

But Miss MacDonald was nowhere to be seen at the elegant ball that Isabella was currently enduring.

Both Isabella's brothers, too, were absent, as the Season was not yet anywhere near its height. As she took her seat beside Prudence—who was busily engaged in conversation with Mrs Edgecombe, who had been one of Mama's closest friends—Isabella allowed herself to recall chestnut hair, broad shoulders and blue-grey eyes. Or had they been green-blue? She would have to check next time she—

There might not be a next time. For all she knew, the MacDonalds might not be high enough to move in the circles she was limited to. Was he a soldier, from one of the Highland regiments, perhaps? His sister had mentioned a matter of business in London. Both had seemed intelligent, mannerly and respectable, but they had also carried themselves with an air of confidence, suggesting they had not been raised to serve. So, if they were gently born, perhaps she might yet see them at one of these interminable evenings.

'Miss Wood? My dance, I think?'

'Oh! Lord Embury.' She rose. 'Yes, of course.' Forcing a smile, she asked him how he was enjoying his evening, but being a man of advanced years and rather deaf, he could not hear her. Allowing him to take her through the steps, she reflected that he had really danced rather well for a man so near his dotage and thanked him with inward relief once the dance was over. Could she really marry a man old enough to be her grandfather?

Thankfully, supper was called and she joined Prudence in the long line of people snaking through the supper room. Half-listening to Prudence's gossip, she gasped inwardly as her eye was caught by two gentlemen in kilts. Her gaze sharpened, taking in the pattern in the tartan, the lines of their shape, their hair. One fair, one redhead. Neither chestnut. Her heart sank. Well, what was she to expect? That having met Mr MacDonald once, she was fated to see him again? There were many thousands of people in London. Why should she randomly re-encounter someone, just because she wished to?

Her mind whirred on and she almost *saw* the steps in her logical reasoning fall into place. It was, she mused whimsically, like watching one of the fascinating mechanical automatons she had recently seen in Monsieur Maillardet's Museum in Covent Garden, for the very reasonable entry price of two shillings and sixpence. Highlanders…perhaps, if Mr MacDonald *was* a soldier, they would know of him. Or even if he was not, perhaps Scots sought each other out when away from home? Keeping an eye on the unknown Highlanders, she waited until she saw them speaking to Mrs Edgecombe. Seeing an opportunity, she abandoned Prudence with a quick word, then made her way across to where they stood.

'Mrs Edgecombe! Apologies for interrupting, but it is a delight to see you! You were speaking to my sister-in-law earlier and I was called away to dance before I had the chance to greet you. You must think me terribly rude!'

'Not at all, child.' Mrs Edgecombe smiled at her in a kindly way. 'I declare you are more like your mother every day, Isabella!'

'Everyone does tell me that, so I suppose it must be true.'

'Ah, but everyone did not know her as I did. We were close friends for many years, you know. Through good times and sad times.'

'Yes… I remember' Isabella looked at her thoughtfully. 'She spoke of you with great fondness.'

The older woman's face lit up. 'She was a dear friend. Now, let me introduce you to my companions. This is Captain John Wishart of the Ninety-Second Gordons, and Lieutenant Archie Murray of the same regiment.' They bowed and smiled as Mrs Edgecombe introduced Isabella.

'A pleasure to meet you, Miss Wood.'

'Delighted!'

They all conversed amicably for a few moments, before Isabella saw her opportunity. 'I met two people from Scotland recently. Mr MacDonald and his sister. Might you know them?'

Captain Wishart chuckled. 'There are thousands of people in Scotland, Miss Wood. And many of them are MacDonalds!'

His tone was not unkind, but Isabella blushed. 'Yes, of course! How foolish of me! I suppose it would be like asking me about people in England with the surname Wood.'

'Precisely.'

'In my defence, Mr MacDonald wore a kilt, so I wondered if perhaps he was a soldier.'

'Oh, indeed? Was it a kilt like this?' He indicated his own garment.

'No, it was longer and the colours were different.'

'Ah. Likely not a soldier then. Our uniforms include

the short kilt. He will have been wearing his as a natural garment, not as uniform.'

'I see.'

'Is there a particular reason you wish to find this man, Isabella?' Mrs Edgecombe gave her a piercing look.

Isabella felt her flush deepen. 'Oh, no! In fact it—it was his sister. Miss MacDonald was very kind to me— they both were—and I would wish to thank them.'

'I see.'

Mrs Edgecombe *saw* altogether too much, it seemed. *Time to depart.*

'Anyway. It was lovely to meet you, gentlemen. I am promised for the first dance after supper, so I must go. Mrs Edgecombe, perhaps we could talk more of my mother some time?'

The older woman's face lit up. 'I should like that, Isabella.'

So he is not a soldier.

What then was the matter of business that had brought the MacDonald siblings to London? Eilidh— Miss MacDonald—had also said they were staying in Mayfair. They would likely be staying in one of the many hotels there. But which one? Or perhaps they had hired a house, if they had means? And how would it even help her to know? An unmarried woman could not call upon people indiscriminately. She sighed inwardly.

'Ah there you are, Miss Wood!'

A cold sensation pooled in her gut. She knew that voice, had tried to forget agreeing to dance with him tonight. Turning slowly, she braced herself to endure what was to come. There he was, sickly smile, thinning hair, protruding gut all present and correct. Pasting a polite half-smile to her face, she made a curtsy. 'Mr Barnstable! Is it time for our dance already?'

'Indeed it is! Though for me, the minutes have been ticking by damnably slowly—pardon my language, my dear...' He lifted his monocle, the better to leer at her, and her skin felt as though a thousand insects were suddenly crawling on it. 'Oh, yes,' he continued, dropping the quizzing glass and rubbing his hands together. 'I have been quivering in anticipation of this moment all evening.'

Suppressing a shudder, she ignored this, instead lifting her chin and stepping away. 'Then let us go to the dance floor, sir.'

The sooner we start, the sooner we finish.

Leading the way, she noticed sympathetic glances from a couple of other young ladies. They all knew Mr Barnstable too well.

Each time she danced with the Honourable Geoffrey Barnstable, she liked him less. He made no conversation, apart from comments highlighting her face, her figure, or her general 'delectability'. Since she had heard them all before—and heard him make similar comments to many other ladies—she knew there was little sincerity in them. And despite being, she thought, reasonably fair-minded, she had yet to find any redeeming qualities about him. Freddy would disagree, she knew, because for him that 'Honourable' title was worth more than gold.

The dance was a lively affair of jigs and reels, and the Honourable Geoffrey was struggling with the steps. Huffing and puffing, he nevertheless managed to keep his gaze on Isabella's bosom and she had to consciously prevent herself from crossing her hands across her chest.

'I declare every part of me is jiggling,' he announced as they clasped hands for a turn, making Isabella close her eyes briefly in horror. 'And I see that you are similarly afflicted, Miss Wood.'

Isabella made no answer, mortification flooding through her. If only he had requested her hand for a more sedate set.

How much longer must I endure this?

Finally—after what seemed like an age—her ordeal ended. Escaping as quickly as she could and foiling his attempt to kiss her hand, she made her way to Prudence.

'May we go now, Prudence?' she asked baldly. 'Supper is over and I have danced with everyone you asked me to.'

Prudence frowned, but made no counter-argument. 'Very well. I declare town life with its late hours does not particularly suit me.'

They made their farewells to their hostess and left. Isabella felt the *ennui* and tension slowly seep out of her as she settled into the blessed darkness of the carriage. As it rumbled through the dark streets of Mayfair, Isabella's mind wandered once again to the Scottish pair.

Where are they now and what are they doing?

For the second night in a row, Angus was struggling to sleep. This was something of a surprise, for he could not recall ever being afflicted by such an ailment before. Last night he had put it down to his arrival in London, the strangeness of it all and the enormity of the task before him. While his bruised ribs ached, such an injury should not have interfered with his sleep to this extent. No, tonight, the list of possible reasons had been complicated by a new addition: the beautiful Miss Wood.

There were many pretty young women of his acquaintance back home and, like Eilidh, he had had a sojourn in Edinburgh a few years ago, attending Assemblies and balls and flirting with a lively set of damsels. A few had caught his eye, but he could not recall losing sleep over a lass. Not ever.

It must be the stampede.

At the memory, a rush of cold fear ran through him—almost as though he was reliving the moment, rather than simply remembering it. The terrified herd thundering towards her. His fear that he might not be able to save her. The thump as the animal connected with him. Her hand on his shoulder. Her dark eyes meeting his…

He shook himself, padding across to the window as he had the night before. The stars were obscured by clouds—or was it the smoke that seemed to hang over the city like a pall? The scents and sounds all seemed wrong to his Hebridean senses. The city noise never stopped, not even at night. Just now, he could hear barking dogs, someone shouting in the distance and the rumble and clop of a carriage. He looked down, his gaze following the dark carriage as it passed—late-night revellers going to or from one of the many social events, no doubt.

His neighbour—the conservatively dressed gentleman he had seen the night before—had gone out earlier, seemingly walking for pleasure, before returning to prepare for his evening excursion. The man had crossed the street towards Angus's house and then turned down in the direction of Curzon Street. Then, later, he re-emerged, this time dressed in evening garb of knee breeches and stockings.

Is this their entire existence, then?

Social events, with an occasional walk in a park that was half the size of the machair near the Broch at home? He shook his head sadly at the emptiness of what he was imagining. Tomorrow was Friday and he intended to call on Lord Burtenshaw's man of business. The sooner he got Burtenshaw's agreement on the sale of land, the sooner he could return home.

'What is the time, Sally?' Isabella heard the sleepiness in her own voice. Since Sally had come in to wake her and open the shutters, it must be mid-morning at least.

'It is past eleven, Miss. How was the ball last—?' She broke off, her jaw slackening. 'Are you unwell, Miss?'

'Unwell? No, not at all.' Isabella had jumped out of bed and was now making for the basin of cold water on her washstand. Sluicing it liberally around her face and neck, she instantly felt more awake, the coldness helping shake away the fog of sleepiness from her mind. 'I do not wish to turn into a lay-abed, that is all.'

'Yes, Miss.' Sally looked dubious. 'What are your plans for today, Miss?'

'There is some ridiculous ball or soirée tonight. Lady Anstruther's, I believe.' She shrugged, dabbing at her face with a soft towel. 'And before that, Prudence intends to take me for a series of tedious afternoon calls. If I am to have time for a walk today, I must make haste!'

Sally's brow cleared. 'Ah! Now I understand, Miss. I had taken the liberty of preparing a walking dress, in case you should wish to go out as usual. Now, what should you like to eat this morning?'

Isabella brushed this off. 'I have no *time* for breakfast, Sally! We must hurry!'

* * *

Half past eleven precisely. Squaring his shoulders, Angus entered the offices of Mr Inglis, Lord Burtenshaw's man of business. Taking a keen look around the outer office, he noted the accoutrements of success: shining brass, gleaming panelling, a portrait on the wall. Henry Inglis, Snr, the plaque beneath stated. It showed a broad-shouldered man in sober clothing, with dark hair and a proud expression.

So this is the balach who has no qualms about taking rent from those who can barely afford it? The man who administers the theft of dignity and sustenance from families who have farmed the same land for centuries?

The names 'Burtenshaw' and 'Inglis' were hated in Benbecula, along with the factors sent on their behalf to wring every shilling they could from the people there. Yet, if he were to prevail, he would be forced into civility with both of them.

The clerk rose to greet him in a neutral way and bade him sit while he informed his master of Mr MacDonald's arrival. Angus sat.

Five minutes passed, then ten.

So that is the way of it?

Angus's jaw set at the disrespect. Still, he was forced to swallow it. To distract himself, he tried to imagine anyone behaving with such rudeness in the Islands and what the response might be. Insults and ire to begin with, he imagined, progressing quickly to fists and bloodied noses, and ending, most likely, in mutual drunkenness, as whatever outrage or dispute lay beneath the rudeness was resolved over whisky. Assuming that both parties were basically honourable. It was hard to imagine honour in this case. Certainly there had been nothing honourable in Burtenshaw's treatment of his tenants.

Promising himself a large measure of fiery smoothness just as soon as he was back in the hired town house, Angus counted to ten, twenty, fifty. The door opened.

'Mr Inglis will see you now.'

Nodding to the clerk, Angus stepped inside the inner chamber. Mr Inglis had aged since his portrait, his hair now grey rather than dark and his face lined into a permanent scowl. He was though, still a large man—not in height, but in girth. His visage was ruddy and puffed with age and the effects of too much wine. Unsmilingly, he gave a formulaic greeting, half-rising, and offered Angus a seat. Eyeing his large wooden desk, he deliberately tidied some papers, then leaned back, bringing his hands together, finally meeting Angus's gaze again. 'You wished to see me, Mr MacDonald?'

'Actually, I wished to see Lord Burtenshaw. You may be aware that I and my cousin have written to him through you on a number of occasions.'

'Ah, yes. The matter of the small estate in north Britain.'

'Where?'

North Britain? Really? He refuses to even say the word 'Scotland'?

Mr Inglis affected to be confused. 'Somewhere on a tiny island, I believe.' He shuffled through some papers and pulled one out. Angus recognised his own handwriting. 'Here we are! Lidistrome estate, Island of Ben-bec-ular.' He sounded out the island's name as if it were alien, adding an unnecessary 'r' at the end as if deliberately mangling the word. Setting the letter down, he eyed Angus evenly. 'Lord Burtenshaw thanks you for your interest. However, he is not minded to sell.'

'But why?' Angus could not keep the exasperation from his voice. 'What possible reason could he have for keeping it? It makes almost no income and is too far away for him to use it.'

Mr Inglis shrugged. 'I am not privy to His Lordship's reasons. Nor would I expect to be. But Lord Burtenshaw was very clear. Very clear indeed.' His tone dripped with condescension. 'My advice, my good man, is to forget this.'

Angus bristled. *My good man?*

'You are aware, Mr Inglis, of my title. I am Laird of Broch Clachan and you should address me as "Sir"!' Never having had reason to do this before, Angus was surprised just how angry he felt. In belittling him, Mr Inglis belittled every islander.

'Of course, *Sir*.' There was an unrepentant gleam in the man's eye. 'And being a…*laird*, you will no doubt be able to raise these matters with Lord Burtenshaw directly—perhaps when you next see him at his club, or at a soirée?' There was no mistaking the man's insolence.

Angus rose. 'Good day, Mr Inglis.'

And be grateful that I did not punch you in your wine-swollen nose.

It was only when he saw the startled expressions on the faces of the Londoners he was passing on the street outside that he realised that his scowl must look fearsome indeed. Schooling his features into a more civilised expression, and one that belied the decidedly *un*civilised anger raging within him, he stomped his way back to Chesterfield Street, gradually venting his anger a little by vigorously striding through Mayfair as though he were in Creagorry.

About to cross the road to his own town house, he turned when he heard the door behind him open. There was the gentleman he had seen numerous times—the one who carried himself more soberly than most of the coxcombs Angus had seen in London. The gentleman must be emerging for his daily walk. Their eyes met and Angus instinctively acknowledged the gentleman with a polite nod.

As usual, the man was dressed more conservatively than many of the London bucks Angus had so far encountered, with a well-fitting black coat, a snowy-white cravat, and gleaming boots. His nose looked as though it had been broken at some time in the past, but everything else about him whispered class and elegance, and civilisation. Beside him, Angus felt like a mountainous yokel, even though he knew such feelings to have no basis in rationality. Islanders, he knew, were just as civilised as the most fashionable of wealthy Londoners.

Remember, we are in the Age of Enlightenment! he adjured himself. *Reason is paramount.*

Turning back, he was forced to pause, as the narrow road was particularly congested just now, with a mix of carts, carriages and jarveys. He heard the man come up beside him and looked towards him again. The man grimaced, before muttering, 'I do not know how I am supposed to cross without soiling my boots.'

Angus could not help it: he grinned. 'Aye, well there is plenty of horse dung to polish them today.' He eyed the man's gleaming Hessians. 'I'll wager your valet will not be best pleased if you ruin those boots, for I reckon he was up half the night getting them to shine like that!' He smiled ruefully, indicating his own serviceable leather boots. 'Mine are clean, I swear, but they look nothing like yours!'

The man eyed him assessingly. 'If you will permit me to say so, my boots would not sit well with your Highland garb. Your boots are perfect as they are.'

'I am glad to hear it!' After a pause Angus added, in a confiding tone. 'I am new to London and know not what is expected of me.'

'Indeed?' The man hesitated, then nodded to himself. 'Permit me to introduce myself. The name is Brummell.' Fishing in his pocket, he handed Angus his card and Angus reciprocated.

'Angus MacDonald, Laird of Broch Clachan. A pleasure to meet you, Sir.' He indicated the card. 'We are neighbours.'

'Indeed. I have seen you and your lady these past days. Are you in town for the Season?'

Angus frowned. 'Yes and no. My sister and I are here on a matter of business. We know no one in town and so it is difficult to know where to begin.' Finally there was a gap in the horse traffic and so they crossed the street together.

'I see.' The man's face remained frustratingly neutral. They had reached the other side. 'I wish you good fortune in your endeavours. Good day!'

'Good day.' Angus watched the gentleman walk off down the street, feeling again that sense of frustration.

How on earth am I to meet Lord Burtenshaw when these clubs and drawing rooms are closed to me? When society is closed to me?

Entering the town house, he braced himself to give Eilidh the disappointing news.

* * *

'For goodness sake be quick, Isabella, or we shall be late for church!' Prudence, disapproving of Isabella's choice of bonnet, had insisted she run and change it, even though it would delay their departure.

Isabella, uncharacteristically cross, was moved to retort, 'Well, which is it to be, Prudence? Leave now, with this bonnet, or delay while I change?'

'Urgh! I suppose it will have to do, though I sincerely hope that none of your suitors will be present at church this morning.'

'Given the amount of brandy flowing at last night's ball,' Isabella returned drily, 'I sincerely doubt we shall see many gentlemen at all this morning!'

This proved to be the case and Isabella's boredom during the service was compounded by the general *ennui* and frustration she was feeling. Oh, it was always there when she was forced to be in London. The picnics and parties meant nothing to her. Bonnets and ballgowns meant nothing to her. Suitors and soirées meant nothing to her. She sighed, glad that her poke bonnet gave her a little privacy. Prudence could not see her face unless she turned towards her—which was perhaps why she had wanted Isabella to change to the neater bonnet.

If she were honest, she was feeling particularly low at present. Her brother Max—as he usually did—had spent his first few days in London catching up with his own friends rather than attending the early Season events and Isabella had only seen him in passing at home. She had been lumbered with Prudence's company much more than usual, as Prudence continued to take her matchmaking role to heart.

Only a few days in London and already I am near fit to scream.

How she would endure the coming months she did not know.

Her sense of powerlessness was compounded by her failure to see the MacDonalds again. She had rushed to the park on Friday morning, hoping they might be creatures of habit and that she might find them near the milkmaids at around the same time. Of course they were not there. Well, why should they be? Besides, she was undoubtedly pinning too much upon a brief, chance encounter. On closer acquaintance Miss MacDonald and her brother would probably have turned out to be just as dull as almost everyone else she knew.

Everything was hopeless.

After the service they emerged, blinking, into strong sunshine, Isabella mentally bracing herself for the day ahead. They were to be 'at home' this afternoon, then tonight Prudence had accepted invitations to Lady Jersey's soirée. No time to walk today then. And it was already past midday, so even if—

'Isabella!'

'Max!' Isabella laughed as her brother engulfed her in a mighty hug, picking her up off her feet. 'Never tell me you did not come home last night!' Taking in his dishevelled appearance, stubble-shadowed jaw and loosened cravat, she was sure of it.

He grinned. 'Fell asleep in an armchair at my club. Woke with the most appalling crick in my neck. Good day, Prudence,' he added, belatedly becoming aware of his sister-in-law's piercing stare. 'How do you today?'

'I was better before I saw you, Max!' She looked him up and down. 'Please tell me you are on your way home for a bath and a shave, for if anyone sees you like this, then I am sure I do not know what would occur!'

'An interesting conundrum, indeed. Perhaps they may faint, or shriek, or even…' he leaned in to speak directly in her ear '…comment that I am your brother-in-law! Now which of these would be the worst?'

'Oh, Max, stop, please!' Isabella, stifling a laugh, glanced at Prudence's set face. 'You know Prudence does not share our wit.'

'Wit? *Wit?*' Prudence's voice was tight with anger. 'I should not call it wit! I should sooner call this muff a cat! Now what have I said?' She eyed them in bewilderment as brother and sister both succumbed to laughter. 'Stop it! Max! Isabella! People are *watching*!'

'Oh, Max!' Isabella declared, once she had dried her eyes, 'How I have missed you!'

'Missed me? It has only been a few days!' Despite his light tone, his dark eyes conveyed understanding. 'Shall we walk out tomorrow?'

'Oh, yes, for walking with Sally is not the same!'

Prudence sniffed. 'I am sure, if you were to ask, that I would happily walk out with you. A sedate promenade in Rotten Row can be an excellent opportunity to—'

'But I do not *wish* for opportunities to meet suitors! Yes, I know that is what you were about to say, Prudence. I need to be free to walk quickly and to rail and jest with Max, and to forget for a whole hour that I must take part in this entire masquerade!' Isabella took Prudence's hand. 'Can you understand, Prudence? Even a little?'

Prudence's brow was creased. 'Well, no,' she said frankly. 'But I suppose I can spare you for an hour in the morning.'

'Midday.' The word was out before Isabella had the time to consider it. 'That is to say, Max, can you take me out just before midday, for that will give you time for a late sleep if you need it and will still mean I can be back for Prudence's afternoon tea visits? Or perhaps we could visit Great-Aunt Morton beforehand if you can come earlier, for I am told she is unwell.'

'A capital notion! Now, may I travel back with you in the carriage? For I undoubtedly look much too disreputable to walk the rest of the way!' Tucking Isabella's hand into his arm, he led the way to where the carriage awaited.

Chapter Four

St James's Park was held to be one of the most beautiful of the London parks. As he and Eilidh walked down its formal avenues and along its impressive canal, Angus's thoughts were not on the shrubberies or carefully tended flower displays. He was, instead, looking for a lady with flashing dark eyes and a slender figure. Hopefully he was being discreet, for he wanted no raillery from his sister.

Miss Wood had now taken to haunting his dreams, which was damnably inconvenient. As if he had not enough to consider, with Inglis's refusal to even consider his offer and now his abject failure to gain even a foothold in polite society. They had no acquaintances in London and were well aware that they could not simply accost Lord Burtenshaw in his home—particularly since it was important to make a good impression on the man.

Although he had not admitted it to Eilidh, Angus's suggestion of St James's for their walk had less to do with seeing and hopefully interacting with members of the *ton* and more to do with a hope that Miss Wood might be in the habit of drinking new milk from the St

James's herd in the early afternoon. It had been Thursday when they had met—it was now Monday.

Disappointingly, when he and Eilidh had purchased their milk around half past twelve, Miss Wood was nowhere to be seen. And why should she be there? Worse, why on earth was he wasting his time thinking about her when he ought to be finding solutions to the problem before him? Searlas had reported back that the servants were adamant about how strict the Upper Ten Thousand were. No one could be admitted to their ranks, nor interact with them socially, without some sort of benefactor to make the initial introductions. So, given his failure to gain any ground with Inglis on Friday, he and Eilidh had fallen back on their only ruse—to focus on public spaces, where they might make new acquaintances. They had also taken the time to visit a dressmaker and a tailor, and some new, fashionable clothing was to be ready in two days from now. Angus had insisted upon his kilt and trews for everyday wear, but had been measured for some ridiculous knee breeches, as well as jackets that would complement the Highland dress, but were more aligned to current London fashions.

Eilidh had provided the dressmakers with lengths of MacDonald tartan with which to fashion some of her dresses, insisting that she was a proud Scot and wished for that to be reflected in at least some of her wardrobe. She was, she had told Angus drily, not optimistic about the outcome.

And so, here they were, meandering along the pathways in St James's, giving a cordial 'good day' to anyone they met and making no progress whatsoever. The muscles in his face were beginning to ache from smiling at strangers and any remaining confidence in achieving his object was leeching out of him. Yet, for Eilidh's sake as much as for his own, he dared not admit his true feelings.

Just keep trying.

It was all he could think to do.

He is not here. Having successfully timed her arrival at the milk herd in St James's to almost exactly the stroke of noon, Isabella immediately scanned around the area, looking for the MacDonalds. Swallowing hard against the disappointment, she then delayed as much as she could, loitering for more than twenty minutes until Max began making his impatience—and some confusion—clear. So they slowly walked away, spending the next half-hour wandering around the park and conversing about little matters. They traversed the entire length of Birdcage Walk, with Isabella as usual bemoaning the captivity of the beautiful songbirds trapped within.

Just like me.

She shook herself inwardly.

I am becoming foolish.

Glancing down at her dress, she could not help feeling a pang of frustration. For the first time ever, she had asked Sally to prepare a particular gown for her to wear—a pretty walking dress in embroidered lemon-and-green muslin with a matching velvet spencer and she knew that it suited her. Never before had she considered choosing to wear something simply because she looked good in it. Comfort was usually her only concern.

Still, she had teamed the outfit with her most comfortable half-boots and it was no inconvenience for her to wear a pretty dress rather than a plain one. Perfectly reasonable, and nothing at all to do with who might see her. So why was disappointment still coursing through her?

Just being in Max's company was usually enough to lift her spirits. Today, though, with the absence of the MacDonalds and the knowledge that another round of parlour conversations followed by another evening of tedious dances awaited, Isabella could not sustain any gladness.

'Why such a sigh, Bella?'

The look in Max's dark eyes suggested he already knew, but she said it regardless. 'Prudence. Freddy. Marriage. All of it. Even visiting Great-Aunt Morton has depressed my spirits.'

'I know what you mean. She is remarkably cheerful, given her circumstances and the fact she has such a cough. That house!' He shuddered. 'A good property in a fine location, but so rundown! She is clearly in straitened circumstances and must not be able to afford to rent anything better. A pity, because her husband had a reasonable fortune when he was alive.'

'She did appreciate our gifts and our company though.' If Cooper was the nearest thing to a true, warm-hearted father they had, then Great-Aunt Morton, their mother's aunt, had been the closest female in their lives since Mama's death.

'Well, she said so, many times. Let us continue to visit her each week. As Mama's aunt, she is the last connection we have with our mother.'

Isabella nodded, adding thoughtfully, 'I wonder that Freddy does not make her an allowance. We are her closest relations, after all. Yet he does not even visit her!'

Max gave a bark of laughter. 'Freddy has no interest in impoverished distant relatives—and no notion of looking after our great-aunt. To listen to him, you would think the Burtenshaw fortune is tiny and all of us close to being paupers. Yet when I was included in matters of business, before Papa's death, it was clear that our wealth is comfortable and Freddy's fortune secure.'

She shrugged. 'Freddy has always leaned towards miserliness—except, of course, where money needs to be spent in pursuit of the Burtenshaw name!'

'To be fair, I do not think he begrudges you your dowry, or either of us our allowance. It is, after all, his duty!'

'Duty, always duty! And do not forget, Max, that Freddy is Head of the Family!' They smiled briefly, a smile of mutual understanding.

'To return to what you said before…you do not wish to marry, Bella? To have children?'

'Some day, yes. Undoubtedly. But…not because my hand is forced.'

'I understand.' He grimaced at her raised brow. 'I *do*.' He spread his hands. 'I would dearly wish to be a father some day, but it will probably be denied me. As you well know I have not the means to marry, being reliant on my allowance from Freddy. It barely supports me, much less a wife or a brood of children. My yacht is my only luxury—though I would argue it is my sanity.' He made a face. 'Nor is there a need for me to marry, being the useless second son, after all.'

The bitterness in his tone drew her attention. 'I know how hard it is to be dependent on Freddy's generosity, for we are the same in that regard, But—useless? No! Never that!'

He shook his head. 'Useless is *exactly* the right word.

I understood my role as "spare" should anything happen to Freddy. But now that he has sons of his own, I am condemned to a cycle of *ton* parties, card games, drinking, and purposelessness. My allowance is enough for me to maintain the yacht and meet the payments to my tailor and my club, but not enough for me to freely pursue my own course. I foresee a future of loneliness and straitened circumstances—just like Great-Aunt Morton!'

'You will never be lonely, for you will always have me, Max. And as for the parties and card games…do you not enjoy them?'

'At the time. Sometimes.' He sighed. 'It may sound good, but it is…empty.'

She caught her breath. 'Empty…yes, exactly! I feel the same way. Oh, why do they not see? But, Max, at least you can escape. After the Season, you are free to sail and hunt and fish all year if you wish. For me, though…' she swallowed, her throat tightening '…if Freddy carries through on his threat then I shall be forced to choose a suitor by early summer and will no doubt be married shortly after.'

'And is there no man who has taken your fancy?'

Pushing away a shockingly clear image of chestnut hair and blue-grey eyes, she shook her head. 'Not one of my suitors inspires me to anything other than tedium— or worse, disgust! And all the time the days tick by and the chains begin to tighten about me.'

'I have no answers for you, Bella, save a hope that something may turn up. It is, after all, how I live my own pointless life.' He grinned suddenly and there was something wild and desperate in his eyes. Stopping, he took both her hands. 'Let us forget such dark thoughts.

I shall challenge you to a race, for that always worked to lift your spirits!'

She gasped, then looked around. 'Here?' There was no one in sight, and… *Oh!* How she would love to run, even briefly. Not just for the glory of running, but also for the sheer rebelliousness of it. 'Very well. Agreed!' She could not help but giggle. 'But I shall require more of a start than usual, as I shall be hampered by this stupid dress.'

At least I am wearing suitable half-boots.

'Fair enough. I shall start here and you may start at yonder oak tree, when I give the word.'

She nodded. 'And our destination? Perhaps that statue, by the rose bushes?' She indicated the end of the walkway, where a dryad statue had been placed, surrounded by a wall of greenery. There were other side paths nearby, but the park was remarkably quiet for the time of day.

'Perfect.'

She moved to her starting position, then, on her brother's call, she let herself fly.

Isabella had always loved to run. Since early childhood she had trailed after Max and had needed to run simply to keep up. Over the years, they had worked out rules for their impromptu races that ensured they each had a reasonable chance of winning. As she pelted down the path towards the rose shrubbery, wind flying in her hair and her skirts gathered indecorously to her knees, Isabella was conscious of a sense of glorious freedom— as if released from a cage. Without slowing, she turned her head slightly, the better to hear Max. He was, naturally, gaining ground, all the time getting closer to her. Summoning all her energy for one last effort, her face screwed up in determination, she focused on the statue, their finishing point.

Yes! I am going to win!

'Oof!' Someone emerged from the side path, just in front of the statue, and she crashed straight into him. Bouncing off a hard chest, she was unable to prevent herself from falling. Emitting a shriek, she landed hard on her bottom. Between the force of the impact and being breathless from running, she found herself momentarily speechless.

However, not all her senses were disordered. The sight of a familiar kilt, and a sporran at eye level, was causing her thumping heart to increase its speed. Her gaze travelled upwards, but Angus was not looking at her. *It is him!* Suddenly her mouth was dry and her pulse fluttering madly, and not just because of the race and the fall. So what she remembered from the day of the stampede was true.

He affects me in a way that no man ever has.

Having seemingly satisfied himself that she was not seriously hurt, Angus was stepping swiftly away from her, drawing a knife from his stocking as he did so. But before she could speak, and before he could get anywhere near Max, she heard a tumble and crash behind her. When she turned, jaw sagging, she saw Max sprawled on the ground and Miss MacDonald with a rather smug expression on her pretty face.

'Nicely done, Eilidh.' Mr MacDonald advanced on Max, knife held threateningly in his right hand. 'Now then, *a bhalaich*, what do you mean by chasing a lady through a park?'

Max, with all the agility gained from spending years of his life on boats, had already scrambled to his feet.

With fire in his eyes and his face twisted in anger, he took up a fighting stance. 'What I *mean* by it? What I *mean* by engaging in a harmless race with my *own sister*? Isabella, how do you?'

Angus glanced towards Isabella, who was rising to her feet with Eilidh's assistance, trying not to rub her poor, sore posterior. 'I am well.' She straightened. 'Max, may I introduce to you Mr MacDonald. My brother, Maximilian Wood.' Her eyes danced as the humour of the situation struck her.

Angus's face cleared. Slipping the knife back to its hiding place, he bowed. 'A pleasure to meet you, Mr Wood. This is my sister, Miss MacDonald.'

Stiffly, Max made his bow to both of them. Eilidh grinned at him. 'Come now, Mr Wood. Surely you can see that our intention was to aid your sister?'

Max remained unmoved, the humiliation of being tripped by a lady all too apparent.

Miss MacDonald was undeterred. 'Indeed, you should be thanking us for coming to your sister's aid again!' She turned to Isabella. 'Miss Wood, are you hurt? You landed with quite a bump just now!'

Ignoring her aching bottom, Isabella gave a rueful smile. 'I believe the harm is only to my pride. How undignified you must think me! Running like a hoyden in a public park.'

'Not at all!' It was Angus, his eyes delightfully crinkling at the corners. 'It is reassuring to see that members of the *ton* may be human after all.' He hesitated. 'May we walk with you a little way?'

'Of course!' Isabella spoke quickly, for fear Max would make some excuse. Her heart was still thumping wildly and now she was unsure exactly why. The race, the fall, seeing *him* again… She indicated the path to their left. 'Shall we?'

He fell into step beside her and she heard rather than saw Max and Eilidh follow them. 'It seems I am once again in your debt, Mr MacDonald.'

'How so? You were not in any danger.'

'But you believed me to be so and I appreciate your intervention—even if my brother does not!'

'Ah, but I understand your brother's ire. Eilidh is well skilled in the art of fighting and knows all sorts of tricks for disarming a bigger, heavier man. In this case tripping him up was the best option—unless, that is, you are Maximilian Wood.' He frowned. 'I should apologise to him.'

'Yes, yes, if you must.' Isabella, well used to dealing with the consequences of pricked male pride, waved this away. 'But tell me, how have you been? Are you finding your way in London?'

'That rather depends.'

'On what?'

'Well, we can find our way around the streets of Mayfair. We know this park and Green Park. We have commissioned the services of a tailor and a dressmaker, the better to fit in with your fashions.'

'I like your Highland clothing very well.'

He grinned at this. 'I thank you and we like it, too. However, in order to achieve what we must, I fear we shall have to blend in somewhat.'

'Blend in?' she echoed, rather dubiously. 'You are more than six feet tall, with broad shoulders and a handsome face. Even without the Highland garb, I cannot imagine you *blending in*. Your sister, too, is beautiful and likely to turn heads wherever she goes.'

He grinned. 'You think me handsome, Miss Wood? Now, do not blush and dissemble. I like your plain speech.'

All confusion, she knew not how to answer this, so instead she attempted distraction. 'If it is not impertinent of me to ask, what is the matter of business that brings you to London?'

'You are not impertinent at all, Miss Wood.' His expression turned serious. 'It is a matter of land ownership.'

'Yes?'

'There is an…estate, I suppose you would call it, that borders ours at home. It is currently owned by an English lord, and I wish to buy it from him.'

'I see.' She did not, not at all, but she was delighting in being in his company, and wanted only to prolong the conversation. All around them, the scent of spring flowers was in the air. Isabella's day had gone from dull to bright and it was all his doing.

'The problem we face,' he continued, 'is that we know no one who can launch us in society. Until we find a way of getting in, we cannot even meet this Lord, never mind persuade him to sell.'

'Oh.' Her instinct was to offer immediate assistance, for she would have no qualms about bringing them about—especially if it brought them more into her company. But, never having studied the unwritten rules of society, she worried about inadvertently making things worse. 'Could you perhaps discuss that with my brother? He would be better placed than me to advise.'

She shrugged. 'Personally, I think it all nonsense. My friend Cooper—he is Scottish, you know—has shown me how we are all equally important. The *ton* and those with titles are no better than anyone else. Surely it is by the goodness of our actions that we may be judged, and not by the conquests of some ancestor?'

'Well, you have only stated what seems obvious to me. But our own servants here have advised us that there is no way to meet this man socially unless we move in the same circles.'

She frowned. 'That is a conundrum indeed and one which I have no answer to.'

I wonder how high his birth is? How would society see him?

She dared not ask for fear of causing offence and instead diverted him by asking his opinion of the London parks.

'All the trees are mightily impressive, that is certain. Trees do not grow easily in the Hebrides, you see.'

'Do they not? It must be wild indeed!'

'We may not have trees, but in summer, when the wildflowers are in blossom in the machair and the moors are blooming with heather, I'll wager there is no more beautiful place under the sky.' The wistfulness in his eye, his heady Scottish accent and the power of his words combined to create a sweet sadness in her chest, a yearning for something unknown. For a moment it seemed to her as though time itself was paused, with everything in her focused on the man by her side and the power in his words.

Shaking herself out of the strange sensation, Isabella realised they had reached the edge of the park. By unspoken agreement they continued together out of the gates and on to the Mall, where the bustle of commerce pierced the cloud of intimacy that had been gathering around them. Max and Eilidh caught up with them as they waited for an opportunity to cross the busy road and, once on the other side, Isabella fell into step beside Eilidh, leaving the men to follow behind them.

They sent each other a shy smile. 'I am glad to see you again, Miss Wood,' Eilidh said.

'And I you. I have been thinking of you both these past days, wondering how you are. Thank you again for your kindness the other day.'

She waved this away. 'Think nothing of it. Why, anyone might have done the same!'

'And again today. How were you to know that I was racing with my brother in a dreadfully hoydenish way, rather than being attacked by an assailant? You and your brother seem to have a talent for being there when I needed you. Twice now.'

'Somehow I think it is less of a coincidence than it might seem,' Eilidh replied drily.

Does she know that I have been loitering in St James's Park, in the hope of seeing them again?

Isabella felt a slow flush grow at the notion. Eilidh, though she must have seen it, thankfully made no comment, instead stopping to comment on some bonnets in the window of a milliner's shop.

Despite herself, Isabella had to agree that the straw bonnet with the blue-satin ribbon was particularly fetching and a moment later she found herself inside the shop with Eilidh, their brothers having resigned themselves to waiting outside. Afterwards, they wandered up to Piccadilly, the ladies stopping frequently to peruse shops and stalls, and Isabella making the astounding discovery that shopping in Eilidh's company was actually *enjoyable*.

She said as much and Eilidh gave her a puzzled look. 'But you are so fortunate to have all of these merchants and wares right on your doorstep. I must order unseen from Glasgow or Edinburgh, then wait for weeks or months for my purchases to arrive.'

'I suppose I take such things for granted, Miss Mac-Donald. Thank you for opening my eyes.' She gave a small laugh. 'I take no interest in matters of fashion and am not womanly enough for my sister-in-law.'

'But your gown! Your hair! You look delightful!'

Isabella shrugged. 'My maid, Sally, sees to such matters.' She smoothed her gown. 'Although I must admit to a little vanity at times. I do like this gown.'

'Our fashions in the Islands are a little different, I must admit.' Eilidh indicated her own gown. 'I shall be glad to see my new dresses on the morrow.' She glanced sideways at Isabella. 'Would you like to come with me to the dressmaker's in the morning?'

Normally any invitation that involved dressmakers and milliners would be anathema to Isabella. Yet she heard herself agreeing to Miss MacDonald's invitation without hesitation.

I like her. I like them both.

All too soon, it was time to part ways, Isabella regretfully informing the MacDonalds that she had social engagements to return to. 'But I shall call on you tomorrow, Miss MacDonald, if you can give me your direction?'

Mr MacDonald produced his card and as she took it from his hand their fingers touched. Even through her glove she felt again that strange tingle at his warmth. Looking down at the card to hide her confusion, she glanced at the details. 'Chesterfield Street. I know where that is.'

Angus had turned his attention to Max. 'Might I have a word with you?'

'Of course.'

They stepped to one side and Isabella's gaze met Eilidh's. At Isabella's questioning expression, Eilidh reported, in a confiding tone. 'I think he wishes to apologise for my tripping him up.'

Isabella rolled her eyes. 'Gentlemen suffer indignity very badly, do they not?'

Eilidh grinned. 'There is little difference, it seems, between gentlemen here and gentlemen back home in that regard.'

A few moments later they parted ways, Isabella surprised by a strong urge to look back for one last glimpse of the Scottish pair. Max, she noted, was unusually silent.

'Well?' Her tone was challenging.

'Well, what?'

'What is your opinion of Mr MacDonald and his sister?'

He shrugged. 'I have no opinion. They seem pleasant enough.'

'Pleasant? Is that all you have to say? When they are both so charming and attractive, and...*Scottish*?' He remained unmoved, so she pushed him further. 'Do you not think that Miss MacDonald is beautiful?' She eyed him slyly. 'I know you normally are very interested in noticing beautiful ladies.'

'I suppose she was fairly handsome.' His voice remained flat and she frowned.

Something is not quite right.

She tried another angle. 'What did you and Mr MacDonald speak about just now?'

He ran a hand through his hair. 'He apologised, and… he wishes to invite me for dinner later. At the Clarendon.'

Her heart leaped. Something within her wished very much for Max and Angus to become friends. 'And will you go?'

'I could not refuse. I wish I had.'

'Why?'

Abruptly, his terseness vanished, replaced by an outburst delivered in a tone of great frustration. ''Isabella, we know nothing about them. Who are they? Why are they in London? Do they have any proper connections? One must always be wary of soldiers of fortune and their allies. She may not even be his sister!'

Isabella snorted. 'Anyone can see from a mile away that they are brother and sister. They are very alike—just as we are.' She laid a hand on his arm and he stopped to face her. 'Max, I know you think me too trusting, but is it not possible that you are too *un*trusting?'

'Look…' he spread his hands wide '…I have agreed to meet him for a short dinner. I shall stay long enough for politeness, but I think it prudent to be cautious until we know more of them.'

Isabella bit her lip. Max, it seemed, would not be open to a suggestion that he might introduce the MacDonalds to society. Which was a great shame, since the only thing that might enliven the dullness of house calls and balls would be the presence of the fascinating Scottish siblings.

Drawing Angus's card from her reticule, she studied it more carefully than she had earlier. 'Max!'

'What is it?'

'He is not a nobody. He is a laird!'

'Let me see.' He took the card. 'The Much-Honoured

Angus MacDonald, Laird of Broch Clachan... Hmmm...
These Scottish titles may be very dubious, you know.'
His tone, however, was decidedly more neutral than
it had been a moment before. 'I shall consult Mr De-
brett's book and ask around for what may be known of
him and his title.'

He refused to speak of the matter further, but as
they walked towards the Burtenshaw town house, Isabella's heart leapt as she thought the matter through.
He is a laird! Surely that meant that, once introduced
by a suitable person like Max, the MacDonalds could
go out in society!

Quite why she found this so important, she could
not say. There were few people she found interesting,
even fewer whom she genuinely liked. Yet that could not
fully account for the strength of the hopes she held. She
shrugged, dismissing the matter. It was enough to even
hope for the *possibility* of seeing more of the Scottish
pair. Mr MacDonald had an opportunity to impress Max
tonight. Isabella prayed he would make the most of it.

Chapter Five

Angus drew a breath, resisting the impulse to straighten his jacket. From being Laird at home and knowing exactly what to do and how to behave in almost every situation, he was still feeling decidedly lost in London. Never had he seen such luxury as that displayed in the private dining room at the Clarendon Hotel.

The furniture and decor was in the French style and Angus could not help but worry that the delicate gilded legs of his chair might collapse beneath him. Being a head taller than most men was normally an asset—though perhaps not when it came to delicate, gilded chairs.

There is nothing wrong with being tall.

Reminding himself that the giants in the old tales were the heroes of the Celt, he adjured himself to be more like the heroic giant Fingal and stop behaving as though any nation could be better than Scotland.

The table was set for two, a liveried footman awaited the arrival of Angus's guest and the clock on the mantel still lacked ten minutes to nine. The sound of its ticking seemed amplified in the stillness of the private room. Perhaps it had been an error to arrive so early. Angus's determination not to be late had led him to arrive at the Clarendon a full half-hour in advance and so he had already been alone with his thoughts for twenty minutes.

Isabella.

Mr Wood had called his sister by her name earlier and Angus, even in the heat and confusion of the moment, had stored the information away carefully.

It is a good name.

Feminine, rather exotic, perhaps a little too delicate for a spirited lady who dared to run a race in a London park…

Iseabail.

The Gaelic version of her name was a better fit. It had the same beauty and femininity, but the sound and feel of it also hinted at her strength of character—a swish and swirl of energy and vitality… He shook himself. Instead of daydreaming of the beautiful Miss Wood, he should be planning how to ingratiate himself with her brother.

A murmur of voices in the hallway alerted him to his guest's arrival. As the door opened he was already rising, greeting the gentleman with a smile and an outstretched hand.

Mr Wood responded to his greeting with polite restraint and Angus noted the decided lack of enthusiasm.

I must go carefully, he told himself, stifling a grin as an image of a timid sheep came to mind—one that had to be shepherded carefully by man and dog working together. *Easy now*, he told himself, much in the same way as he would direct his sheepdogs.

When the footman enquired as to their preferred beverage, Angus ordered generously.

Alcohol might lubricate his stiffness.

'I declare,' he explained, 'I am determined to make the most of the opportunity to sample new wines during my visit here.'

'You are in town only for a short visit then?'

'I am.' He elaborated, feeling as though he had need to carry the conversation. 'A matter of business brought me here, but I mean to experience as much as I can of London while I am here. What would you recommend I do and see during my stay?'

Mr Wood shrugged. 'I know not where your interests lie. All life is here, from fencing and horse racing to cockfights and brothels.'

Angus grinned. 'Much as I fear being denounced as priggish, I have no interest in brothels, beyond a certain ghoulish curiosity. Cock fights are everywhere, but I should welcome an opportunity to practise my fencing—or even my pugilism.'

'I'd say you'd strip to advantage,' returned Mr Wood, eyeing Angus's frame.

'Likewise.' Angus's eyes gleamed. 'Think you could best me?'

Now there was a spark of interest from Mr Wood. 'Ha! I have no notion!'

The footman arrived with their first dishes. Angus refilled both his glass and Mr Wood's as the food was being served.

'This is delicious!' he declared into the silence.

'Yes, Jacquier was chef to Louis XVIII before he came here.'

'Indeed? I have not before tasted such delicate flavour. He is clearly a master of his trade.'

Now, will he say something cutting about Scotland? This is his opportunity...

But Mr Wood only nodded politely, turning the conversation to other hotels and clubs in London where one might procure what he termed 'a decent bite'. Angus, noticing that their glasses were again empty, refilled them.

After the second remove—escalope of veal with truffles, croquettes, white soup and lobster—Monsieur Jacquier himself deigned to visit them, to check that they had everything necessary for their comfort. Both Angus and Mr Wood chatted with him easily in fluent French and Angus could not help but wonder if Mr Wood was surprised at his own level of education. While that gentleman had made no pointed remarks, Angus had often heard of the disdain with which some Scots were treated by London society. Disdain that had been evident in Mr Inglis's treatment of him. He was entirely unused to feeling unsettled like this, but London with all its unwritten rules was entirely alien to him.

By the time the fourth set of dishes had been served and enjoyed, the air between the gentlemen had settled to something rather more tranquil. Angus was under no illusions as to the cause. Mr Wood remained wary of him, he believed, but the effect of the Clarendon's fine wines was potent. As he settled the account, he was aware that Mr Wood was taking the opportunity to scrutinise him, as he had on a number of occasions during the evening. Carefully, he avoided making of it an issue, knowing that the progress he had made so far was fragile.

Outside, the cool air hit him like a wave in the sea, causing him to rock slightly on his feet. Mr Wood, he noticed, was swaying gently in a similar manner. 'Now then, MacDonald,' he declared briskly, his speech ever so slightly slurred, 'the night is young. Where to next?'

'It is?' Angus was momentarily bewildered, before recalling the late return every night of his neighbour and the nightly activity of well-sprung carriages in the streets. Usually it was almost dawn before the noise settled, only to be replaced a half-hour later by milk carts and coal merchants beginning their daily rounds. 'It is!' He bowed with a flourish. 'I am at your command, Mr Wood. Show me London!'

Mr Wood grinned. 'Call me Max—and I know just the place!' He frowned, as if a thought had just occurred to him. 'Forgive me for raising such a delicate matter, but are you—er—under the hatches?'

'Under the—? Oh, no, I have plenty of blunt! Well...' Angus shrugged '...enough to get by. I should not like to waste my money foolishly.'

Mr Wood—Max—leaned forward to whisper in an exaggerated fashion, 'A little foolishness is the greatest treasure and worth more than gold. Trust me!'

Angus grinned. 'Very well. I shall be foolish for one night. Lead on!'

'That is the spirit! You know...' he clapped Angus on the shoulder '...perhaps you are a good sort of fellow, after all!'

'Angus. *Angus!*'

'Go away, Eilidh!' He groaned, suddenly conscious of his thumping head. 'Too early!'

He heard her tut in exasperation, then cross to the window. Blinding light filled the room, piercing his closed eyelids and arcing directly into his skull.

'You need to get up, Brother. For two reasons.'

He opened one eye. There she was, sitting primly in his armchair, hands resting neatly in her lap. Clearly, she had no intention of leaving him in peace.

'First,' she continued, 'I wish to hear all about your evening with Mr Wood.'

Sighing, he pushed himself up into a sitting position, throwing her a frustrated look. 'There is little to tell. We had dinner, then afterwards played cards at some sort of gaming club.'

Eilidh's eyes widened. 'Never say he took you to a gaming hell!' She straightened her shoulders. 'Tell me truthfully, how much did you lose?'

His eyes gleamed. 'My pocketbook is on the table.' He indicated it with a nod of the head.

She opened it, then turned to look at him in confusion. 'But where did all this money come from?'

He grinned. 'I won. I bate them all. You should trust me, you know. I am not as green as I am cabbage looking!'

She snorted. 'Aye, and a good thing too!' Her brow creased. 'But Lydia warned us how newcomers to London are brought to such places so they may be fleeced by Captain Sharps!' She swallowed. 'Did Mr Wood try to fleece you? Tell me honestly.'

'Of course not!'

She sagged in relief. 'Good.'

'Why so relieved?'

She looked down, suddenly busy smoothing the skirt of her gown. 'Mr Wood and his sister are our best option to be introduced into society. Our only option, in truth.' She looked directly at him. 'And I think I like them. I certainly like Miss Wood. I should not wish to discover that they are unworthy of our respect. But stop attempting to divert me, Angus. How did you defeat the cheats? Especially since you were undoubtedly drunk.'

'Drunk? I had had quite a fill of wine, it is true, but their wine is nothing to whisky. By the time we reached the gambling place my head was already starting to clear. Plus I had the sense to stay away from the faro and hazard tables and stick with whist and piquet.'

'Games we play in the Islands all through the dark winter evenings… I begin to understand. Then—you are well enough to wake up?'

He yawned. 'I have the headache, I must admit, but otherwise I feel well.' Frowning, he added, 'I do not like this business of staying out so late, or sleeping so late. It is unnatural!'

'Which may be precisely why the *ton* like it so much.'

'What is the second reason?'

'Pardon? Second reason?'

'You said there are two reasons why I must get up.'

Her brow cleared. 'Ah, yes. Miss Wood will be here in—' she glanced at the small clock on the mantel '—a little more than an hour. You will recall she agreed to accompany me to the dressmaker's today.'

'Of course!' At the very mention of Miss Wood, his heart had unaccountably quickened. 'Let us hope she does not require rescuing again!'

'Oh, I think, Brother, that you quite enjoy rescuing her!' With this, she rose and was gone before he could think of a suitable rejoinder.

Despite having less than four hours sleep, he left his bed with no regrets, suddenly finding a liveliness and vigour that had not been there even a few moments before.

Isabella stood outside the door to Number Eleven Chesterfield Street, her heart pounding and her hands feeling much too warm inside her kid gloves. Behind her, Sally waited patiently. She had made no comment about Isabella's continued—and entirely uncharacteristic—

interest in her appearance, but had spent longer than usual dressing her hair, and ensuring that her spencer was a perfect match for her pretty sprig-muslin gown. If she wondered why Isabella was taking such care for a visit to a dressmaker's with another young lady, she did not say.

The door opened and a few moments later Isabella was being led into an elegant drawing room, having been relieved of her bonnet, gloves and spencer by a polite maidservant. Sally left her there, having been invited below stairs for tea with the servants.

'Miss Wood!' Eilidh rose from her chair, both hands outstretched in welcome. 'My, how delightful you look!'

Isabella thanked her, blushing, and Eilidh let go of her hands, inviting her to sit.

'Now, should you prefer to go immediately, or shall we have tea first?'

'Tea would be delightful, thank you.'

Tea and a helping of your handsome brother, if you can arrange it.

Eilidh turned out to be every bit the gracious, welcoming hostess that Isabella had expected. Before long they were chatting in a relaxed way, including discussing their brothers' outing the night before.

'Max had not yet arisen when I left,' Isabella confessed, sipping her tea, 'so I have no information about where they went or how they might have enjoyed one another's company.'

'As to the latter I cannot say for sure. Men can be less than open about such matters. But when I saw Angus earlier, he seemed to me to have the air of a man who has enjoyed his evening.'

'I am glad to hear it. Where did they go, do you know?'

Eilidh told her, adding frankly, 'I admit I was concerned when he mentioned the gaming hell, for one of the horrors of London we were warned about was Captain Sharps who prey on newcomers, fleecing them of their cash with weighted dice and sleight of hand.'

Isabella put a hand to her mouth. 'Never say your brother lost heavily! If this was Max's doing, I declare I shall—'

'Oh, no, no! Please do not be concerned. Angus has no complaints about your brother. Indeed, he rose from the card tables with more in his pocketbook than when he began.'

'I am relieved to hear it.' There was a pause. 'Is your brother already out on an engagement?'

'No, he is still here. In fact—' she tilted her head, listening '—I believe I hear him approaching even now.'

Eilidh proved to be correct. A moment later, the door opened and there he was, in all his chestnut-haired glory. His smile made her heart skip, and that was nothing to what she felt when he bent over her gloveless hand. His lips were soft and warm against her skin and sent a delightful tingle through her whole body, making her stammer in confusion as she tried to answer his polite enquiry as to her well-being. As they all retook their seats Isabella thought she saw a fleeting look of concern on Eilidh's face, swiftly smoothed away.

Angus, on Isabella's query, regaled them both with an account of the dining experience at the Clarendon and how they had been honoured to meet the great man, Jacquier himself. 'I shall tell the tale for years to come back home,' he concluded, a twinkle in his eye.

'Aye, and I have no doubt it will be well embellished, too!' added Eilidh.

'I noticed on your card,' Isabella offered, 'that you are Laird of Broch Clachan. Am I pronouncing that correctly?'

Angus smiled, setting off an inconvenient burning sensation in Isabella's chest. 'It's actually pronounced like a soft "k" rather than the English "ch" sound. Brohh Clahhan,' he murmured, the sound halfway between a soft 'h' and a harder 'k'. Listening intently, Isabella was unsurprised when his words caused an actual shiver to run through her. There was some sort of magic in his voice, she was sure of it.

'I assume that is a place?' Thankfully, her voice sounded remarkably steady.

'Indeed. A broch is a tower—a round tower, specifically. It is very old. We honestly do not know how old. But it is home.'

'You live in a tower? How positively Gothic!'

He laughed at this and he and Eilidh went on to describe how their castle had been built around the tower, over many generations and hundreds of years. 'It seems to me,' he mused, his blue-grey eyes unfocused, 'that it grew out of the land. Of course people moved the stones and built it tall and safe, but it is *of* the island, somehow.'

'As the people are,' Eilidh added.

A lump formed in Isabella's throat. 'How wonderful! That you should feel such a connection to your home, I mean.'

'And you do not?'

'Not at all.' She laughed lightly. 'If I am honest, the only time I feel a sense of belonging is when I am out at sea. Although…' she thought for a moment '…certain *people* are important to me. Perhaps, in the end, that is what home means.'

'We are blessed, I think,' said Eilidh thoughtfully, 'for in the Islands the people and the place are one and the same.'

'Then…you could never settle to live outside Scotland?'

Both confirmed it and with clear conviction. 'Even Scotland would not be enough,' Angus offered. 'I would not live long away from the Islands, I think.'

Isabella nodded, understanding his words held great meaning.

There is no chance of him staying in England, then, even if he…liked me.

As to whether she could see herself leaving behind everything she knew to go and live so far away…no. It did not bear thinking about. The idea was too…*enormous* for a parlour tea with people she barely knew.

'Miss Wood.' Refocusing, she realised that Mr MacDonald was looking directly at her and there was something particularly focused about his gaze. 'There is something I should say to you.'

'Yes?' Suddenly breathless, she could not help fleetingly wonder if he would use just such a tone if he were making a declaration to a lady. Mentally, she shook herself. She had never in her life been fanciful.

What on earth is happening to me?

'I mentioned to you that we are here on a matter of business, to do with an estate we wish to buy from an English lord. In truth, he is refusing to even see us and—as I indicated previously—we need someone to introduce us to society so that we may consider how best to approach him.'

'Yes? You must forgive me, for I have never taken an interest in such matters. There are dozens and dozens of lords and I personally know only some of them. My brother Max would be much better placed to assist you.'

'No, you misunderstand me, Miss Wood. I am saying this not in an attempt to seek your assistance, but rather—' He broke off, running a hand through his hair. 'Well naturally, I would welcome your assistance, but that is not—'

Eilidh intervened. 'What my brother is attempting to say, in a remarkably incoherent way, is that we *like* you, Miss Wood. And we quite like your brother, too. And so our pursuing this acquaintance has as much to do with that, as the hope that you might advise us or assist us.'

They like me! He likes me!

The warm glow that had taken hold of Isabella's chest intensified at Eilidh's words.

'Yes!' Angus's eyes bored into hers. 'And I have been feeling increasingly uncomfortable with knowing how much we need an entry into society and how we deliberately walk in the parks and go to various public places in the hope of striking up friendships… But that is not…' He eyed her steadily. 'Whether or not you and your brother are able to assist us, I am glad to know you.'

All she could do was nod, for her throat was too tight to speak.

'Enough!' Eilidh stood, brushing down her skirts. 'Today is for simple pleasures, not business woes. We are going *shopping*, my dear!' She grinned and Isabella, rising, echoed it.

Mr MacDonald wished them well, adjuring his sister to not stint on finding treasures in the bazaars, shops and dressmakers' salons. He himself, he declared, would be visiting his tailor again later, to see if that worthy gentleman had been able to create suitable clothing for what he described as his 'Scottish frame'.

Isabella, who had been trying desperately not to stare at his tall, muscular frame and his exposed knees this past half-hour, merely smiled, gulping inwardly, but she said all that was proper in terms of their formal farewell.

He took Isabella's hand again and kissed it, making Eilidh roll her eyes, exclaiming, 'Yes, yes, Angus, but we must *go*! I am impatient to see what the dressmaker has done with my precious tartan cloth.'

'Perhaps I can meet you once your shopping is done,' he offered.

Naturally, Isabella acceded to this and on her recommendation they arranged an assignation in Gunter's for two hours hence. The very thought of seeing him again so soon made Isabella's innards flutter in excitement.

Five minutes later the ladies were outside in Chesterfield Street and walking to their destination via Curzon Street. Sally followed, chatting in low tones to Miss MacDonald's serving maid, Mary.

At the dressmaker's they were served tea and sweetmeats, while the dressmaker showed Eilidh the two gowns she had so far completed, as well as the progress she was making on three more. Eilidh tried them on and Isabella found herself genuinely engaged with matters such as whether the amber-coloured silk should be finished with a V-shaped or square neckline and whether the green velvet gown Eilidh had brought from Scotland for improvement should be completely remade or just altered a little.

In the end Eilidh, with Isabella's and the dressmaker's advice, decided to keep the sumptuous gown starkly unadorned, simply lifting the waistline in keeping with current fashions. Isabella found herself tempted by some divine cream-coloured silk and the dressmaker agreed to make her up a lace-trimmed gown, for which she would return for a fitting a few days hence.

As Eilidh disappeared behind the curtain to try on the first of her tartan gowns, Isabella took another sip of tea and allowed herself to remember Mr MacDonald kissing her hand. He had done it twice today and both times the same frisson of delight had tingled through her. His eyes had met hers in the same instant his lips had touched her hand and the combination had made her foolish heart pound, her pulse race, and her senses sing. Angus MacDonald. Even his name was to her exciting.

'Ooh!' Eilidh emerged from behind the privacy curtain and stepped up on to the low platform before the mirrors. Isabella's jaw dropped at the sight of her dress. The underdress was of tartan and the result was stunning. The predominant hue was green, crossed with narrow lines of white, black and red. The effect was dramatic, highlighting Eilidh's creamy skin and deep-red hair. 'Miss MacDonald, you look—you look *wonderful*!'

'Do call me Eilidh,' she replied, turning this way and that. 'Do you really think it suitable for London? It is not too much?'

'Too much! Never!'

'Thank you. They say a friend's eye is the best mirror and so I shall trust your judgement.' She stepped down, thanking the dressmaker. Ten minutes later they were on their way to the bazaar, where they bought gloves, stockings and ribbons, all the while talking, laughing, and building a stronger acquaintance.

Finally it was time for Gunter's. Mr MacDonald was already there and had secured a good table from whence it was possible to see and be seen while enjoying ices, conversation and the simple felicity of watching others. Isabella was seated directly opposite him and, once, her foot accidentally bumped against his beneath the table. She flinched in a way that seemed overdramatic even to herself and he frowned slightly.

I need to be calmer in his company.

The difficulty was that she had no idea how to achieve such a thing, for her mind, heart and body were anything but calm. Never had she experienced anything like it.

Isabella was able to introduce them to two of her acquaintances, Miss Bell and Miss Sandison which, given the MacDonalds' need to go out in society, was very satisfying to her. The young ladies' eyes gleamed with interest as they declared themselves pleased to make Mr and Miss MacDonald's acquaintance.

Hrmmph! They are not interested in Eilidh at all, just in...him!

'Thank you!' Eilidh leaned forward to utter her thanks in a low tone, as the ladies walked away. 'Perhaps we can yet make connections enough through this sort of casual encounter to achieve an introduction to Lord Burtenshaw!'

Isabella paused in shock, her spoon halfway to her lips. 'Lord—Lord *Burtenshaw*! Did you say Burtenshaw?'

'Yes. He is the man my brother needs to do business with.' She eyed Isabella dubiously, taking in her shocked reaction. 'Do you know him?'

'Know him? He is my own brother!'

Now it was the MacDonalds' turn to look shocked. 'Your brother Max is Lord Burtenshaw?' Mr MacDonald sounded astounded.

'No, not Max. My brother Freddy. He is the eldest.'

They all paused, simply looking at one another and allowing the information to register fully.

'Then…we knew the family name was Wood, but I did not dare to hope that you would be so intimately connected to him.' Mr MacDonald gave a short laugh. 'Being a MacDonald in Scotland, one grows tired of people asking if we are connected to some other random MacDonald from Edinburgh or Aberdeen or Inverness! I never dreamed…'

'But this is wonderful!' Eilidh's eyes gleamed with excitement. 'Do you know what it means?' They both continued to gaze at her. 'It gives me hope, for such a coincidence cannot be chance alone. Do you not think so?'

Her brother's jaw hardened. 'I am not one who believes in fate. We make our own luck in this world. However, I shall take the coincidence and welcome it.' He looked directly at Isabella. 'If your eldest brother is anything like you and Max, Miss Wood, then I would be very hopeful of a good outcome. I shall dare to hope that he will hear my case and consider my offer.'

Isabella grimaced. 'As to that, my brother Freddy is not at all like Max or me.'

'How so?' Eilidh set down her spoon, her ice seemingly forgotten.

'He is…' Isabella chose her words carefully, anxious not to disrespect Freddy. 'He takes his duties and responsibilities as head of the family very seriously. Max and I—we cannot know or understand the burdens he carries.'

'I see.' Eilidh's expression suggested she remained confused, despite her words. 'But he is a sensible man? A man of honour?'

'Of course! Indeed, the family's honour is one of his

preferred topics of conversation, particularly with regard to me and Max.' She clapped a hand to her mouth. 'I should not have said that. I do not wish to appear ungrateful. Max and I can enjoy ourselves in ways which Freddy, as Lord Burtenshaw, cannot.'

Mr MacDonald looked thoughtful. 'I understand that, being in a similar role in Broch Clachan. Our own *papaidh* raised me to understand the burdens and responsibilities I would one day carry. As Laird, I must be the first man into danger and the last man out of it. I must know of the needs and burdens of every person under my care and ensure their needs are met. I must carry the name and title with honour and pride, but not self-aggrandisement. It can indeed be a heavy burden.'

Isabella nodded dubiously. Mr MacDonald's notion of lairdship seemed more noble—and less self-important—than the lords of her acquaintance. Including, admittedly, Freddy.

'So your brother Max has no responsibilities?' Eilidh's question seemed light, but there was something behind it that Isabella could not quite fathom.

'No. As the second son he was raised to understand something of the responsibility, for fear something would happen to Freddy. But now that Freddy and his wife have sons, Max is…' She shrugged. 'There are many such young men in the *ton*. Without duties to attend to, they seek their amusement as best they can.'

'I see.'

Isabella frowned, hearing an edge in her tone. 'Max is a good person. It is not his fault that society has nothing for him.' Her gaze became unfocused. 'He feels it, I know.'

'And is your eldest brother in town?' Mr MacDonald's keen question brought them all back to the matter at hand.

'Not until next week, for he had matters of business to attend to at home. But Prudence—his wife—is here. She is my chaperon.' Even to her own ears, the final word sounded rather flat.

'So…may we call on you? Would that be reasonable?'

'I—yes!' She frowned. 'I do not see why not.' Yet inwardly, she felt a little apprehensive, not ever having had cause to consider such matters before.

Will Max say I should not have agreed to this?

'Splendid! When will you be at home?'

'Er…tomorrow. We are making calls today, so tomorrow I expect Prudence will have informed her acquaintances we can receive visitors.'

They parted soon after, Eilidh giving her a brief hug. Despite it being unexpected, it fitted the girl's warm spontaneity and made Isabella feel again that this attachment could only be good. Disappointingly, her brother did not this time kiss Isabella's hand, merely bowing and wishing her a good day. Determined not to read anything into it, Isabella found Sally and floated all the way home.

Chapter Six

'Leave it, Eilidh. I do know how to dress!' Angus spoke shortly, despite knowing his sister would refuse to listen.

'There!' She finished brushing invisible dust from his new jacket, worn with his usual MacDonald kilt, then turned for a final look at her own reflection. 'Very well. I think I could pass for a London lady—although there is no disguising your origins, Angus!'

'You have no need to pass for a London lady,' Angus growled. 'Remember, we are proud Scots.'

She snorted. 'Proud Scots with a need for approval from London's elite.'

'Our need is temporary, Eilidh. Once this business is done we are straight back to Benbecula.' She agreed with alacrity, reassuring him. The last thing he needed was for Eilidh to begin to like their life here, preening over dresses and whatnot. Ignoring the unsettling feeling that he, too, needed the reminder, he focused on the fact they were finally making a house call. And with the Burtenshaws, no less!

They travelled the short distance to the Burtenshaw town house by carriage, since apparently to walk would be unseemly. And yet Miss Wood had walked from her house to theirs when she had called yesterday. It was all too confusing. But taking a carriage for such a short journey? It made no sense. Yet another example of the empty purposelessness of many of the *ton*.

They think themselves better than us, yet would not walk the length of themselves, unless specifically 'promenading'.

Suppressing a shudder, he reminded himself once again of the matter at hand.

Mary, Eilidh's maid, had masterfully questioned Isabella's personal abigail and dutifully reported everything back. Had Miss Wood not revealed her kinship to Lord Burtenshaw at Gunter's, they would have discovered it through Mary as soon as they arrived back at their house.

While Sally, Miss Wood's maid, had refused to be drawn on her opinions of the Family, she was quite content to advise Mary on London customs, revealing as she did so some of the habits of Lord Burtenshaw and his family. His lady was apparently taking her responsibilities with great seriousness and intended to assist Miss Wood to choose a suitable husband, at which intelligence Angus's heart sank. Well, naturally she would be thinking of marrying. Why would she not?

The news that Miss Wood was Lord Burtenshaw's younger sister had been a shock. While he naturally welcomed the good fortune that they had managed to become acquainted with so close a connection, it sadly meant that he would have to cease his harmless flirtation with the young lady. One did not jeopardise so important a matter of business by antagonising the brother of a maiden.

Back home he had frequently had to intervene or adjudicate on matters involving a suitor and his beloved's disapproving kinsmen. To pursue Miss Wood now, even lightly or casually, would be foolhardy, given the importance of his mission to acquire the Lidistrome estate from her brother. The last thing he needed was to complicate matters.

And so, not without some regret, he had resolved to change his demeanour towards Miss Wood. No more flirting or hand-kissing or fevered dreams... The latter, to be fair, he could not fully control, and last night his thoughts had been particularly lively. Still, in the cool light of day he had confidence in his ability to treat her with nothing warmer than friendship. The task would not be easy, he knew, given the way in which something about her had called to him from the first. Still, he had to at least *try*.

Some adjustment to his own feelings might be required, he conceded. It had cost him a pang of regret not to kiss her hand on leaving Gunter's yesterday. Had there been disappointment in her eyes? No, probably not. A beauty like Miss Wood surely had many suitors. And she would likely choose from among them very soon, if the maid's chatter was to be believed.

His thoughts turned to her character. Both she and Max had impressed him with straightforward likeability. It was not their fault they lived in a time and place where they were condemned to be decorative rather than purposeful. Although Max was, he guessed, around his own age, he seemed younger—probably due to the fact he had no responsibilities.

Isabella seemed sensible and fairly grounded in reality. Neither of them were anything like the picture he had created in his head of the evil Lord Burtenshaw and his family. It gave him hope that Burtenshaw would be as sensible as his siblings. Still, he could not help feeling his shoulders stiffen a little as the carriage pulled up outside a large, four-storey town house. Within was Lady Burtenshaw. And Miss Wood.

Here we go.

'What on earth ails you, Isabella? You are as restless as a puppy! Come, sit. Our callers will begin arriving shortly.'

'Yes, Prudence.' Isabella sat, knowing exactly why she was restless. Would they come? How would Prudence respond to them? Her heart skipped as the footman opened the door, announcing their first visitors, then sank again as she realised it was only Mr Craven. She made polite conversation as Prudence poured the tea, trying to focus on what the man was saying. Something about the ball they had lately attended and which she could now barely remember.

'Oh, yes,' she offered generally. 'Such an entertaining evening!'

The footman reappeared and once again Isabella was doomed to disappointment. 'Mrs Sandison, Miss Sandison,' he announced, 'and Miss Bell.'

Stifling a surprised expression, for she was not particularly intimate with the young ladies, Isabella rose and greeted them politely. Prudence introduced Mr Craven to them and they all took their seats again.

The next ten minutes was spent enduring a rather stilted conversation, punctuated mainly by Mr Craven making himself acquainted with the young ladies. Prudence, naturally, was not best pleased, clearly cross that

a suitor she considered to belong to Isabella was showing an interest in other ladies. Isabella suppressed a
sigh, wishing, as she often did, that Prudence's thoughts
were not so clearly writ upon her face. Thankfully, the
footman reappeared and this time, finally, he was followed by a tall, handsome Highlander and his beautiful sister.

Despite her suddenly thunderous heart and racing
pulse, Isabella could not mistake the look of triumph
that passed between Miss Bell and Miss Sandison. Suddenly the reason for their presence became clear. And if
she were honest, Isabella could not blame them.

This time it was Isabella who made the introductions, being sure to give Mr MacDonald his full title
and honorific, which she had memorised from his card.
The young ladies' smiles became even broader and even
Prudence now had a gleam of interest in her eye.

Mr Craven, his eyes large and round as he took in
Miss MacDonald, stuttered as he attempted to state how
charmed he was to meet her and Isabella suppressed a
wry grimace.

*So much for his pursuit of me! He is as distracted as
a baby, his head turning to every new sight and sound.*

They all seated themselves again, Mr MacDonald
and his sister choosing a sofa near Prudence. The young
ladies lost no time in expressing how delightful it was to
see Mr MacDonald and Miss MacDonald again, leading
to Prudence developing a thoughtful look.

*Prudence believes them to be out in society, because
the ladies know them.*

She should probably correct her sister-in-law later,
yet she knew full well she had no intention of doing so.

Prudence ordered more tea, commenting about how

busy her little drawing room was today. Her pride was palpable, yet Isabella, who did not set much store in being popular, remained focused only on the Scottish pair.

I want them for myself, she thought fiercely, knowing her smile had become rather fixed as she watched the young ladies engage Mr MacDonald in animated conversation and Mr Craven attempt to flirt with Eilidh. *She is my friend, and he is...he is* mine, *for I knew him first!*

Surprised at both the intensity and direction of her feelings, Isabella chided herself inwardly. Why, she was no better than a child, fighting over who was best friends with whom. Reminding herself that she was a grown woman and sister to a viscount, she joined in the conversation. The young ladies, having discovered that the MacDonalds were new to London, were busy regaling them with a list of sights they must see and places they must go. Not to be outdone, Mr Craven, spontaneously, it seemed, invited them all to share his box at the theatre two nights hence, if they were not otherwise engaged. Mrs Sandison agreed instantly on behalf of herself and her daughter, while Miss Bell undertook to check with her mama if they would be free and the MacDonalds accepted the invitation with calm thanks.

They carry themselves well.

Isabella could not help a spurt of pride, as if she were personally responsible for her new friends' success.

Prudence, with all of the conservative shrewdness of her name, promised to check if she and Isabella were already engaged, saying that she would send a note to Mr Craven later in the day.

'Splendid, splendid,' he replied, rubbing his hands

together, then, as if suddenly remembering Isabella's existence, turned to her again, a speculative look in his eye. 'Are you much addicted to balls and soirées, Miss Wood?' He spread his hands wide. 'The delights of London are no doubt plentiful, but could you live in a quieter way, do you think?'

Instantly recalling what she had heard of Mr Craven's remote estate in Yorkshire, Isabella saw the trap before her. Still, she could only be honest. 'Balls and soirées are entertaining at the time, Mr Craven, but they are decidedly not essential to my life. Indeed, I am sadly unmoved by such things. Oh, I can enjoy a dance as much as any maiden, but if I were to learn on the morrow that I would never attend another ball, I believe I would not mourn the loss.'

Instantly, Miss Bell and Miss Sandison clamoured to disagree with her and to state that a London ball was surely the greatest of all experiences. Appealing to the MacDonalds for confirmation, they were shocked to hear that the Scottish pair had not yet experienced the felicity of a London ball or soirée, being only lately arrived in the city. Miss Bell, rather boldly, asked for Miss MacDonald's direction, promising to see if she could secure an invite to a soirée her mama was planning, while Mrs Sandison promised to write to them about her own event, planned for a few days hence.

Not long later, and careful not to overstay on their first visit, the MacDonalds rose to leave. They thanked Prudence, repeated how delightful it was to meet everyone, bowed and left. As the door closed behind them, a feeling of flatness came over Isabella. Glancing around, she saw it mirrored on the faces of both young ladies, and even Mr Craven. The MacDonalds had seemed to bring sunshine with their presence and dreariness when they departed. It was no surprise when the remaining visitors also left, just a few moments after the Laird and his sister.

'Well!' declared Prudence, almost as soon as the door had closed behind them. 'So many visitors!' Her eyes narrowed. 'Why should Miss Bell and her friend visit you? I have already told you that befriending other debutantes may risk you losing suitors and once again I am proven right.'

'What do you mean?'

'Both of them, flirting outrageously with Mr Craven and Mr MacDonald. In my day girls would never have behaved in such a forward way! Young ladies must flirt, naturally, but some subtlety would not go amiss!'

Isabella opened her mouth, then closed it again. The very notion of Prudence flirting in what she deemed a subtle manner was unthinkable.

Prudence straightened the lace on her left sleeve, then the right. 'Still, you can regain the ground you lost with him today at the theatre, Isabella.'

'Then—you mean for us to attend? I thought you said—'

Prudence patted her hair. 'Of course I intend to accept Mr Craven's invitation. There are many more opportunities for you to fix his interest in an intimate setting such as a theatre box than there are at any ball.' Her gaze became thoughtful. 'Plus there is the Scottish gentleman. These Scottish titles are not quite the thing but still, he may be worth considering.'

Stifling the surge of hope blazing within her at Prudence's words, Isabella could only reply, 'I do not believe he is on the hunt for a wife. I am informed they are in London on a matter of business.' She bit her lip. Given that the business matter involved Freddy, ought she not to have said anything? And besides, even a man not on the hunt for a wife might change his mind, if the notion took him.

Still, she needed to be careful. Prudence was altogether too direct regarding these matters. If Mr Mac-Donald were to take an interest in Isabella, it would likely happen gradually, and hopefully quietly. The last thing she needed was for Prudence to spoil things with bluntness.

'Ah. A pity. Still,' she added, echoing Isabella's thoughts, 'we should not discount him. Men have been known to change their minds.' With a dismissive wave of her hand, Prudence moved on to more pressing matters. 'As you know my husband is to arrive this afternoon and he will wish to see his sister looking her best. What gown are you planning to wear for dinner?'

Dinner was predictably tedious. Freddy was in fine form, looking forward to being out and about in London and seeking progress in what he deemed 'Isabella's quest for a husband'.

Trying not to flinch, she answered him in what she hoped was a measured tone, 'Freddy, it sounds vulgar when you say it like that. I am not following a quest of any kind. Rather, I am treating your request with seriousness. As Prudence will confirm, I am doing my best and am considering a number of different possibilities.' Ignoring his 'Splendid!', she pressed on. 'But I should warn you, Freddy, that so far none of them has proposed to me and I am not yet sure I would want any of them to do so!'

'Ah, the Season is barely begun, Isabella. Plenty of time to reel one in!'

Isabella closed her eyes briefly at his turn of phrase, while he guffawed loudly at his own wit. 'Prudence, give me the chatter, then. Who are the runners for my sister's hand?'

'Freddy, please…'

'Pfft! Such sensibilities, Isabella. And you should call me Frederick. Prudence?'

'There are, I believe, at least four clear possibilities and one outlier.' Isabella listened in deep discomfort as Prudence dispassionately outlined the situation and fortunes of Mr Craven, Lord Embury, Sir Geoffrey Barnstable, and Lord Welford. Interestingly, Sir Horace Lazenby—the man whose wealth was built from his plantations—was not mentioned.

Perhaps she understands my objections to him, after all.

A small victory, but one that meant much to her. She could not imagine living off the proceeds of slavery. After all, despising one's husband was not a good basis for a successful marriage.

'And the outlier?'

'A Scottish gentleman, who called upon us today, as did Mr Craven.'

Freddy was frowning. 'Scottish? Not ideal then.' He turned to Isabella. 'I encourage you, sister, choose a good English man. These Scots are barely civilised.'

Stung, she found herself protesting. 'How can you say such a thing about an entire race? Surely there are good and bad Englishmen and the same with the Scots?'

He harrumphed. 'The English do not rebel against their betters every five minutes. The Scots are wily.

They bide their time, but they will surely rise again, and attack us all with pitchforks and claymores! Jacobites, one and all!'

'Nonsense!'

'Ah, Isabella, you are so unworldly. If only you knew half of the things I do…' He tried to look mysterious, but managed only a sort of knowing pompousness. Even though he had spoken to her like this for years, Isabella found herself gritting her teeth. Continuing the argument would not help, she knew. It would only serve to bring Freddy into a more extreme state of mind and she desperately did not want him to say she *must* not choose any Scot as a husband.

Not that Mr MacDonald was a suitor of hers, anyway. Yes, there had been a certain warmth in his eyes at times, but she well knew not to refine too much on such things. And if he were a suitor…could she really leave behind all she had ever known to spend the rest of her days on a remote Scottish island?

She frowned in concentration, but struggled to imagine a change so dramatic, so fundamental. *So thrilling.* Unfortunately her mind had abruptly abandoned its focus on practical matters, instead presenting her with an image of herself as wife to the handsome Highlander, enjoying his kisses, his attention, and more…

'Pardon me? I was not attending.'

'I was saying,' Prudence repeated, 'that attending the theatre with two of your suitors on Friday will hopefully give you a better sense of them, Isabella.' She turned to her husband. 'Three young ladies, as well as Isabella, have also been invited to attend. She will have to make an effort to shine.'

Isabella paused, cutlery in hand. 'But I have no *wish*

to shine. I wish to get a better sense of them, yes, but not by playing flirtatious games!'

'Come, come, Isabella,' Freddy urged her in a paternal manner. 'There is no harm in a little innocent flirtation while finding a husband. Why, even my dear Prudence—' He glanced at his wife, whose visage looked as though it might have been carved from stone. 'Yes, well, perhaps better not to speak of that. Go to the theatre and make sure they know you are considering marriage. Sometimes gentlemen need a little encouragement. Is that not so, Prudence?'

Prudence agreed with him in a mild tone, then began speaking of her preparations for the Season. Dresses had been ordered, a dancing master engaged, and the house, having been spruced up over the winter, was now a credit to the family name. Thankfully, this diverted Freddy away from the topic of Isabella's marriage, at least for now.

Isabella, left once more to her own thoughts, was conscious that she was not in truth considering a number of possibilities, for her mind and heart was full of one man and him only. Angus MacDonald, Laird of Broch Clachan.

'Max! Are you to accompany us?' Isabella, in the act of donning her long evening cloak, abruptly realised that Max was wearing knee breeches, signalling his intention to go out in company tonight.

'Indeed, yes. I procured an invitation from Craven. I believe he was happy to have more of a balance of guests tonight.'

'I had wondered. In terms of gentlemen, there are but

three, with five—or possibly six—ladies, as I understand Mrs Bell may also accompany us to the theatre.'

He gave a short laugh. 'Some of my friends would consider me lucky, I suppose, with Miss Bell, Miss MacDonald and Miss Sandison to entertain! I suppose—' he eyed her keenly '—that Craven will attempt to monopolise your attention.'

'Well, I should hope I know not to let him! For I am no green debutante, ready to have her head turned by a smile or an empty compliment!'

'True.' He shook his head ruefully. 'Keep both feet on the ground and be ready to see the difference between gold and gilt. Mama raised us well in that regard. As did Cooper.' They exchanged a warm glance at this mention of the people who were so dear to them both, then he offered her his arm and they followed Prudence outside and into the carriage.

Fortuitously, they arrived at the Haymarket Theatre at the same time as the MacDonalds and Isabella's heart made a now entirely predictable leap on seeing the Laird, looking resplendent in a short evening jacket teamed with his usual kilt. She greeted them both with enthusiasm, conscious that Max's greeting seemed strangely stiff.

I had thought that he and Mr MacDonald had enjoyed their night out together.

Max had been uncharacteristically reticent about his evening with the tall Scot, leading Isabella to wonder if they might have got up to some or other mischief that night. Yet she knew from Eilidh they had simply played cards and got drunk—perfectly unexceptional activities for young gentlemen.

Max, Isabella knew, remained sceptical about the Scottish pair. He had been shocked when she had told him of their desire to buy land from Freddy, and was determined to discover if their proffered friendship was genuine, or whether they were simply cultivating a relationship with Freddy's siblings simply in order to gain an advantage in terms of their business matter. At the same time, she suspected he liked the MacDonalds just as much as she did, and so decided to simply ignore his scepticism in the hope it would disappear by itself.

Mr Craven had managed to secure a large box to the right of the stage, and Isabella was pleased to note that the two young ladies, along with Miss Bell's redoubtable mama and Mrs Sandison, had arrived ahead of them and claimed most of the chairs in the front row. She herself was much more comfortable in the hind row, where she felt less observed.

With a flourish, Mr Craven led Prudence to the last remaining front row seat, then indicated that he would seat himself in the centre of the hind row, with Isabella to one side and Eilidh to the other. Since siblings did not normally sit together, this meant that Max took the empty seat to Eilidh's right, while Mr MacDonald, to Isabella's delight, seated himself on her left. Along with the others, Isabella took a moment to look about her. The pit was almost full, the people there craning their necks to ogle at the ladies and gentlemen in the boxes.

Massive chandeliers hung from the ceiling and, together with the tall candles in the sconces, gave great light to the whole auditorium. The furnishings were rich and opulent—velvet hangings in the three tiers of boxes, and silk fabric on the chairs. It was all quite lovely and Isabella felt a thrill of anticipation at the evening ahead.

Tonight's play was an old one by Fletcher. It was called *Rule a Wife to Have a Wife*. Isabella, reading the title, prominently displayed on paper hangings around the walls, could not resist a sceptical comment. '*Rule* a Wife? I think not!'

Mr Craven was suddenly all ears. 'You do not believe a wife should submit to her husband, Miss Wood?'

'I certainly believe that the most felicitous marriages are those where neither the man nor the woman can be said to rule.' With a pang, she remembered her own parents. Her father, demanding, constantly criticising. Her mother, unhappy every time he was home. Mama had had some relief when he was away in London and of course after Papa had died of apoplexy the year Isabella turned nine. From then on Mama had blossomed into contentment, being no longer *ruled*. She had enjoyed eight years as a widow before a fever had carried her off, the winter before Isabella was due to make her debut.

Perhaps that is why I never valued the Season and its pleasures.

Even a year later, making her debut after her period of mourning had ended, Isabella had struggled to enjoy the balls and parties, forever wishing Mama was with her.

What would she think of my new Scottish friends?

'But it is the proper order of things for a man to be master in his own house,' protested Mr Craven. 'Mr MacDonald,' he appealed, 'surely you will support me on this?'

Isabella turned towards the Highlander, only then realising just how close his chair was to hers. Blue-grey eyes met hers and his were dancing with amusement. 'He can certainly be Master...'

Mr Craven smiled in satisfaction.

'…as long as his Lady is Mistress.' The smile faded on Mr Craven's face. 'I come from a long line of strong women, Mr Craven. Indeed, the Islands are full of them, as my sister can confirm. It does not make a man weak when women are strong, for they have a different kind of strength to us.'

'How so, Mr MacDonald? How does a woman's strength differ from a man's?' Isabella heard the question erupt from somewhere deep within her. This was important. How he saw women was…important.

Suddenly he was serious. Serious and breathtakingly close. 'A man can withstand physical pain—the pain of hard work, or wounds from battle—but a woman endures childbirth. A man may hide his fear on the eve of battle, but at least he can act. The women must hide their fear from the children and the old ones, while being strong enough to endure the waiting.' His eyes lost focus, as if another thought had occurred to him. 'Men fear ridicule and rejection, while women fear assault and violation.'

Mr Craven's jaw dropped. 'Surely, Sir, you do not intend to suggest that all men are capable of such—such abhorrent acts?'

'Not all men, no.' Mr MacDonald had refocused on Mr Craven and there was a teasing glint in his eye. 'But I'll wager those who feel the need to rule have the greater likelihood.'

Isabella, watching Mr Craven's reddening face with interest, also noted, behind their host, that Max was stifling laughter, while Eilidh looked displeased at her brother's inflammatory comments.

'I think,' she offered, her soft Scottish accent drawing Mr Craven's attention instantly, 'that where there is a meeting of minds, the notion of one ruling the other is less relevant. It is certainly true that men and ladies have different expectations put upon them. And yet I could not see myself choosing to marry a man who was too soft, for example. A man should be…manly.'

'What then, is your definition of "manliness", Miss MacDonald?' There was a tart edge to Max's tone as he asked the question. Eilidh turned to answer him, but Isabella could not hear what she said.

A few moments later the play began and Isabella soon found herself caught up in the farcical situation being played out on stage. A rich woman agreeing to marry as long as she could take lovers when she wished. A poor woman pretending to be rich, in order to trick a man into marrying her.

It is all very cynical. Does no one, even in plays, enjoy a truly harmonious union?

At the end of the first act Mr Craven presented them with the refreshments he had ordered. Isabella accompanied Eilidh to the ladies' retiring room and on the way back Eilidh confessed how much she was enjoying the evening. 'It is the first time I have been in so large a theatre,' she said with a smile.

'And my brother is being attentive towards you?'

At Isabella's words, a strange expression flitted across Eilidh's face. 'He is all kindness,' she replied neutrally. Isabella frowned, but before she could pursue the matter they had arrived back at their box. There they found Miss Bell, Miss Sandison, their mothers and Prudence being entertained by all three gentlemen, though it had to be said that Mr Craven, as host, seemed to be leading the conversation. Mr MacDonald looked to be listening intently, while Max's expression was strangely unreadable.

Something is bothering him.

They joined the group, passing an idle ten minutes with meaningless chatter. All the while Isabella was supremely conscious of the tall Scot. She was sure she had never seen anyone so handsome—apart from her own dear Max, of course, and he did not count, for he was her brother.

For the first time it occurred to her to wonder what he and Eilidh thought of each other. Reviewing the interactions she had observed, she was puzzled by the fact that she did not know. Was Max still suspicious of the MacDonalds? Had they told him yet that it was Freddy they wished to do business with? Before she had the chance to draw him aside, the second act was announced and they all took their seats again.

Chapter Seven

Yet again, the nearness of Mr MacDonald was consuming Isabella's thoughts, feelings and attention, so much so that she was finding it hard to focus on the play again. During a scene in which a maidservant played by a man, to the great hilarity of the audience, was contributing to the fanciful events unfolding, Isabella felt her fan suddenly slide off her knee from pure inattention on her part. She reached to catch it, only to discover that Mr MacDonald had done the same. She froze, discovering that their faces were inches apart.

'Good evening, Miss Wood,' he offered, his eyes dancing.

'Oh!' She straightened, her heart thumping so loudly she feared the entire box would hear it.

'Your fan.' He had leaned further towards her, his lips close to her ear, and the sound of his voice sent a tingle from the back of her neck all the way down her spine. It was the most curious sensation and one she had never before experienced.

She turned her head, a 'thank you' on her lips, but found that he was right there, so, so close, and she could not breathe with the wonder of it.

Wordlessly, she reached out for the fan, dropping her eyes to his strong hand holding it gently. His fingers touched hers as she took it and her eyes flew to his. Had he done that deliberately? Seeing the intent look there, she was certain he had.

He is flirting with me! Is he actually flirting with me?

Her eyes remained glued to the stage for the remainder of the act, although she was conscious of every movement he made. On her other side, Mr Craven twice tried to engage her in conversation, but she replied only briefly, seemingly caught up in the story being played out before them.

During the second break, Mr MacDonald departed for a few minutes—to the men's retiring room, she assumed—and when he returned it was to Miss Bell that he gave his attention. Isabella swallowed, responding to Mr Craven's conversation with what she hoped were sensible answers, but all the while she was feeling as low as she had earlier been in alt.

What a fool I am to allow a man I barely know to affect me so greatly!

Now, what would her mama say if she were here?

While Mama had died before Isabella was of an age for courtship, she had instilled in Isabella a sense of her own worth and value.

'Never forget, child, that you are the only Isabella Jane Margaret Wood in the entire world. No one else can ever be you. So be proud, but not haughty, calm, but not disdainful. Know yourself, your gifts and your flaws and do not allow anyone to make you feel worthless.'

Even then, Isabella had known that her mother's wisdom had come from years of pain. Somehow, Mama had found beauty within herself, despite Papa's harshness towards her, and she had tried her best to instil in Isabella a sense of sureness, of self-reliance, of belief in her worthiness. Drawing upon it now, Isabella forced herself to maintain an air of calm, as if it mattered not at all whom Mr MacDonald deigned to speak to. Yet when they sat again for the final act, Isabella was undone by a lone boy, singing a heartfelt plea in the centre of the stage.

'Could you but on me smile,' he pleaded, his clear sweet voice ringing around the theatre, 'but you appear so severe that, trembling with fear, my heart goes pit-a-pat, all the while.'

Her heart had certainly gone pit-a-pat for Mr MacDonald tonight and when he smiled at her it seemed fit to burst, but when he had turned his attention to another lady she had the lowering realisation that it *mattered* to her, that she wanted his eyes and his thoughts and his words to be focused on no one but her.

The boy sang on, wrenching emotion from her with every word. 'You make no reply, but look shy, and with a scornful eye kill me by your cruelty.'

Mr MacDonald had not been scornful towards her. Indeed she could hardly call it cruelty for him to share his attention with the others in their party, for it would be rude of him not to do so. But just the imagining of him being scornful towards her had tears starting in the back of her eyes.

What am I become? she wondered dazedly. Such imaginings had never happened to her before.

In truth, she had never even had a *tendre* for any young man before—no, not even in the heady days of her first triumphs as a debutante, when she had been the recipient of compliments and flowers, and even poetry. Yes, she had been flattered, but her equilibrium had remained in place—to the extent that she wondered at times if she even had a romantic heart at all. It now seemed that she had and it had announced its presence in her life like a thunderstorm.

Sensing him glancing in her direction, she schooled her features into neutrality, hoping that her distress was not showing. Thankfully, he did not question her, and by the time the play had come to its conclusion Isabella was ready once again to smile and make conversation and hide her fascination with Mr MacDonald. While seemingly in conversation with Mr Craven, who had suggested they wait for the pit to clear before making for their carriages, she could not help but overhear the Scot accept an invitation from Mrs Bell to the soirée she was hosting two days hence.

Miss Bell must have asked her to do it, as she said she would.

Gradually, the Scottish siblings were beginning to successfully make their way into polite society. Naturally, she was glad for them. They would certainly have a better chance to persuade Freddy if they impressed him socially to begin with.

Freddy, she mused, set much store by reputation and social niceties, and by the opinions of others. Max and Isabella had often commented in private that he frequently had no opinion on a topic until he had a chance to see what way the wind blew among his cronies. Despite this, his prejudices were myriad—Scotland and its people among them. The MacDonalds would need to tread carefully if they were to persuade him to sell the island estate to them.

'Max!' Before she even knew what she was about, she had called her brother.

Max, who had been lost in a reverie, gazing abstractedly across to where Miss Sandison and Miss MacDonald were conversing, turned to her. 'Well, Bella. Did you enjoy the play?'

She shrugged. 'It was entertaining, I suppose.' She lowered her voice. 'I am certainly enjoying the company of Mr MacDonald and his sister. Is there nothing we can do for them? You know how Freddy hates the Scots.'

'Hate is too strong a word. He was certainly fed a diet of anti-Scottish sentiment by our father. I remember Papa ranting at length about Jacobites and ingratitude, and the need to be ever watchful.'

She acknowledged this, but added, 'Still, someone should warn Mr MacDonald. Prepare him. Advise him.'

'By "someone", you mean me, I suppose?'

She nodded. 'Will you do it, Max? They are good people and Freddy can be so…mercurial when making decisions. It is nothing to any of us if Freddy sells this small estate. But it would mean much to the people there.'

Max sneered. 'Why should I put myself out for strangers? After all, I am nothing but a good-for-nothing layabout!'

Isabella recoiled, shocked by the vehemence in his tone. Rallying, she decided to push back on him. 'For goodness sake, Max! Stop being so self-critical. You know full well you are better than that. And here is your chance to do something that has meaning. Will you not take it?'

He had the grace to look rather chastened. 'I suppose…' His jaw hardened. 'But any such conversations will remain private to me and Angus only. No one is to know—particularly Mi—particularly our sisters. So you are not to ask me about it after tonight. Agreed?'

'Agreed. Thank you, Max.' She touched his arm. 'So when will you speak to him? Tonight? Tomorrow?'

He grimaced. 'You are too impatient, Isabella. I shall choose the time and place—' she opened her mouth as if to argue '—or I shall not do it at all!'

Clamping down on what she was about to say, Isabella contented herself with a nod of agreement.

Angus. The casual way in which Max had said his name had warmed her heart. She desperately wanted them to be friends, just as she and Eilidh were fast becoming friends.

Putting aside all thoughts of men, Isabella made her way across to Eilidh and Miss Sandison, joining in their conversation with easy grace. Was there a slight furrow on Eilidh's brow? Perhaps she had not liked the play. Or perhaps she had the headache. The theatre was stifling with candle smoke and the heat of so many people. Not wishing to embarrass her by quizzing her in front of Miss Sandison, she set out to distract her instead and soon had both ladies laughing at the remembered antics of the comical serving maid from the play.

Just a few minutes later Mr Craven announced the hallways were now reasonably clear and they all made their way downstairs and out to where the carriages awaited. He offered her his arm as if it were a great honour and she took it without comment, trying not to crane her neck to see whom Mr MacDonald had chosen to accompany outside. Mr Craven handed her directly into the carriage, making it impossible for anything but the briefest of waves to the rest of the party, as they, too, emerged into the cool night air.

Feeling far too disappointed at not having one final moment of conversation with Mr MacDonald, Isabella replied as best she could to Prudence's satisfied comments. Despite the presence of the other ladies, Isabella had, Prudence felt, handled the situation well, her coolness in contrast with what she described as the 'fawning' of Misses Bell and Sandison towards the gentlemen.

Isabella, feeling this was unjust, was immediately moved to defend the young ladies. 'Fawning? No! I did not see them fawning, Prudence. They were simply more interested in Mr Craven's opinions than I was.'

'I was coming to that. That was the one moment where I thought you let yourself down a little. You might do better to keep your ideas to yourself, Isabella. Gentlemen do not like opinionated women.'

Isabella snorted, stung. 'And I do not like gentlemen who do not like opinionated women, so we are at a standstill, it seems!'

Prudence remained serene. 'Mr MacDonald, it is true, did not seem to object to your ideas. But Mr Craven looked affronted.'

'He did, did he not?' Isabella's satisfied tone was, it seemed, too much for Prudence, who lapsed into silence.

As the carriage rumbled through the darkened streets, Isabella's thoughts returned to her last glimpse of Mr MacDonald. Having handed Miss Bell and her mother into their carriage, he had stood in shadow, seemingly waiting for Max to finish his conversation with Eilidh. Max had not requested a ride home with

Isabella and Prudence and Isabella guessed it would
be hours yet before her brother sought his bed. Despite
his hedonistic life, Isabella felt sure that Max, beneath
it all, was deeply unhappy. She sighed.

I do not know how to mend this.

Frowning, she stared sightlessly out of the carriage.
Why could circumstances not be straightforward? Between Freddy's insistence she marry this Season, an
unhappy brother and the arrival in her life of the Mac-
Donalds, she was sure she did not know one end from
the other.

'And so your brother may refuse to sell, simply because we are Scottish?'

Max took another sip of brandy, shrugging. 'Freddy
is entirely predictable in many ways.' He frowned. 'And
occasionally unpredictable.' He narrowed his eyes.
'What I can say is, tread carefully. Once he makes his
mind up, it is difficult to change it.'

They were seated in a comfortable corner of Max's
club, in the quiet part of the night. Max had signed
Angus in as his guest—a clear sign that Angus had his
approval. A boisterous group of young men had lately
departed and the clock had struck three times just now.
Finally, they were speaking of Angus's business.

It is the time of night for confidences.

'So, your advice?' Angus prompted.

Max shuffled uncomfortably. 'He is my brother. I
cannot advise you too strongly. But I see no harm in him
accepting a fair price for an estate that he has never even
visited.' He thought for a moment. 'He sets much store by
the views of the *ton* and I do believe he is more likely to
do business with an acquaintance rather than a stranger.'

Angus snorted. 'Then he is no different to anyone else in that regard!' He took a swallow of his own drink. 'Still, I am making some headway in terms of *ton* events. Eilidh and I were invited to the theatre tonight, we have Mrs Bell's soirée next, and after that, who knows?'

'Prudence—my brother's wife—might host a soirée or something this Season, for there is Isabella to be fired off. She may well invite you—' Max grinned briefly '—though not if you turn Isabella's head from her suitors!'

Angus's heart suddenly smashed a strong tattoo in his chest.

I can turn her head?

'And why should anyone think I would or could do that?'

Inwardly, his heart was soaring. Perhaps his instincts, the ones that told him Isabella was drawn to him just as much as he to her, were right. The usual conflicts raised their head once again. The need to be with Isabella, to see her, to touch her, to dream about her…and yet, the hard-headed knowledge that courting her was not sensible if he wanted to secure Lidistrome from her eldest brother. Head and heart were at war, leaving him torn inside.

'I know Prudence of old,' Max was saying. 'She can be tigerish in her pursuit of a goal and any barriers to it are dealt with ruthlessly. She may not yet be aware that you are not in town to find a wife. Once she is, expect yourself to be struck off her list and ruthlessly ignored. Her one aim this Season is to see poor Isabella leg-shackled!'

'*Poor* Isabella?' Angus managed to say. Abruptly, his mind was awhirl. 'She will be *forced* into marriage?'

Max grimaced again. 'I cannot imagine so. But they will pressure her, yes. Freddy has told her she must marry this year.'

'And if she does not? What then?'

'He will choose her husband himself.' He raised an eyebrow. 'You shake your head, but it is not as bad as it sounds. Isabella is more than ready to leave behind the life of a spinster, ready to be mistress of her own household.' He frowned. 'It is hard for her, living under Freddy and Prudence's eye. I at least have some freedom.' His mouth twisted. 'Such as it is.' He remained silent for a moment, then added, 'What of your own sister? Do you not have a duty to see her settled?'

Angus laughed shortly. 'Nay, she knows her own mind, our Eilidh. She will choose a husband when she wishes to, or remain unmarried if she prefers. It is of no matter to me, for I want only her happiness.'

'Yes. I see.' Max's expression was shuttered. 'That is very different to the expectations of Isabella. Freddy seems to take it as a personal slight that she is unmarried. I believe he thinks it reflects badly on our house and lineage.' There was a hint of bitterness in his final words.

'It is good to be proud of one's name, surely?' He smiled. 'We MacDonalds are known for fighting each other, until a common enemy unites us.'

'A common enemy? Like the English?'

'I was thinking more of the MacNeills or the Campbells. But, yes, oft times it has been Scot against English.' He paused. 'I bear no ill will towards individuals who have done no harm to me and mine.'

'I am happy to hear it!' There was a silence. 'I am

promised to Gentleman Jackson's tomorrow for some boxing practice. Should you like to join me?'

'I should and thank you.' He grinned. 'If only all our woes could be settled by fisticuffs, the world would be a better place!'

Two hours later, Angus made his way home in the pre-dawn light. Max was cautious with him yet, he felt it, but he was allowing a friendship to warily develop between them. Angus found himself pleased with developments and not simply because they might assist him to influence Lord Burtenshaw. No, he wanted this friendship for its own sake.

And for more contact with Isabella?

He stopped in the middle of crossing a quiet road, then resumed. Honesty forced him to acknowledge that he had, despite his best intentions, flirted again with Isabella at the theatre. Oh, he had done his best to resist her, forcing himself to converse with the others in their party, but in truth his attention had been directed to Isabella all of the time. His conscience was pricking at him.

What are you doing? There can be no future with her, and it would be unfair to lead her to believe in the possibility.

His thoughts drifted to his cousin Alasdair, whose first wife—not an islander—had been deeply unhappy. Engaging with marriageable females who were not from the Islands was pure foolhardiness. Plus Isabella was, he reminded himself ruthlessly, Lord Burtenshaw's sister.

Will she attend the soirée?

The thought randomly crossed his mind. Lord, he hoped so.

And therein was the problem. No matter how much he adjured himself to be cautious, how much he reminded himself of all of the reasons to keep a distance from her, his traitorous heart paid no heed whatsoever.

He took a breath, needing to find a way to reconcile his heart and his mind, for the conflict between the two was slowly driving him to madness.

If I do not take this too far, it need not interfere with business.

Yes, perhaps it had been unrealistic to expect himself to deny completely his attraction to Miss Wood. Perhaps the more sensible thing to do was to manage it, temper it, control it.

I can do that.

Feeling unaccountably better, he strode on, but now with a quickened step and a lighter heart.

Chapter Eight

Isabella could not recall all of the soirées she had attended, nor even hazard a guess as to their number. She did know, however, that she had not looked forward to one before in the way she was looking forward to this soirée. Having persuaded Prudence that it was better to attend than avoid Mrs Bell's event—for all of the gentlemen on Prudence's list were likely to be there—she found herself ready on time and eager to go. Once in the carriage, Prudence could not help commenting on her unusual punctuality and eagerness.

'I declare, Isabella, it is good to see you taking your quest for a husband with such seriousness and dedication. It is a serious matter and you are approaching it with much more good sense than I had anticipated.'

'Er…thank you.'

I do not deserve her praise, well-meaning as it is.

Isabella's eagerness had little to do with good sense and everything to do with a fiery *tendre* for a certain tall gentleman with a penchant for exposing his knees. Shaking herself out of her dreamy reflections when she heard a familiar name, she asked sharply, 'Cooper? Did you say Cooper?'

'Yes. My husband has summoned him to London. There is some trouble, I think.'

'Trouble? Does Freddy need Cooper's assistance with something? I cannot see how, for Cooper has rarely been to London. Surely the grooms or the footmen could assist with whatever the matter is?'

Prudence looked thoughtful. 'That's not it.' She shrugged. 'It is a matter for Lord Burtenshaw. We should not interfere.'

'And yet you were the one to mention it. Why?'

Prudence looked out of the window. 'I shall say nothing more on the matter.'

She would not be budged and, as the carriage stopped outside the Bell mansion, Isabella put it to the back of her mind. She could do nothing about it tonight, anyway.

They took their places in the receiving line, Mrs Bell greeting them graciously, her portly husband by her side. 'My daughter will be absolutely *delighted* that you are here, Miss Wood,' she gushed, her smile not quite reaching her eyes. 'You will find her in the salon.'

With a murmured 'thank you' they passed on and sure enough Miss Bell came to greet them in the salon. 'Lady Burtenshaw! Miss Wood! I am so happy to see you!'

They replied in kind, though perhaps without the same degree of enthusiasm, and Miss Bell ensured they were served with ratafia. 'We shall have some music later,' Miss Bell continued, a glint in her eye. 'May we count on you for a performance, Miss Wood?'

Isabella agreed, having played her piano pieces at

similar events on many occasions. She knew herself to be a decent musician, without being outstanding; it sufficed. Miss Bell, she recalled, fancied herself a songbird and had been known to sing for rather longer than her audience might have wished on occasions such as these. With the Bell family hosting tonight, Isabella foresaw that they might be destined to endure a ten-verse epic this evening and gritted her teeth at the prospect.

'Mr MacDonald and his sister have not yet arrived,' Miss Bell offered. 'I do hope they will manage to be here.'

'Oh, I believe they have every intention of attending,' said Isabella smoothly, unable to prevent a hint of studied confidence in her tone.

They are my friends, it said, *and I know of their plans.*

'I am glad. And what of Lord Burtenshaw?'

'He is committed to meeting friends at his club,' Prudence stated, 'but hopes to drop by later.'

'Splendid, splendid! Now, if you will excuse me...'

They all dipped a shallow curtsy, then Miss Bell was gone, leaving Prudence and Isabella free to mingle. The salon was rapidly filling and Isabella took in the guests with a single sweeping glance. All her suitors but one were here, along with the usual stalwarts of such events—those members of the *ton* most addicted to the social events of the Season.

What if he—what if they—do not come?

But no, this was exactly what Angus and Eilidh needed—the chance to mingle with the *ton*, the chance to meet Freddy in an environment where he might be disposed to approve of them. *They must come!*

As she moved through the room with Prudence, Isa-

bella's mind was only half on the empty conversations.
The more important part of her mind was thinking of
the Scottish pair and the response they might receive,
and how much she wished for them to be welcomed.
Her heart was fluttering with nerves for Angus and for
Eilidh—almost it felt as though she was with them, part
of them, wanting that acceptance. They needed it for
their matter of business. She needed it for…she knew
not what, exactly.

Friendship was all she could hope for, for Angus,
she reminded herself firmly, was not on the hunt for a
wife. Despite her own wishes on the matter—wishes
that she dared not even fully articulate—that was the
way of it and so she must ignore the pangs of pain that
went through her each time her mind recalled the hopelessness of it all.

Yet even friendship was something. In Angus and
Eilidh she sensed kindred souls—people she understood in some way. People who were not foreign to her,
as much of the *ton* was. She glanced around. There they
were, in their glitter and silk, laughing and chattering
as though the evening *mattered*.

While she was similarly uniformed, she did not belong. She was, had always been, an outsider here. Not
because anyone was unkind to her. But because they did
not understand her. She put no value in wealth and position, wanting only the freedom of the sky and the sea.

Am I ungrateful?

Better to be sister to a viscount and suffering the
ennui of Mrs Bell's salon than being born to poverty
and disadvantage… Yet the familiar litany had no power
to soothe her tonight. No, not with the MacDonalds
about to arrive.

* * *

Angus handed Eilidh down from the carriage, unsurprised to notice a slight tremble in her hand. They both understood that success tonight might have a significant impact on their quest to restore the Lidistrome lands to the Benbecula people. Max's words had given him much food for thought and he understood he would have to tread carefully with Lord Burtenshaw.

'All will be well,' he murmured in Gaelic, and she replied in the same vein. Both knew their assertions contained more bravado than belief, yet saying the words was just the shot of fire he needed in his veins to enable him to mount the steps to the open doorway of the Bell mansion.

In the hallway was their hostess, smiling and welcoming, and beside her, her husband. Greetings done, they were directed through to a large salon filled with people and Angus caught his breath. The value of the jewellery on display would feed the entire island for ten years or more, he estimated, again wondering why Lord Burtenshaw was so determined to hold on to a relatively small and low-value estate on the edge of the old world. His eyes swept around the room and he was conscious that he and Eilidh were attracting a great deal of attention from the other guests. There was even a brief lull in conversation as people turned to eye them.

'Mr MacDonald! Miss MacDonald!' It was Miss Bell. 'I am delighted to see you here!'

With a sense of relief, Angus lost himself in the familiar ritual of small talk and greetings, Eilidh also doing her part. By the time everyone had confirmed they were well and that the evening was indeed delightfully mild, and Eilidh and Miss Bell had complimented one another's gowns, conversations in the room had begun again, albeit with an air of interest—or specula- tion, perhaps, that had not been there before.

We are like strangers at a Gathering, he mused. *Peo- ple who are accustomed to the same faces might rea- sonably be more interested in outlanders.*

Taking another look about the room, he was glad to see Lady Burtenshaw seated near the piano with some other middle-aged matrons, which hopefully meant that somewhere—

There she is!

His heart leapt as he spotted the now familiar dark head of Miss Isabella Wood. She was currently talk- ing with Miss Sandison and so he was able to enjoy the beauty of her profile—that perfect little nose and long slender neck, an elegant white shoulder peeping above a lace-trimmed evening gown. His gut kicked at the sight of her, while, had he been a few years younger, another part of his anatomy might have threatened to embarrass him. Hastily he looked away, bringing his attention back to Miss Bell, who was asking if he or Ei- lidh might like to perform a musical piece later. Eilidh accepted on behalf of them both and Miss Bell called a footman to bring them drinks.

'Now,' she declared, all briskness. 'Let me introduce you to some of our other guests…' Leading them around the room, she performed numerous introductions and Angus was conscious of a feeling of relieved delight.

We have cleared the first fence!

He made himself amiable and affable, exchanging pleasantries with a range of titled and high-born ladies and gentlemen, while Eilidh charmed them all.

'What a pleasant young man!' he heard one dowager declare as they moved off. 'And the sister is quite the diamond!' He exchanged a quick glance with Eilidh and they shared a moment's devilment—he knew his sister's thoughts would be along the same lines.

They would not think me so pleasant if they saw me playing shinty, or working at the harvest!

Parlour-room conversations were all very well, but he could not imagine this being his only diversion. Hard labour and whisky shamed no man.

Eventually, they reached Lady Burtenshaw, who was all affability, introducing them to her companion Mrs Edgecombe, who declared cryptically, 'Ah, so you are the MacDonalds I have heard about!'

'Good things, I hope.' Eilidh twinkled and Mrs Edgecombe sent her a warm smile.

'Naturally!' She turned to Angus. 'Have you been to London before, Mr MacDonald?'

'No, this is our first visit.'

'Well, I do hope that Isabella will show you both around, as I understand you have struck up something of a friendship. You may wish to visit the Tower, or the Palace of Westminster perhaps?'

'Perhaps.' While he naturally welcomed the notion of outings with Isabella, he did not wish to put his new friends under any sort of obligation.

Liar! his brain told him. *You would take any opportunity to be near her.*

'And here is my brother-in-law come to join us,' said Lady Burtenshaw. 'Oh, and my husband!'

Lord Burtenshaw! Finally!

Eilidh stiffened a little beside him and Angus sent her a reassuring glance. 'We have met Mr Wood already,' he offered smoothly, 'though not Lord Burtenshaw.'

'Good evening!' It was Isabella and his heart skipped at least one beat at the sight of her so close by.

By the time they had exchanged greetings, the two men had joined them. 'Angus!' Max greeted him in a friendly way before turning to Eilidh. 'Miss Mac-Donald.'

'Mr Wood.'

Was there a coolness between them? Angus had no time to think, for Max was finally introducing him to Lord Burtenshaw. Shaking his hand, Angus was conscious of the hardship done by this man and his ancestors to generations of islanders, but adjured himself not to think of such things when he needed to win this battle with amiability, not fierceness.

And so he and Eilidh smiled and pleased and made pleasantries. Mrs Edgecombe repeated her suggestion of them seeing the sights of London and Isabella and Max agreed to bring them to see the Tower on the morrow.

They continued in a similar, friendly vein until supper was called. Isabella helped the conversation flow, as did Max, and Angus—though he could not be certain— quite thought that as an introduction it had not gone too badly. Lady Burtenshaw said little, but her companion Mrs Edgecombe was warm and amiable and so the conversation continued nicely. Lord Burtenshaw, while a little prosy, seemed perfectly reasonable and hope was beating strongly in Angus's chest. Maybe, just maybe, they might succeed!

After a few moments they were joined by two other gentlemen, who both made it clear from their demeanour that they were particularly interested in Miss Wood. One of them, the Honourable Mr Barnstable, was quite the buffoon, but the other, a sober gentleman introduced as Lord Welford, had a sort of quiet dignity that, Angus thought, might appeal to some women.

Watching carefully, he could not tell from Isabella's demeanour if she favoured the lord in any way. Was he imagining it, or was there a brittleness to her smile and her occasional comments? A brittleness that was absent when she conversed with himself and Eilidh in a relaxed way…

Recalling his conversation with Max about Isabella's oldest brother pressurising her into choosing a husband, he could not help but frown. It did not seem right to him that anyone could be forced to wed. And Isabella's happiness was becoming increasingly important to him.

He himself was aware of feeling some pressure in that regard—people always wanted to see the Laird 'settled'—but he was determined to not act hastily. His cousin Alasdair had married in haste, to Hester, a beautiful girl he had met in the ballrooms of Edinburgh. The marriage had not been a success, for Alasdair's new wife could not adapt to island life.

Angus grimaced internally. *No.* Best to think carefully and take his time. After Hester's death it had been years before Alasdair had finally remarried. Although his second wife, Lydia, had managed to adapt to life in the Hebrides, that did not mean it had been easy for her.

He glanced at Isabella again and a pang went through him at the notion that she would have to bear her wedding vows with stoicism rather than happiness. As if she sensed his regard her eyes turned to his and he felt that now familiar heart-skip.

'How are you after yesterday's pummelling, Angus?' Max had a teasing glint in his eye as he deliberately referenced the pounding Angus had received at Jackson's boxing club.

'Ha! Better than I expected and keen for a rematch! Once I become accustomed to your rules, I expect to acquit myself well.'

'Urgh, pugilism!' Isabella grimaced. 'Max, you have not changed since you were ten years old and getting Cooper to teach you how to punch better!'

Max was grinning. 'Cooper was the best teacher—and not just for boxing!'

'Yes, well, let us not speak of servants in company,' adjured their older brother, who turned the conversation to the weather, while Max and Isabella glanced at each other in a look that spoke of countless similar tellings-off.

Anxious not to seem over-eager, Angus spent some of the time at supper conversing with the Bell family and Miss Sandison, as well as other new acquaintances. Afterwards, the piano was opened up, a full-sized harp brought out from a corner and Mrs Bell asked them all to be seated in preparation for the musical performances.

Settling himself into a delicate chair near the window, Angus took the opportunity to survey the gathering. As the others began seating themselves he caught Isabella's eye and nodded her towards an empty chair nearby. As she approached he rose, moving the chair closer to his own. Thanking him, she sat gracefully, asking him if he was looking forward to the performances.

'Naturally. How could anyone dislike music?'

'There are some who find it uninspiring, or flat,' she replied, looking at him from under her lashes.

'You astonish me. For islanders, music is—it is vital and more than just entertainment. It is a thing of the soul, of the stars, of the land and its people.'

Her eyes were wide. 'You have a wonderful way of saying things.'

He shrugged. 'It is the truth. Singing, storytelling, and dancing to wild jigs and reels is an integral part of who we are as islanders. The winters are long and music is practised and performed through all the dark nights and short days.'

'And will you and your sister perform tonight?'

She was so close that he could smell her scent—a clean freshness that filled his senses and made him desperate to kiss her. Right here, right now, in this drawing room, in full view of all of London society. How would it be if he simply leaned forward and pressed his lips to hers?

The notion was preposterous of course. Aware of the danger, he forced himself to focus on her question. 'Probably. From a young age all island children take their turn at playing or singing, each according to their talents, and so by adulthood no one has to worry about performing. Not everyone has the same level of talent, but everyone contributes.'

'So music has an importance in the Islands that may be even more significant than here?'

'Since I do not know how important music is here, I cannot say.' He paused for a moment, adding thoughtfully, 'What I can share with you is some wisdom contained within old Gaelic words: *Thig crìoch air an t-saoghal, ach mairidh gaol is ceòl.*'

Her eyes widened. 'That sounds beautiful. What does it mean?'

'The world will end, but love and music will endure.'

She caught her breath as their gazes held and he felt the world shifting about him. Almost he felt as though he were drowning. Drowning in her eyes. Or perhaps she was his rescuer. Or his anchor.

The gentle sound of a harp pierced his consciousness, bringing him back to the present. Miss Bell had the honour of performing first, when ears and minds were fresh, and she did a creditable job—although her performance was rather extended. Afterwards came a stream of young ladies and one or two gentlemen, entertaining them with harp, piano and singing, each according to their preference.

Isabella played a complex piano piece by Mozart, but while Angus enjoyed the opportunity to gaze at her beauty, he sensed that her playing was lacking something. It was technically excellent, but she was not connecting to the music in the way that…that he *believed* she could. There was nothing of passion in her playing. Nothing of the rebelliousness he had sensed within her. No, she was every inch the demure, polished young lady of the *ton*.

Quite why this frustrated him, he was unsure. London society to him was beginning to feel like something of a prison—albeit a prison filled with wealth and excess, and a furious refusal to acknowledge the reality of the rules with which they had imprisoned themselves. Isabella, he sensed, was more aware than most of how society's strictures limited them, yet she had kept herself contained while playing.

'Well done!' he murmured as she retook her seat. 'You are clearly very accomplished.'

She shrugged. 'Thank you. At least my turn is done. Oh, look, your sister is next!'

He turned to see Eilidh beckoning him. 'Excuse me.'

As he rose, she asked him, 'Do you mean to perform also, or simply to turn pages for her?'

He twinkled at her, enjoying her teasing smile. 'Wait and see.'

After a brief conversation with Eilidh agreeing what they would sing, he took the seat at the piano. Softly he played while Eilidh sang Burns's 'Red, Red Rose', her voice clear and pure, causing a hush to fall over the assembled company. He needed no sheet music, for the tune was a favourite at home, and as she sang he closed his eyes briefly, almost imagining himself transported back to the Great Hall in the Broch, with the scent of peat smoke in the air and a glass of local whisky in front of him.

As the last notes faded into silence he waited. There it was—the pause as those listening took a collective breath before applauding.

'Delightful!'

'That was beautiful, my dear!'

'Wonderful!'

Eyeing the assembly, he was pleased to see smiles almost everywhere. Miss Bell looked a little put out, Isabella was clapping fervently, while—

Lord! Isabella's brothers, standing together near the fireplace, were wearing near-identical frowns. *What on earth—?*

Maintaining what he hoped was an unruffled demeanour, he exchanged places with Eilidh, who started playing the opening bars of another favourite from the Burns collection—'Ae Fond Kiss', the sad tale of parted lovers. He sang well, he knew, his voice true and free of artifice, and managed to get all the way through it while only looking at Isabella a couple of times.

Afterwards, amid the general clamour of congratulation and thanks, he made sure to look particularly towards that part of the room where Max stood with his brother. This time, Max was clapping politely, but Angus was almost sure he saw Lord Burtenshaw mutter the words 'What next, I wonder? "Scots Wha Hae"?'

He really does not like Scots—even when we sing and are merry. A wave of self-disgust went through him. *Am I betraying my heritage and my ancestors by appearing so compliant towards those who have nothing but disdain for us?*

If Burtenshaw was determined not to sell, regardless of how much Angus and Eilidh smiled, and pleased, then what was the point? Why was he bowing and scraping to the *ton*, to the very class that had oppressed his people? A surge of rage shuddered through him, cloaked in self-loathing.

Gritting his teeth, he silently answered his own question. The point was that, until such an outcome was certain, he had to try. Had to suppress his anger and play the role of pleasant visitor, compliant conquest, smiling house guest. Stifling a sigh, he returned his attention to the present and to the surprising acclaim with which his performance and Eilidh's had been received.

They are so used to fakery that they could not resist being moved by a heartfelt performance, even though Eilidh and I are far from being the most talented of our people.

Despite the pleas of many, Angus and Eilidh refused to perform again, making their way back to their seats amid general fêting. Conscious that Isabella had been among the most enthusiastic of listeners, he yet could not prevent an almost boyish hope that she had enjoyed his performance. At the same time, given Lord Burtenshaw's disapproval, the last thing he needed was to annoy the man further by flirting with his sister.

He could be watching me this very instant.

And so it was with simple politeness in his demeanour that he enquired as to whether he could procure her another lemonade.

'Oh, no, but thank you,' she returned, almost shyly.

They had no time for more, for Mrs Bell herself performed next, playing a delightful piece on the harp with great dexterity. When she finished she declared the musicale at an end and advised that her servants would now set up card tables for anyone who wished to play.

Cards? Perhaps he could manage to get himself included on Lord Burtenshaw's table… *Lord!* Stepping outside events for a moment, he was conscious of the level of agitation in his mind.

Tonight really mattered. He and Eilidh had invested heavily in their venture—not just in terms of money, but also effort and planning, and sheer *hope*. They carried not just their own hopes, but the hopes of all the islanders on their shoulders. He needed to remain focused on their task and less distracted by a beautiful woman.

Easier said than done was the thought that followed, but somehow he had to succeed. Isabella could not be for him. Despite the mysterious attachment that had seemed to bond him to her, despite the intensity with which his body and his heart responded to her, he somehow had to find the strength within to focus on the task at hand. Playing cards with a group of gentlemen—

particularly if he could worm his way on to Lord Burtenshaw's table—was exactly what he needed just now.

Isabella had been deeply moved by Eilidh and Angus's performances, which had unsettled her in ways she could only dimly understand. 'That music was wonderful,' she murmured as servants swooped in to remove the harp and piano stool and as people began rising to allow the footmen to move furniture. 'Robert Burns, I think?'

'Yes, indeed. Our bard and very proud we are of him.'

'I do not know those pieces to play, for I was encouraged to play only classics while I was a girl.'

'I would argue that the pieces written and collected by Burns are just as superior as anything by Beethoven or Handel.'

He sent her a piercing look—one that went all the way to her toes and left her breathless.

How does he do that?

'And now?'

'Now?' She had quite lost track of the conversation.

'Now that you are a woman, do you have more freedom to make your own choices?' He was eyeing her intently, as though her answer truly mattered to him in some way.

She shrugged. 'In unimportant matters, yes. I may choose what music to play, I suppose, and which dress to wear—from limited options—or whether to walk in the park, or what to eat at dinner time. But I have not got the choices or the freedom that men have. You may choose where to live and whom to marry, and even *whether* to marry.'

And there is no changing it. Like every other young lady, I must accept reality.

Grimacing, she added, 'As long as you can afford it.' She cocked her head on one side, as a horrifying thought occurred to her. 'All this time I have been assuming you are unwed—probably because your sister accompanies you. It is entirely possible that you may have a wife and a clutch of children at home, yet still enjoy the freedom to travel to London. Gentlemen have freedoms that ladies do not.'

He chuckled. 'There is no wife or children and my sister does her best to curtail my freedoms. But I should not jest about such matters, for I see that you are in earnest.' He frowned. 'It just seems strange to me that ladies are so restricted here. It is aimed at more than simple protection, is it not?'

She considered this, conscious of an overwhelming sense of relief at the knowledge he was unwed. 'Some of it is undoubtedly rooted in a genuine concern for my— for women's well-being. But it is also, according to my brother Freddy, about how a family is perceived. It is a performance, in a sense.' Her eyes widened. 'Performance! That is what struck me about your singing, and Eilidh's. You were not *performing* in the usual sense.'

His brow creased. 'Oh? It certainly felt like we were performing.'

'Well, of course you were, but not—oh, dear, I am not explaining this very well.' She thought for a moment, then tried again. 'Despite the fact that your piano playing was excellent and that you both have good voices, it seemed as though your intention or your *object* perhaps was not to perform for the sake of it.'

'I think I understand you,' he said slowly, 'and I am pleased that you, like me, sensed a different approach from myself and Eilidh to the performing.' He thought for a moment, as if searching for the right words, and she revelled in the moment, in the opportunity to simply *observe* him intently.

'We wanted to tell the story of the songs,' he continued, 'to allow the words and the music to touch people.' He shrugged. 'That is how it is done at home. Sometimes the most polished singer has less impact than another who may not hit all of the notes perfectly, but who allows those listening to *feel* the music and the words.'

'Yes! That is it, precisely!'

He hesitated, then asked, 'Did you *feel* the Mozart piece as you were playing it earlier?'

Her eyes widened as his words struck true. 'No, not at all.'

'Yet I could still admire your skill and talent as you played. Performance has its place. And tonight, I did feel as though I was "performing"—much more than usual, for we are among strangers, including one in particular whom we would wish to form a positive impression of us.'

'Not all strangers, surely?' she asked softly, holding her breath while she awaited his answer.

He flashed her a brief smile. 'Strangers and a few friends.' At this, Mrs Bell arrived to take him off for cards, and Isabella was left with hope burning in her heart and his words ringing in her ears. Yet as quickly as it had started the flame died within her, leaving confusion in its place. *Friends.* It was precisely what she had wanted—to be his friend, was it not? His and Eilidh's? Why then, did she feel so...empty?

* * *

Friends. As he allowed Mrs Bell to lead him towards the card tables, discreetly requesting that he be placed with Lord Burtenshaw, his own word had lingered in his mind. Isabella and her brother seemed like friends in a sense, and yet…

'With Lord Burtenshaw?' Mrs Bell glanced towards Isabella, a knowing expression on her face. 'I see.'

'There is a matter of business I mean to discuss with him,' Angus replied firmly, 'and so I should like to make his acquaintance first.'

'Of course,' she responded smoothly, but he could tell she had her own opinion about his intentions. *Damnation!* Now he was drawing the worst sort of attention to Isabella. He had little doubt that Mrs Bell had assumed he was one of Isabella's suitors. Her many suitors. It would be unhelpful for Lord Burtenshaw to see him in that way, for it called for the man to judge him. No, it was best if he remained unremarkable to Lord Burtenshaw. Surely that would give him the best opportunity for persuasion? Once again he reminded himself of the wisdom of the Islands.

One does not attempt to do business with a man at the same time as courting his sister.

Complications complicated business and everyone knew it.

Mrs Bell, to her credit, placed Angus at the corner table, along with Lord Burtenshaw, Max and the Honourable Mr Barnstable—'Call me Geoffrey!' They settled down to play and before long it became obvious that the Honourable Geoffrey had some ploy in mind.

He spent the entire time flattering Lord Burtenshaw with insincere comments about his card-playing skill—

comments which were as undeserved as they were false, for it emerged that Lord Burtenshaw had little talent for cards. As the night progressed and they played hand after hand while Mrs Bell's footmen kept them well-lubricated with good wine, gradually all four gentlemen became a little easier, a little less formal. *In vino veritas*, the old saying went, and while it could not be said that all four gentlemen showed their hand, during the course of the evening Angus certainly formed more of an opinion about the others. Barnstable was little more than an *amadan*, courting Burtenshaw with the clear intention of winning his sister. He alternated praise for Burtenshaw's prowess at cards with praise for Isabella's beauty, demeanour and spirit.

'Her spirit?' Max, it seemed, had heard enough. 'You know nothing of my sister's spirit!'

'I know her to have more liveliness and quickness than many of the other young ladies,' retorted Geoffrey.

'I must declare,' interjected Burtenshaw, somewhat ponderously, 'that if there is a suitor who has seen our sister's liveliness and is not dissuaded, then he may be just the man for her!' Guffawing at his own witticism, he seemed not to care that his comment was decidedly unflattering towards Isabella.

Max's expression made it plain he did not agree with his brother, but knew better than to prolong the argument in company. Geoffrey, naturally, was looking delighted and Angus squirmed uncomfortably.

Does Lord Burtenshaw genuinely see Isabella's liveliness as an impediment? How could he?

And would the man genuinely pair her with a fool like Geoffrey?

If Isabella dislikes him, no good brother would force

such a marriage, he mused, as Geoffrey apologised for belching.

The notion was unthinkable. And yet Burtenshaw did seem to be enjoying the man's flattery.

His thoughts turned to his own purpose.

If I were better at deceit I would do the same—not to win Isabella's hand, but to win an agreement to recover the lost land.

Yet Angus could not. It was enough that he and Eilidh were involved in this charade of pretending to enjoy life in the *ton*. He could not force himself to drip empty compliments to Burtenshaw, who was revealing himself to be lacking in discernment, unimaginative, and decidedly pompous. Not someone whose company Angus would normally seek—and a decided contrast to his lively, quick-witted brother and sister.

Not for the first time, his gaze sought out Isabella. There she was, talking in an animated way with someone, and looking so dashed beautiful that he was forced to look away again. She was becoming something of an obsession with him and he did not like it one bit.

Chapter Nine

Isabella and Eilidh moved around the party, sometimes together, sometimes apart, speaking with acquaintances and meeting new ones, while the gentlemen—and some ladies—enjoyed cards at the various baize-covered tables Mrs Bell had had placed around the room. Eventually, however, they gave up any pretence and just went about the party together, with Isabella delighted to have her friend's company. Daringly, she said so aloud. 'I am so happy to have you here, Eilidh. Without you and your brother, this evening would be so dull!'

Eilidh looked at her curiously. 'Is there no one here whose company you enjoy?'

'Well, there is Max, naturally—although he does not usually stay very long at these sorts of events. There is a…a restlessness within him, particularly in London.'

'Then outside London he is different?'

'He is more settled, yes.' She thought for a moment. 'Like me, he is happier in the countryside, or out at sea. Does that seem strange?'

'Not to me, for *this* is what is strange. It looks a little like a Gathering such as we have at home, but the air is altogether different.'

They shared a glance of mutual understanding, then Isabella exclaimed. 'Oh! There is someone else here for whom I have a great liking. Mrs Edgecombe, who was my mama's dearest friend. You met her earlier, remember? Shall we go and speak to her, for I see she is alone at present?'

Eilidh agreed and together they sat with Mrs Edgecombe, chatting for more than half an hour. She was as warm and as sensible as ever and Isabella was pleased to see that she seemed to approve of Eilidh.

'So, Isabella,' Mrs Edgecombe asked with a knowing smile, 'I am glad to see that you managed to find your friends and that they are here tonight.'

A slow flush began to build on Isabella's face, but she decided to brazen it out. 'It is wonderful to have them here tonight. We also went to the theatre together on Friday, as part of Mr Craven's party.'

'You did?' She glanced across to where Mr Craven was conversing with Miss Bell. 'Mr Craven seems a very worthy gentleman.'

'Worthy. A good word.' She grimaced.

'He is not to your liking?'

'I like him well enough, I suppose.'

'But you do not *like* him.'

'I—no. No, I do not.' She sighed. 'Which is a pity, for I cannot say what is wrong with him. He is everything that is…worthy.'

'Is there anyone that you *do* like, Isabella?' Placing a hand on Isabella's arm, she added, 'I do not mean to pry, my dear, but I think your mother would want for me to watch out for you.'

Isabella felt mortification flow through her. Eilidh was right there and listening to every word, and so she could not be open with Mrs Edgecombe. 'None of my suitors are particularly inspiring,' she replied carefully.

And Angus is not one of my suitors, more's the pity.

'Your taste runs elsewhere? You are your mother's daughter in that regard.'

'What do you mean?'

Mrs Edgecombe leaned closer. 'Your mother, despite doing her best to comply with society's strictures, was something of a rebel—a trait that was not appreciated by her husband.'

Isabella considered this. Her memories of Mama had been gained through the eyes of a child, but Mrs Edgecombe's words made her view them through an adult lens. 'No. I see that. I remember them arguing when Mama refused to travel to London for the Season. Papa went without her after that.' Parallels with her own situation were clear to her. 'Freddy is very like Papa, I think.'

'Like peas in a pod—in looks as well as character. Freddy has your mama's eyes, but in every other aspect he is his father's son. You and Max were your mother's children, and your papa had eyes only for his heir.'

Swallowing, Isabella acknowledged the hit. She and Max had indeed been Mama's children, while Freddy had been Papa's. Why had she never thought about it in that way before? And Papa had encouraged Freddy in all his small-minded pompousness.

Aloud, she said only, 'It is true! Papa's portrait could well be Freddy in old-fashioned clothing—apart from the eyes. We all have Mama's dark eyes. People always used to comment about how alike Papa and Freddy were. They have never said that about Max and me.'

'You both favour your mother.' Mrs Edgecombe took her hand. 'She would be proud of the young woman you have become, Isabella.'

'Thank you.' Isabella's throat was suddenly tight with emotion. To her great relief Mrs Edgecombe then turned her attention to Eilidh.

'I assume since your brother is Laird that your father is gone, but is your mother yet living, Miss Mac-Donald?'

'No. She is also deceased. Miss Wood and I have this in common.'

'And what brings you to London? Are you on the catch for a husband, perhaps?'

'Oh, no! I do not think of marriage—I have plenty of time for such things in future.'

'Then, has the Laird come in search of a suitable lady?' Mrs Edgecombe's eyes twinkled with humour and Isabella felt heat flood her face again.

'Lord, no! I expect when the time comes that he will marry a girl from the Islands. He definitely has no such intentions here.' Eilidh glanced at Isabella as she spoke and Isabella's breath froze in her throat. In the kindest possible way, Eilidh was trying to warn her against developing any hopes or expectations. A cold knife seemed to pierce Isabella's heart.

I think it is already too late for me.

Half-listening as Eilidh spoke of Angus having business matters to deal with in London and their expectation that they would only be in town for a couple of months at most, Isabella felt a cold dread seep through her. While she had been trying to tell herself that Angus was not here to find a wife, she had nevertheless dared to hope that something might happen between them. To hear from his sister that he would marry an islander felt like a blow to the gut.

And soon they both would be gone. Not only had she been indulging in foolish daydreams about Angus, even Eilidh's friendship would soon be lost to her.

And when they are gone and Freddy makes me choose a husband, my misery will be complete.

The months and years ahead were laid out before her in a cold, dreary plain of emptiness and at this moment she saw no hope for happiness. None.

Max sent Angus a knowing look as the Honourable Geoffrey once again praised Burtenshaw for playing a good card, even though the man would have been better playing it in the previous round. Burtenshaw's lack of insight meant that he seemed to genuinely believe himself to be a skilful player. It was absurd and entirely risible, yet naturally Angus could not even hint at his feelings on the matter. Instead he responded to Max with a quick glance, unwilling to risk being caught laughing at their two companions, although the situation was becoming more preposterous by the minute. It being a social gathering they were playing for penny points—which was just as well, as Burtenshaw would have otherwise lost heavily. Angus had taken to deliberately playing bad cards at times, in order to make Burtenshaw's limitations less obvious. Naturally, Max knew full well what he was doing and it seemed to cause him great hilarity.

Max took another sip of wine. 'So, Angus, shall we

return to Gentleman Jack's on the morrow, so you can try your hand at besting me again?'

'Yes, why not? We can go before accompanying the ladies to the Tower.' Angus grinned. 'I am keen to learn more of the "science" of pugilism as practised in London—if only to defeat you, Max!'

'Ah, boxing!' The Honourable Geoffrey sighed. 'I was a reasonable fighter in my day. What of you, Plank? Did you enjoy a round of fisticuffs in your youth?'

'I am not yet in my dotage, Geoffrey! And I do not like to be called Plank,' Burtenshaw retorted. 'But since you ask, such vices have never interested me. I leave such activities to men like my brother.'

'What do you mean by that?' There was a martial light in Max's eye.

Burtenshaw sniffed. 'Simply that I have more weighty matters with which to fill my time.' He sighed. 'The life of a second son must be truly blessed. They know not the burdens we carry.' It was unclear whom he included in the 'we', which was uttered in a sad, almost mystical tone.

Max was in no mood to let this pass, it seemed. 'Angus has time for boxing, yet he is head of his family and Laird of—what is the name of your place, Angus?'

'Broch Clachan,' Angus muttered, wanting no part of their debate.

Burtenshaw raised an eyebrow. 'A Scottish title? Not at all the same thing, Max. As Papa always said, the Scots are half-civilised at best—and that only because of English influence. The Burtenshaw line is long and noble and its preservation and continuation rests with me.'

Gritting his teeth, Angus saw Max's knuckles were

white with anger—entirely understandable anger. Burtenshaw's disdain for his younger brother could not have been clearer. His disdain for Scotland was equally evident. If anyone dared utter such nonsense north of the border, they would soon discover the severity of their error.

Here, though, Burtenshaw was in his own lair and was clearly so convinced of his being right that it perhaps did not occur to him that others might disagree with his views. He also had clearly been raised with a different view on what constituted simple good manners.

So, biting down on possible responses ranging from a long treatise on how much more civilised Scotland was in contrast to the marauding Angles and Saxons, to hitting Burtenshaw a satisfying punch in the nose, thereby proving the man's assertion, Angus simply sipped his wine and pretended not to have heard the man's insult.

'And now you plan to marry off your sister, eh, Burtenshaw?' The Honourable Geoffrey, showing a severe lack of judgement, decided this was a good moment to press his case. 'What are you looking for in a suitor for her, eh?'

Burtenshaw lifted his chin. 'Someone of impeccable breeding. A family who deserve to be aligned with mine.'

'Ah! Well, you may look no further. The Barnstables came with the Conqueror, you know!'

A gleam of interest lit Burtenshaw's eye. 'They did?'

As Barnstable began listing his noble connections—throwing into his litany the fact that Henry VIII was reputed to have spent a night at their country estate, Max and Angus exchanged a look of disgust. Was Burtenshaw genuinely considering this buffoon as a suitable husband for Isabella? Why, anyone could see how unsuited they were.

'One last hand, gentlemen?' Max, seemingly barely able to disguise his anger and frustration, drew an end to their playing. The last round was blessedly brief and Angus rose from the table relieved to have survived the encounter without speaking plainly or thumping anyone.

'Such a pity we cannot play on!' The Honourable Geoffrey was displaying a petulant look. His face cleared. 'Ah, gentlemen, I have it! I shall host an evening of cards at my house this Season. Next month, perhaps. Will you all come?'

They agreed and Geoffrey undertook to write to them with the details. Angus almost had to force himself to accept, for all his instincts wanted to be as far away as possible from both Geoffrey and Lord Burtenshaw, neither of whom had impressed him. But he must not forget his quest and being in Lord Barnstable's company suited his purpose.

In his mind's eye he could envision MacDonalds of old, being required to show bravery and persistence in adversity. The card table was a different form of battlefield and navigating the *ton* a different form of warfare, but the qualities required of Angus were simply more subtle versions of those needed to triumph in battle. Fortitude. Courage. Strategy. Some of his ancestors had given their lives for their people. The least he could do was to endure bad company.

Isabella's heart skipped as she saw the four gentlemen rise from their card table. *Finally! Now I might see him and talk to him again.* Sensing Eilidh's gaze upon her, she glanced towards her friend. Eilidh was eyeing her evenly, a sort of sad kindness in her gaze, and Isabella felt a slow flush suffuse her face. *What am I doing? I have become so lost to reason that I persist in dreaming of Angus, even after his sister has given me the clear message that he will not seek a wife from anywhere but his home.* Yet she could not seem to help herself.

Eilidh's exact words came back to her now. *'He will marry a girl from the Islands.'* Well, naturally he would. He was a Scottish laird after all, not an English gentleman. He could probably have his pick of ladies in the Islands or Edinburgh—or wherever it was the Scottish Marriage Mart took place. Pretending to look for something in her reticule, Isabella reminded herself to be sensible. She had never dreamed she would become the sort of maiden to develop such a *tendre*.

Why, it was so much more intense, more all-consuming than she could ever have anticipated. Oh, she had listened to many songs and stories about love, but never had she imagined that this was how it would feel in reality. If she had considered the matter at all—which she had not—she might imagine that being 'in love' with someone might involve a sort of dreamy wonder. Not this, this…she looked inward, seeking words to describe it.

It was like hunger, but *more*. Like the greatest thirst she had ever felt. Like the need to breathe. Her stomach griped with a strange near-nausea when she saw him, almost like fear, and yet she was in no way frightened of him. When he was nearby, her heart started a loud tattoo, while her blood thrummed in her ears till she could barely think straight.

When he was *not* there, her body and mind remained in a state of agitation. Waking or sleeping, the world was utterly changed because he was in it and because he would occasionally smile at her, or kiss her hand, or call her friend.

Yet there was nothing to suggest he felt anything for her beyond a common liking or mere flirtation. His sister, who knew him well, had seen fit to indirectly warn her and Isabella ought to heed such well-intentioned counsel. Yet she seemed unable to prevent herself from feeling what she felt.

Dreamy wonder, she realised with a brief flash of humour, was there, too, for how else could she account for the fact that she liked to conjure up his image in her mind's eye when travelling in the carriage, or sitting having her hair pinned up by Sally, or lying in her bed? No, she was a fool and no better than a hundred lovesick maidens she had seen during previous seasons, and she must own it.

Thinking back, she realised she ought to have had more sympathy for the forlorn debutantes she had observed in ballrooms and drawing rooms all over London. They gave themselves away by their demeanour, clearly favouring their preferred gentleman above all others. When he would engage them in conversation the young ladies would sparkle and flirt and *shine* in a way that did not happen when they spoke with other gentlemen. And so, determined to reclaim her privacy and dispel any rumours, Isabella determined to treat all of her suitors in the same way. That would mean shining rather less for Angus and sparkling much, much more for the others.

'Let us join my brothers and their companions,' she heard herself say, her tone suitably neutral. 'I believe they have finally finished their card games.'

Eilidh and Mrs Edgecombe agreed and they made their way to join the gentlemen, who were standing near one of the window embrasures. Prudence had also moved to join them. 'Well, Freddy,' Isabella offered lightly, 'did Max win every hand?'

Freddy stiffened slightly. *Oh, dear.* 'Not at all! Indeed we all won and lost some hands. I dare say I would have come away the clear winner overall, but for some dashed ill fortune with the turn of the cards.' Prudence was frowning, Isabella noted. Did she disapprove of Freddy's card playing?

'For certain!' To Isabella's great surprise—for Freddy had not the understanding to do particularly well at cards—the Honourable Geoffrey Barnstable came to his aid. 'Why, your brother is as quick-witted a player as I ever saw!'

Had she imagined the briefest of glances passing between Angus and Max? Before Isabella had the chance to say anything, Mrs Edgecombe intervened.

'I have not the patience for cards,' she offered mournfully, 'although your dear mother was a notable whist player.'

'She was?' Always hungry for information about her mother, Isabella lit on this with great interest. 'Did she play here?'

'Oh, yes. She even hosted card parties for ladies at her home. Her husband was not particularly supportive, however, even though he himself had a weakness for gambling.'

'Quite right!' said Freddy, his chest puffing out with pride. 'It would be unseemly for a lady to indulge in gambling. Besides, they have not the faculty for it.' He tapped the side of his head. 'Not like my papa would have had. Or such as I myself have.'

Isabella, determined to be serene, chose to ignore this insult to womankind. Nor did she retort that perhaps many women had too much common sense for gambling—a pastime that, in her mind at least, was entirely different to the card playing itself. In the one, the focus was on the simple enjoyment of the game. In the other, the elation or despair of betting on the outcome.

Instead she played her part as the conversation meandered on. She sparkled and shone for everyone, showing no favour towards Angus and not allowing herself to rest her eyes upon him a moment longer than necessary. Mr Craven joined them then and she sparkled anew. She sparkled so much that by the time they reached the carriage she was sparkled out and could only respond to Prudence's soliloquy about her evening with monosyllables.

Holding the last of her light within her, she made it to the sanctuary of her chamber, and theatrically yawned her way through Sally's ministrations. Alone at last, she hid beneath the covers and cried bitterly.

Chapter Ten

'Angus, get up! I must speak with you.' The Gaelic words, uttered sharply, penetrated Angus's dream—a delightful dream with confused images of a triumphant homecoming, grateful islanders and, strangely, him introducing Isabella to his cousin Alasdair.

'Hrmph! What time is it? And why do you persist in disturbing me so early in the morning, Eilidh?' Blinking as she released the shutters, he brought an arm to cover his eyes.

'It is almost midday. If you slept this late at home you would rightly be judged as being a disgrace to our ancestors! We have a busy day ahead, for I am promised to Isabella and you to Max, and then we are to visit the Tower. Now, I shall meet you in the morning room in twenty minutes!'

He groaned. 'An hour.'

'Twenty minutes and no later!' She swept out and a few minutes later his valet arrived, presumably under instruction from Eilidh. In this mood, she was formidable.

He yawned, stretched and rose. To be fair he did not wish to develop the habit of keeping such late hours—

shockingly, it had taken a relatively short period of time for his usual habits to be completely destroyed.

How on earth did I manage to sleep until midday?

It was a little over thirty minutes after his sister's foray into his chamber that Angus arrived in the morning room, now wide awake and hungry. She was at the small desk dealing with correspondence when he entered and he made his way immediately to the sideboard, where a simple breakfast had been laid out.

Helping himself to porridge, eggs and toast, and accepting a cup of tea from the waiting footman, he waved the man away and sat at the polished oak table to enjoy his repast. As soon as the door had closed behind the servant he addressed his sister. 'Well, Eilidh, how was your first evening at a *ton* party?'

She indicated the messages before her on the desk. 'You know how they say that going to a wedding is the making of another?'

'Aye?'

'Well, in our case going to a soirée has led to…' she counted the missives before her '…five new invitations!'

'No! Really?'

'Yes! And the first is an outing tomorrow afternoon with the Sandisons.'

'Surely the first is our assignation to visit the Tower with Mr Wood and his sister?'

She frowned. 'I do not count that as a social engagement, somehow. Not an event where we must perform and wheedle, and not be ourselves. I see it more a pleasant outing—although naturally, our new friends are Burtenshaw's closest family.'

'It is true.' Angus felt a now familiar tightening in

his gut as he thought of Isabella. 'They seem *real* to me in a way that no one else in London is.'

She nodded, then paused a moment. 'I hope you did not say anything to Lord Burtenshaw last night about the land.'

He snorted. 'I am not as foolish as I look!'

'And a good thing, too!' she countered and they shared a smile at the exchange, which they had rehearsed many times over the years.

'We played cards, talked of nothing and I was able to form something of an impression of him.'

'And?' Her look was intent. 'What manner of man is he, Lord Burtenshaw?'

Angus thought for a moment. 'Well,' he said cautiously, 'we know already how agreeable and pleasant Max is. His sister, too.'

She sniffed. 'I am not so sure. They are certainly *real* with us, as you say—a refreshing contrast to the false smiles and simpering we have encountered in some of the others—but in this case it may be as much a curse as a blessing. Isabella is a darling of course. Which reminds me—you really ought not to flirt with her, you know. She is being forced to choose a husband over the next few weeks and if she thinks you are eligible it may prevent her from…from seeing other men clearly.'

Her words landed uncomfortably with him and just now he did not wish to consider such matters. He had taken an age to fall asleep last night, troubled by images of kissing her in Mrs Bell's well-appointed drawing room.

I must be rational and sensible! We are here to buy back Lidistrome for its people.

Anything else was simply a distraction.

Instead of addressing Eilidh's point directly, he sought refuge in timeless brother–sister raillery. 'What? Are you giving me an indirect compliment, Sister? You think me more eligible than the dour Mr Craven? Or the delightful Honourable Geoffrey Barnstable?'

'Ha! The ladies have apparently dubbed him the "Dishonourable Geoffrey" because of his habit of wandering eyes and wandering hands.'

Angus's jaw slackened in shock. 'Indeed? Do let me know if he attempts any such thing with you, Eilidh. He shall have my fist to answer to!'

'I shall make it my business to avoid him—as do most of the young ladies, I am told. Isabella, Miss Bell and Miss Sandison all warned me about him on separate occasions.'

'I see. Such a man would soon be banished at home, if he could not learn to behave himself.' He frowned. 'Would Lord Burtenshaw know of this? Or Max?'

She shrugged. 'I know not. Possibly not, for they seem to have unwritten rules about matters that can be discussed with gentlemen and matters that are for women's ears only.'

'Well, that is no different to home, for there's many a conversation that we get shooed out of, for it concerns "women's business".'

'Aye but here, there's much less plain speaking generally. Everything is done with a nod of the head or a tilt of an eyebrow. Have you not remarked upon it?'

'True, but something like a dishonourable man should be spoken of plainly to the menfolk.'

'We will be here for only a matter of weeks, Angus. We cannot change them. Now, you were about to tell me your impression of Lord Burtenshaw.'

He took a sip of tea. 'I was and I had just stated that Max and his sister are both likeable. You agreed in respect of Isabella, but am I to understand that you dislike Max?'

Her jaw fell open. Clamping it shut, she replied 'Dislike him? No, at least I think not. But he…vexes me.'

He frowned. 'But why? He is perfectly amiable. Has a quick mind and a ready wit. Boxes well, too,' he added ruminatively. 'He will probably best me again today.'

'He is—he is like a pretty boat adrift on the ocean. He looks good, but is unmoored and lost, and you just know he will sink beneath the waves eventually.' Her gaze became unfocused. 'This *ton* life is cruel to second sons.'

'Aye, but he cannot help his birth. None of us can.'

'But I am not speaking of his birth. I am speaking of his *life*! He does nothing, besides…besides *being* a second son all day long. He does not even *try* to find something purposeful. Isabella, too, seems sometimes possessed of a certain *ennui*…' She shuddered. 'I could not stand to live in that way.'

'I see and hear your frustration, but you have already pointed out that we will only be here a matter of weeks. We cannot fix the ills of London society.' She shook her head, but he refused to be distracted again.

'My point is, Lord Burtenshaw is nothing like Max and Isabella. He is as unlikeable as they are likeable, as lacking in humour as they are witty, as mutton headed as they are bright and rational. In short, they are nothing alike—a fact which makes our task much more challenging.'

She sighed. 'I knew it. While I spent much less time than you in Lord Burtenshaw's company, that was my impression, too.' She grimaced. 'It also explains why Isabella and Max are so close to one another and why they seem to avoid his company as much as they can. Their nature seems similar to ours and to people we know at home, rather than many of the *ton*.'

'Their older brother also detests Scotland.' Briefly, he told her of Burtenshaw's scathing comments.

'What an *amadan*!' She shook her head. 'This is worrisome indeed. Still,' she added, more brightly, 'we are not yet defeated. These invitations will help, for even if Burtenshaw does not attend the events himself our acceptance in society—which is by no means assured— must be something to strive for. He is a man much given to conformity, I think.'

He nodded. 'Aye. Maintaining and enhancing his family reputation seems to be his main spur, his duty as he sees it.'

'Very well.' She picked up her pen. 'I shall accept all of these and hope for more.'

'So how did you enjoy your first *ton* soirée?' The two young ladies had met in Gunter's and were idly watching the other parties present while enjoying delicious ices. The gentlemen were boxing and would come for them in an hour, for they all intended to visit the Tower together.

Eilidh smiled. 'Well, I did enjoy it, Isabella. Meeting new people is always diverting. The music was excellent, as was the company.'

Isabella felt a warmth in her chest. 'I do not know how I shall manage when you return to Scotland. You think as I do on so many topics and I have never met anyone like that before. At least, apart from Max. But you are the first true friend I have had. Most of the other young ladies think only of gowns and compliments, and dancing. I care little for such things.'

Eilidh's eyes gleamed with humour. 'And yet you and I also spend time together looking at fashion plates and even visiting dressmakers.'

'That is true! And I am learning to appreciate a pretty gown. But those are not the *only* things we speak of. Why, today we have already discussed the creation of the Regency, the need for both rationality and sensibility, and Napoleon's antics in the Peninsula! And I have loved hearing more about your home.'

'And now I am going to risk having you judge me for an excess of frivolity—'

'Oh, no! Never!'

'I am glad to hear it.' She took a breath. 'I wish to ask you about dancing.'

Isabella could not help it. As soon as Eilidh had said the word a vision had appeared in her mind of dancing with Angus, her hand held in his… She swallowed. 'What of dancing?'

'We have our own jigs and reels in the Islands and I learned some dances at school in Edinburgh, but I think that Angus and myself probably need to familiarise ourselves with dances popular in London at present.' She shrugged, a rueful expression on her face. 'Not that we can be sure of being invited to any balls. But if we are, I do not wish for us to disgrace ourselves. Can you suggest perhaps a school or a dance teacher who might—'

'I know the very man! Monsieur Dupont is quite simply the best dance teacher in London. I did some classes with him a few weeks ago to catch up on the latest steps, so that Prudence could satisfy herself I was able to hold my own on the dancing floor without disgracing the family name.'

'Thank you! I knew you would advise me. Could you possibly get me his direction?'

'I shall do better than that. He is in such demand, you see, that he is unlikely to take on anyone new this Season. But, given the fact he has already completed some lessons for Prudence and me, I shall simply book a few more and you and Angus can join me.' Hopefully her excitement was not showing, for now she really, really wanted dance lessons with Angus and Eilidh.

Her friend looked a little dubious. 'Naturally I am grateful for your kind offer, but would Lord Burtenshaw or his wife not object to finding a couple of Scottish cuckoos in their elegant nest?'

'Oh, stuff! Why would they object? Indeed, Freddy does not trouble himself with such things and would not care in the slightest!' Trying to disguise her enthusiasm as best she could, she added in a more measured tone, 'Monsieur Dupont may not even be available, but I will ask.'

'And can you check that your sister-in-law agrees?'

Isabella nodded. 'Monsieur Dupont has an assistant who plays piano during the lessons. He must be fifty if he is a day and has the most diverting eyebrows—as though two caterpillars had crawled up his face and decided to rest on his brow.' This provoked a smile. 'Oh, I do hope you get invited to a ball!'

'Well, I do, too—even if it has little to do with our purpose in coming here, I admit to a certain curiosity about a *ton* ball. It is an experience I shall never have again, so I do not think it an unreasonable wish.'

'No, indeed! And in the meantime there are soirées and the theatre, and tomorrow's jaunt to Greenwich.'

'Yes, tell me, what shall we do there?'

'The Sandisons will have invited thirty people or more. We shall drive out in carriages to the place with a view over London and the servants will bring food in wicker baskets for us to enjoy outdoors. It is a way of enjoying the natural landscape.'

'I see,' Eilidh replied in a dubious tone. 'Well, I do not fully understand, but no doubt it will be an interesting experience. Tell me, will your suitors be there?'

Isabella sighed, as the weight of expectations once again settled about her shoulders. 'I expect so. The thing is—' She bit her lip. 'May I speak plainly?'

'I should welcome it.' The teasing light had gone from Eilidh's eye.

Gathering her courage, Isabella finally spoke some of what was in her heart. 'My difficulty is that I have this foolish notion of wishing to *like* my husband. And there are no gentlemen I like half so well as Max and Angus and I cannot marry either of them!' It hurt more than she had expected to acknowledge out loud that Angus would never be her husband, but she managed to say the words with her voice only trembling a little, which was something of a relief. The last thing she wanted was for Eilidh to realise how deeply her *tendre* for Angus ran.

'I understand you. Angus is by no means perfect, but he is a good man. Max is…he is definitely far from being perfect, but I am coming to like him, too. And frankly, if I try to imagine myself married to the worthy Mr Craven…' She shuddered. 'And as for the Dishonourable Geoffrey…!' They eyed one another in mutual understanding. 'What will you do, Isabella?'

A wave of bleak futility washed over Isabella. 'I do not know. Would living with Mr Craven be worse than living with Freddy? Perhaps not, but why should I have to choose among impossible options?'

'When must you choose?'

She shrugged. 'It is by no means guaranteed that any of them will even offer for me. Manly pride being what it is, it is expected that a lady shows a gentleman some encouragement and the truth is that I do not wish to encourage any of them.' There was a brief silence. 'But enough of my troubles. The sun is shining, we are eating ices in Gunter's and, today, all is well!'

'And here is where Anne Boleyn met her grisly end!' With a flourish, Max indicated a particular corner of the courtyard. Isabella shuddered at the very notion.

They had spent an hour making their way through the winding stairs and interlinked rooms of the old Tower, encountering helpful Yeomen and enormous, quite frightening ravens in the process. Isabella cared not, simply enjoying the company of their new friends. Each time she looked at Angus, it gave her delicious flutterings in her heart and stomach. He was so handsome! And so tall. And so… Struggling for a word, she realised that she was not simply attracted to his face and form. Recalling her conversation with Eilidh earlier, she nodded inwardly. She *liked* him. And what was more, she felt an affinity to him and to Eilidh—almost as though she had always known them.

'As did the Fox!' Angus returned, grimacing, and Isabella returned her attention to the conversation.

'Do you mean Lord Lovat, the last Jacobite?'

'Aye.'

'I believe he was held here in the Tower, but was actually executed on Tower Hill, not far from this spot,' Max explained. 'There were very many spectators, you see.'

Angus and Eilidh exchanged a glance. 'Of course there were.'

'Was this following the Jacobite rebellion?' Isabella, memories of history lessons returning, wished to be part of the conversation and Angus duly obliged, reminding her of the details of that time, over sixty years ago.

'We call it an uprising rather than a rebellion,' he said and she searched his face.

My, he is so handsome when he is serious!

'The Scots and English disagree yet about who was the rightful king.'

'And still,' Max offered softly, 'we may put such things aside on a personal level.' A wave of relief passed through Isabella at Max's perfectly weighted words. Naturally they would disagree about Culloden, which neatly encapsulated the strife between England and Scotland, but it need not mean there had to be strife between their peoples.

Moving across the courtyard, they stood in the space where Anne Boleyn had died. 'She lived here in the Tower for more than two weeks, awaiting her trial and execution,' Max explained, changing the subject rather neatly. 'They brought a swordsman from France to do the deed.'

'The swordsman of Calais,' Angus murmured. 'Kings were ever merciless.'

'Some say Henry was being merciful—ensuring Anne had a quick death,' Max offered. 'Thankfully we live in more civilised times.'

'I am not so certain of that,' Eilidh retorted, her eyes blazing. 'Were there not nearly a hundred people executed in London last year? The list of capital offences brought through by the Whigs grows ever longer.'

'Well, I must say I agree with you there,' Isabella declared. 'When they hang a woman for stealing a small amount of food to feed her family, as they did recently, something is not right!'

This stimulated a great deal of conversation and the gentlemen—though asserting that there needed to be a rule of law—agreed that the current statute was oppressive. Finding a shared passion for justice and the need for social reform, they discussed this at length, cementing Isabella's sense that the MacDonalds were good people and that their views were likely to align on many matters. Eilidh—almost defiantly—raised again the spectre of injustices visited upon the Scots after the Battle of Culloden.

Conscious that the shadow of Lord Lovat's execution hung over them and that they were dancing around a troublesome period in history—one that could potentially prove a barrier between them—Isabella felt a little anxious, but she and Max both indicated a willingness to listen.

Angus and Eilidh went on to speak of their father and grandfather and all the men being prohibited from wearing the Highland dress. A small punishment, some might say, and yet it was clear to Isabella how deeply that wound had pierced and how proud Angus was to once again wear the ancestral dress.

And very well he looks in it, too! I think it could be argued that all men should wear the kilt.

Isabella and Max both responded with openness and sympathy and expressed a curiosity to hear more about the impact on the Scots. Their Scottish friends duly obliged and, hearing of clearances and killings and the Gaelic language being frowned upon, Isabella felt a little sick.

'There has been bad blood between our nations,' Max offered soberly.

'Aye, but it need not echo between us.' Eilidh's voice was low.

'Indeed not!'

They shared a glance and something in it—some edge—made Isabella momentarily frown. *Do they like one another or not?* Despite Eilidh's positive words about Max earlier, Isabella was never quite certain.

Moving on through to the far side of the keep, once again they meandered through hallways and rooms, some in terrible disrepair. By this stage they were moving in two pairs, with Max and Eilidh keeping a little way behind Angus and Isabella. As they descended the stone staircase towards the gate, Isabella, hampered by her long skirts, slipped and would have fallen, had Angus not caught her.

He had his hands on her for just a moment, yet Isabella was entirely confused, her insides fluttering and her mind agitated. Their faces had briefly been close together and Isabella had been conscious of a wish he might kiss her. A wish she had held with ever-increasing frequency. A wish that was as futile as it was nonsensical, given Eilidh's warning.

Naturally he had not kissed her—indeed, he *could* not—and they had continued on, his hands falling away from her waist where he had caught and steadied her. He did place her hand in the crook of his arm as they walked on and Isabella thrilled at the sensation of his warmth through his sleeve and the closeness with which they were walking. They had fallen into step with one another and she glanced briefly at him, feeling warmth insinuate through her body as their eyes met.

Does he feel it, too? This thing, this unexpected, wondrous, terrifying thing?

Once again she found herself lost in wishes, rationality forgotten. Somewhere in the back of her mind was a memory of last night's tears and the knowledge he would never marry her, but in this moment, enjoying the thrill of his company, Isabella cared nothing for such pointless reasonableness. Her hand was in Angus's arm, the sun was shining and all was well.

The journey to Greenwich took more than two hours, so Angus was grateful that he and Eilidh were seated in Max and Isabella's carriage, along with Prudence. Lord Burtenshaw had declined the invitation, at which news Angus did not know whether to be glad or sorry. While they needed to continue to build their acquaintance with him, the thought of an entire day in Isabella's company without having to worry about her pompous older brother could only be welcome.

The three ladies, naturally, had the front-facing seats, while he and Max could only see the passing scenery a little at a time. Angus cared not, for there, directly in front of him, was Isabella, looking delightful in a gown of sprig muslin, with a matching spencer and pretty bonnet, tied under her right ear with a blue-satin ribbon. He himself was in full Highland dress, having decided that in Lord Burtenshaw's absence he could dispense with the trews, pantaloons or unmentionables he had been forced into wearing during some of their previous social engagements.

As the carriage rumbled on—part of a long line led by the Sandison coach—they passed the time in talk. Even Prudence joined in as they spoke of matters high and low—of the good weather and their hope for a pleasant day ahead, of the new Regent and how he would manage, of the sea battle with the French that had happened a week ago. Word was just coming in indicating that the French had been firmly repulsed, which Angus freely acknowledged was a good thing. Despite the Auld Alliance, he had no love for Napoleon and worried that the Emperor's ambition had no limits.

Throughout the conversations, Angus's eyes were continually drawn to Isabella. Continually he noted how beautiful she was, how warm and how clever. Like Eilidh, she took a full part in the discourse on politics and European affairs. Unsurprisingly she was well informed and had sensible opinions to offer and he could not help but reflect on her being close to his ideal. If only she had been born an Islander!

Despite all of his good intentions he could not prevent the way his heart leaped and stuttered in her company, or the way he constantly imagined kissing her. Her lips were tempting and perfectly pink, with a Cupid's bow on the upper and a fullness to the lower that would have made him groan aloud had they been alone.

Naturally there could be no future for them, for how could he even think of taking a delicate London lady to the harsh wildness of the Islands? His heart sank as he ruefully acknowledged that she had taken his fancy in a way that no other maiden had ever managed. Yet he knew he must be strong and resist all temptation.

His thoughts wandered again to his cousin, Alasdair, with clear memories of how he had married in haste and come to regret it. Alasdair's first bride, Hester, had been a beauty and he had fallen under her spell in the ballrooms of Edinburgh. His lady had not even tried to see the goodness of the Island community and they had both been dreadfully unhappy. Alasdair had been widowed young and left to raise his young daughter alone, but his first experience had made him—and Angus, too—wary of the notion of marriage.

Angus's mind wandered again to Alasdair's current happiness. After many years alone, Alasdair had recently married again—to an English lady, ironically. Lydia had come as governess to Alasdair's child and had adapted beautifully to Island life. Recalling Lydia's evident happiness was now making Angus hope for impossible things.

Until now Angus had never met a woman who had tempted him into considering marriage, but unfortunately he had to acknowledge that Isabella was the wrong woman. Unlike Lydia, Isabella was a lady of the *ton*. How would she ever cope without the social whirl of aristocratic society and the convenience of London shops and markets? He squirmed slightly in his seat, recalling that she had declared a disinterest in such things and a preference for a rural life.

Ah, but the reality would be much harsher than she could ever know.

A lack of interest in shopping did not necessarily translate into the ability to survive months of waiting for ordered goods and the need to reuse and reshape everything they had.

Life in the islands could be frugal at times, although there was plenty of good plain food, fuel for the fire and good company. For an instant he tried to imagine Isabella in the Great Hall at Broch Clachan, mingling with the people and caring for them as their Lady. His heart skipped a beat. She could absolutely do it, he knew—if she was happy and contented there. Yet taking her in hope was a risk too great for him to even consider. For her sake he must forget any notion of marriage.

That did not mean that he was forbidden from enjoying her company. Could he even steal a kiss perhaps? Would it be unfair to her to do so? His heart leapt as he imagined holding her in his arms. Once the notion entered his head he could not shake it. While he certainly did not wish to give her false expectations of his intentions, surely a single kiss could not hurt? Or perhaps he should speak to her openly about his feelings—including his concerns about her ability to adapt to Island life?

A shout from the carriages ahead brought him back to reality. Max leaned out, confirming a moment later that their destination was in sight. Instantly everyone sat up straighter, the ladies checking for their reticules and smoothing their skirts. Instinctively his eyes followed the sweep of Isabella's hands as they brushed down her legs. With determination, he averted his gaze.

Despite enjoying the company on the journey, they were all keen to stretch their legs and explore their destination. A few minutes later the carriage drew to a halt and Max and Angus jumped down to lower the step and hand the ladies out. It was a task normally carried out by the footman after descending from his perch at the rear and it was a courtesy for the two gentlemen to perform this small service for the ladies. Lady Burtenshaw seemed particularly gratified by their gallantry. 'Thank you, Max. Thank you, Mr MacDonald,' she murmured as they each took a hand and assisted her out of the carriage.

Eilidh was next and Angus gave way as Max offered both hands to her. Seeing her slight flush, Angus stifled a grin. He was not the only one to be affected by Burtenshaw's siblings, it seemed! Despite her protests, Eilidh was clearly drawn to Max. Any chance of a future between them, he knew, was as doomed as that between himself and Isabella. More, for among the *ton* he understood a wife was generally expected to leave her household and become part of her husband's family. Eilidh would never leave the Islands and Max had no reason to go there.

Finally it was Isabella's turn. Mimicking Max, he held out both hands to her and she placed both her dainty hands in his as she jumped down lightly. His heart soared and once again his thoughts turned to the possibility of kissing her. What had begun as a wish was fast becoming a necessity.

All around them ladies and gentlemen were pouring out of carriages, gentlemen donning beaver hats and some of the ladies opening parasols as they greeted one another, all the while exclaiming at the surroundings. A few people commented on Angus's Highland dress, but in a complimentary way. He did his duty by all his acquaintances—including Miss Sandison and Miss Bell—before returning to Max and Isabella. Prudence had been immediately claimed by one of her friends and had wandered off contentedly, leaving just the four of them.

It was certainly idyllic, Angus acknowledged. Under the warm spring sunlight the trees were greening, the grass thick and luxuriant, and dotted here and there were spring wildflowers—primroses, daisies, and dandelions mingling with delicate clusters of lilac speedwell and, under the trees, bright celandines and nodding daffodils. It was not the island machair, Angus thought, but it was certainly pretty.

Mrs Sandison and her husband were busy greeting their guests anew and directing the footmen currently unloading multiple wicker baskets from a second coach. Lemonade was poured and they all drank their fill, then Mr Sandison glanced at his pocket watch. 'We shall make all ready here, so we can eat in an hour. Before then, my friends, feel free to explore the woods and fields. For those keen for exertion there is a pretty stream about half a mile in that direction and for those who wish to sit and rest, we shall have cloths laid out immediately. The views, as you see, are spectacular.'

Indeed they were. For the first time since arriving in London Angus was able to properly breathe, or so it felt. Wandering to the edge of the hilltop with Isabella, Max and Eilidh, he paused, drinking in the scene and the clear air. Up here atop Greenwich hill the sky was enormous and one could see for miles.

'It reminds me of home,' Eilidh murmured and Angus sent her an understanding glance.

'I was just thinking the same.'

'How so?' Max seemed genuinely interested. 'Is the landscape similar?'

'Not at all,' Angus responded. 'We have very few trees and at this time of year the heather and bracken give the landscape as much bronze as green. But, yes—' he nodded to his sister '—it reminds me of home, too. It is the bigness, I think.' He laughed lightly. 'That is not a real word, I know, and yet...'

'If your islands are anything like as picturesque as this, I wonder why you would ever leave it,' Isabella murmured.

'Needs must.' Eilidh shrugged. 'But I confess I shall be glad to be home again.'

A wave of sweet memories washed over Angus. The view from the top of Rueval, the Island's highest hill. The smell of peat fires in winter. The colours of the machair when the orchids, yarrow and all the other wildflowers were in bloom. If only Isabella and Max could see it!

'I, too,' he said. Turning to Isabella and Max, he bowed formally. 'I should like to invite you both to visit Benbecula, as my guests, should you ever wish to travel there. It is very far away and I do not expect you to come, but I make the offer nevertheless.'

'But I should love to come!' Isabella exclaimed. 'To see Broch Clachan, which I have heard so much about, and to visit your cousin's castle at Ardmore! To see the hill and the heather and the beaches…it would be a dream come true!'

Max was frowning. 'I thank you for your offer, Angus, although as you say it is far away and it is unlikely we shall be able to take you up on it.'

Isabella had a decidedly crestfallen expression on her beautiful face. 'Yes, of course, Max. One must be sensible.' She looked directly at Angus, adding softly, 'But it was a lovely notion.'

He swallowed. What he felt was almost like grief. Grief for the loss of something that could never be. A life not lived. A life with Isabella. The intensity of it shocked him. Had he really become so taken with her?

'Now!' Eilidh was all briskness. 'I have a fancy for—what did Mr Sandison call it? Exertion? So I should like to suggest we find the pretty stream he mentioned.'

'A capital notion!' Max concurred.

They finished their lemonade and returned their cups to the Sandison servants, Isabella declaring that she could not imagine a life where lemonade was denied her.

Before Angus could think too much about the implications of this, Max offered Eilidh his arm. 'Shall we?'

Isabella and Angus fell in behind and they made their way down the narrow path that Mr Sandison had pointed out. At first they stayed quite close together, but the awkwardness of being able to overhear each other's conversations meant that, before long, Max and Eilidh had walked steadily further ahead, while Angus and Isabella strolled slowly behind, Angus enjoying the privacy of these precious moments alone with her. 'I do enjoy walking!' she declared as they strolled through the idyllic setting, green light filtered through the canopy casting everything in a magical glow.

'And running, too!' he reminded her and they shared a smile at the reminder of one of their early encounters. How long ago it seemed and how well they knew one another now.

'Do you still walk with your neighbour?' she asked and he confirmed it. The man who had commented on his boots tended to take a brisk walk at the same time each day and Angus often joined him.

'I miss being active,' he confessed. 'At this time of year there is much to be done at home, for there are lambs and calves, spring planting and, of course, in the better weather we repair any damage from the winter storms.' He laughed lightly. 'Much more of this fine dining and late sleeping, and I shall have become soft!'

'I sincerely doubt that!' she returned wryly. 'How bad are the winter storms in the Islands?'

'Bad,' he replied. 'The wind can be so strong there's

an old saying that it would blow the horns off a goat! *Sheideadh e na h-adharcan de ghobhar,*' he translated.

She smiled at this, and echoed the last word. '*Ghobhar.* That is the word for goat, yes?'

'It is and you said it very well.' He had been teaching her some Gaelic words and loved to see her brow furrow in concentration as she attempted to master the pronunciation.

'*Mo ghràdh, mo ghràdh, m'aon ghràdh,*' he murmured now, overcome by the sight of her serious face as she spoke in his native tongue.

My love, my love, my only love.

His heart ached. The grief he had felt earlier now forced him to admit the truth. He loved her. Never had he felt anything like this, for any other lady. This was the one chance he would probably ever get to say those words to her and he was fiercely glad he had taken it.

Well, of course I love her.

The knowledge had been building slowly within him, released just now by hearing her speak in the tongue of the Gael.

A love that cannot be.

She tilted her head on one side. 'What does that mean?'

'Ach, it's nothing,' he lied. 'Just a wee phrase from the Islands. Now tell me, can you remember how to say "good morning" in Gaelic?'

She replied with a creditable attempt and on they walked through the trees, all the while following the path through the ferns and grasses, their way dotted with golden celandines. Ahead of them the path twisted and for the moment, Max and Eilidh were out of sight. *Now is our chance!* He had to kiss her. Nothing in his life had ever come with a stronger imperative. And yet…his principles forced him to think the matter through.

He caught his breath. Could he really just kiss her, in the knowledge that she liked him very well? While he could not know how strong that liking was—and there was no indication that she believed herself to be enamoured of him as he was of her—his sense of honour forced him to speak.

'Isabella, there is something I should like to say to you.'

Was that hope in her eyes? *Dash it all!*

'Yes?'

'I did not come to London to seek a wife and I know I must marry a woman from the Islands. I do not wish to give anyone false notions of me, or my intentions.'

Even to his own ears his words sounded blunt. Yet her light-hearted statement from earlier now returned to him with full force. She could not imagine a life where lemonade was denied her. Isabella clearly had no idea that a luxury such as lemonade was almost unknown in the Islands and could only be enjoyed with the greatest of expense in procuring citrus fruits from the mainland. *And it is not just lemonade.*

In truth, there were no luxuries in the Hebrides, save the joy of land and sea and sky, of good company and fiery whisky and a sense of belonging. He shook himself. How arrogant of him to even think that such intangibles could ever make up for the loss of luxuries and comforts that a lady of the *ton* would take for granted!

Her expression became shuttered. 'I understand. You have always been clear about your reasons for being here.' She laughed, a hint of bitterness in it. 'While I am forced to choose a husband from among a list of suitors that I cannot like.'

Taking her hand, he uttered the words that were in his heart. 'But I can say that I *wish* you were from the Islands. Is that unfair?'

She looked at him blankly and he waited, his pulse throbbing madly.

How will she respond?

Around him, the breeze stilled and the sounds of birdsong receded—almost as if nature itself held its breath.

Isabella felt her mind was frozen, as his words penetrated her consciousness. *'I wish you were from the Islands.'* A few short words, yet so much meaning behind them.

He would marry me if I were from the Islands! He likes me well enough to consider marrying me! Then the lowering realisation. *He cannot, will not, marry me because I am not from there.*

Feeling as though her very life depended on her answer, she thought carefully, her mind flying from elation to fear to despair and back again. She was not an islander and could not pretend to be so. Although only a few seconds had passed, time itself seemed to wait on tiptoes for her reply.

'And I can say that I, too, wish I were from the Islands.' Her voice cracked, as she finally allowed him to see a little of what was in her heart.

'Oh, Isabella!' Finally, his arms were around her as she lifted her face for his kiss.

Chapter Eleven

Isabella still felt as though time was standing still. He paused, a hair's breadth from her mouth, giving her the chance to move away if she chose. For answer, she slid her hands around his strong back and pressed him closer, lifting her chin a little to claim his lips with hers.

Instantly, she was lost. Finally, Angus was kissing her and she was kissing him right back. His lips were warm, bewitching and urgent and she gave him her mouth, their tongues circling and dancing as they explored one another. He squeezed her tighter, making her gasp as desire flamed even higher within her. Of their own volition her hands went northwards to finally bury themselves in his thick dark hair, while his went southwards to knead her bottom and press her hips tightly against his.

'Isabella!' he groaned and her heart felt as though it turned over.

'Angus,' she returned, 'Angus.' Her head felt as though it were spinning and she had lost all sense of time and place. Only Angus was real and only Angus mattered. On and on they kissed, she thrilling with delight as his hands wandered from her bottom to her breasts and back again. Her body felt as though it were ready to burst into flames. Never had she experienced anything like it.

Now his hands were on her hips, steadying her as he moved slowly against her, while his tongue continued to drive her to madness. A high-pitched moan emerged from her as he left her lips to trail kisses across her cheek, down her neck, all the way to her bosom.

Returning to her lips, he kissed her once more, this time a slow, reverent salute. It felt like a farewell and so it proved. They stood together, forehead resting against forehead, until their breathing steadied a little. Finally he stepped back, his breathing still a little noisy and his handsome face twisted with what looked suspiciously like anguish.

His gaze fixed hers, his hands sliding down her arms to take her hands in his. 'Isabella, you are—' He swallowed. 'You are the most beautiful lady I know. Your heart is kind and your mind quick. I am almost lost with desire for you, but thank the heavens I was able to stop myself before I completely compromised you.'

Her heart soaring from his compliments, Isabella could not stop herself from dimpling at him. 'Permit me to say that I wish you had, for then Freddy would make us marry and that would suit me very well!'

His eyes danced as he dropped one of her hands and indicated the path ahead. 'What?' he asked lightly, matching her tone. 'You do not prefer the Honourable Geoffrey Barnstable?'

She pretended to consider the matter as they began walking again, this time hand in hand. 'I am sure he has some admirable qualities!' Her pulse was still racing and she discovered her bonnet to be slightly askew. As she straightened it with her free hand she could not help but think that her insides were much, much harder to straighten. Whatever it was that Angus had done to her had been delightful and disconcerting, and simply wonderful.

'I feel as though I should apologise, Isabella, but the truth is that I do not wish to, for I enjoyed our kisses very, very much.'

'I, too! No one has ever kissed me like that before. It was very interesting.'

'Interesting?' He raised an eyebrow.

Laughing, she squeezed his hand gently. 'Disconcerting and confusing, and—and delightful!' Flushing as his eyes seemed to darken, she added quietly, 'I should very much like to do it again.'

He shook his head. 'Much as I agree with you, I know it would be foolish to do so, for in a few short weeks I shall be gone, and we shall never see one another again. Kissing you today has made a memory I shall treasure all my life, but we would be foolish to make a habit of it, as we might both suffer if we become too attached during my visit here.' He frowned. 'It feels unfair to you to even say such things, but I am at my wits' end, Isabella. Truly, I am torn between doing what is *right* and doing what I…what I truly desire.'

She nodded, a painful lump in her throat making it difficult to speak. *I believe him.* Not that it made it any easier to accept what he was saying.

'Oh, Isabella! I do not wish to cause you pain! That is exactly why—' He broke off, exclaiming as a tear escaped, rolling down her cheek. *Never see one another again!* With a muttered expletive, he pulled out a clean handkerchief and wiped away her silent tears. 'I feel it too, Isabella,' he muttered fiercely. 'Never doubt that! But it cannot be.'

'Why not?' she managed to say, feeling as though the words were being torn from her very soul. 'Why not, Angus?'

He nodded grimly. 'Let me tell you of life in the Islands. Not the dreamy summer's day with the orchids in bloom and the sun shining on a white beach. No, let me tell you of the long winters, the dark cold days, the Atlantic storms.'

He proceeded to do so, painting a picture of dreary winters, frugal springs and short summers. Of the need to order supplies and wait weeks or months for their arrival. Of lives lost to the sea and young people lost to emigration. 'Everyone works there,' he added finally, 'and we work hard. There can be no easy life, even for a laird or his lady. Your life there would be as different to—' he gestured vaguely '—all of *this* as it is possible to be.'

He looked directly at her, seemingly reading the words that were on her lips. 'Oh, I know that you wish to say you will do it, anyway. But how can you possibly imagine it? How can you understand just how hard it will be? How can you possibly say whether you would take to that life, or not?'

Isabella felt as though she were standing on the edge of a tall cliff. One slip and she would fall, lost for ever, separated from him for ever.

What can I say to him?

'Naturally, I cannot imagine that life. But what I *can* imagine is a life with Mr Craven, or with the dis—with Mr Barnstable. Tied to the *ennui* of London. Forced to obey my husband. Forced to share his bed—at least until I have delivered one or two healthy children.' She shuddered anew. 'I have always disliked London and shopping, and the social events of the Season, much preferring to be out on the boats and working there. *Working*, Angus.'

He shook his head. 'It is not the same. When you are in Sussex and have planned a day on the boat, what would happen if you were ill, or tired that day?'

She frowned, knowing he had scored a hit. 'I suppose I would not have to do it if I did not wish to. But I *know* I could.'

'How? How do you know, if it has never happened?' He stopped, taking her other hand in his. 'I know you for a strong woman, and full of determination. But Eilidh—daughter of the last laird—has been milking cows and helping outside and inside since she was very wee, while you have been raised to make conversation and dance.' She winced. 'You are more, so much more than that, I know, but I could not bear to make you unhappy.'

A thought occurred to her. 'Would you worry that the islanders might not welcome an English wife? I mean, with Culloden and everything.'

Is that perhaps his real concern?

He shook his head. 'There would certainly be a few raised eyebrows, but they would all come to accept you in time. My cousin's second wife, Lydia, is English and the Ardmore people love her. No, this is about you, Isabella. How could I be so selfish as to take you away from your home and family, from this entire life, the only one you have ever known, to a place on the very edge of the world? It would be madness.' His eyes narrowed. 'Tell me, if a young lady you knew—Miss Sandison, perhaps, or Miss Bell—agreed to marry a Scot from the Islands and leave here to go with him, would you not worry for her?'

She could not argue. Put like that, it seemed foolish indeed to consider doing such a thing. Yet her heart remained unmoved, knowing what it wanted. Whom it wanted.

'Please tell me you understand, Isabella. I do not mean to be unkind, or to hurt you, but I see no answer here.'

She nodded, and her heart felt as though it cracked in two. 'I understand. I do not like it, but I understand.' She lifted her chin. 'Let us continue, for Max and Eilidh will be wondering where we are.' Deliberately, she let go of his hands.

He fell into step beside her. 'Isabella. *Isabella.*' She turned her head. 'I am sorry. I never intended any of this.'

She shrugged, trying desperately not to *see* him, not to give way to the crashing wave of agony that threatened to engulf her. 'Neither of us did. You have done nothing wrong, Angus.'

'I know we are to have dancing lessons together. Apart from that, it is probably best if I keep some distance from you in future. Your brother—your eldest brother—intends that you marry this Season and I should not prevent you from building a connection with the gentleman of your choosing.'

But you are the gentleman of my choosing, Angus. Only you.

All around them, birds sang, the breeze whispered and spring sunlight pierced the shade of the green woods. But inside Isabella, winter had returned. Her broken heart was ice cold, her mind frozen. She was blessedly numb and absurdly grateful for it. Somehow, she had to survive the day, knowing what she now knew. All hope was gone.

Chapter Twelve

March soon gave way to April and the Season continued. Isabella whirled and waltzed, sparkled and shone, and all the time her heart was frozen. By night and by day she worried at the conundrum before her. In the short time she had left with Angus, could she find the words to convince him that she would adapt to Island life? Not just because she wished to. But because she knew she needed to.

The difficulty was that she did not know the words that would break the spell. How was she to convince him with words alone? Every time, her mind came to the same conclusion—that perhaps in the end there could be no words, for only by *showing* him could she truly convince him. And she could not show him without living there, could not live there unless he took her there. Around and around she went, in an exhausting, self-defeating circle.

Angus and Eilidh came for dance lessons and Isabella and Max partnered them as they learned. Isabella loved every moment of it—standing close to him, looking into his eyes, feeling his warmth as they moved together through the figures. Frustratingly, however, he maintained the friendliness with which he had been treating her ever since that day in the woods. Friendliness which was like a drop of water when she needed a river, a candle when she needed a fiery furnace.

'*Bravo, mademoiselle!*' Monsieur Dupont was, it seemed, impressed by Eilidh's mastery of the steps, as she and Max twirled about the room. 'Yes, and you, too, sir,' he added, making Angus grin at the realisation he was clearly an afterthought.

Her heart skipping, Isabella could not help it—she grinned back at him and in that moment felt the briefest moment of communion with him again. A moment later it was gone and her heart sank back into its usual pain.

Angus watched the smile fade from her face, and knew himself to be the worst of men. Knowing it was impossible for them to be together, he never should have encouraged their friendship. Never should have given her any inkling of his feelings for her. Never should have kissed her.

And yet, part of him could not be brought to regret it. Selfishly, he hugged the memories close, while continually reminding himself that succumbing fully to this *tendre* as he wished would only bring pain to both of them. Romantic notions of a wedding and a life of happiness were just notions. The winter storms cared not if the person being battered by wind and rain was a hardy islander, or a delicate London lady.

But what of Lydia? his treacherous heart whispered for the hundredth time. Alasdair's new wife had come from London to the Hebrides and had adapted perfectly well to life there. Might Isabella adapt as Lydia had?

Ah, but Lydia had come as a governess, not a lady,

having been raised in the merchant classes with the knowledge she would likely have to work all her life to earn her keep. No matter how much Isabella enjoyed sailing as a pastime, no matter how much she detested the strictures of London's drawing rooms, she could have no notion of how much she would have to sacrifice if she were to marry Angus. And so he danced with her, holding every detail in his memory as best he could, but desperately maintained the friendly demeanour he had cultivated in recent weeks.

Nearly two hours later, Monsieur Dupont declared himself *almost* satisfied. 'Mademoiselle Wood,' he announced, 'I thank you for bringing me two such apt students. One more lesson, I think, is all that I shall require! The same time tomorrow, perhaps? I regret I have not many gaps in my appointment book, for this year's debutantes…' He rolled his eyes. *'Oh, là-là!'*

One more lesson. I shall have to make the most of it, for I might never dance with her again.

Swallowing hard against the sudden lump in his throat, Angus reminded himself that he was doing this to spare her years of pain in future. The possibility that she might thrive in the Islands was so slim, and the consequences so severe if she did not, as to make it unreasonable for him to indulge his own wishes and desires, no matter how powerfully they were affecting him.

You are a laird, he reminded himself.

Being the Laird required leadership and self-sacrifice, and a commitment to do what was honourable, not what was desired. These were the values he had been raised to uphold. Yet he could not recall a dilemma so severe, so painful as this one. His heart was breaking and he could do nothing about it.

* * *

Isabella kissed Great-Aunt Morton's weathered cheek, then stood back as Max leaned over the old lady to do the same. They sat then, one on each side of her bed, and it struck Isabella anew that Mama's aunt was dying. She had always been so energetic, so vital, and while the familiar light was in her eyes, her body was clearly fading. Great-Aunt Morton's breathing was laboured and she closed her eyes frequently, sometimes for minutes at a time.

Max met Isabella's gaze across the bed and his grim expression showed that he, too, had realised the end would soon come. Amid the sorrow of losing Angus, here then was a new sorrow—losing their once-fierce great-aunt, Mama's last living relative.

'Max. Isabella. You two are my only true family,' Great-Aunt Morton wheezed, echoing Isabella's thoughts, 'and I would see you both happy.' Interestingly, she clearly did not see Freddy as part of her only true family.

Well, why should she, when Freddy never even bothers to visit?

'Isabella—' Great-Aunt Morton turned her head, and Isabella swallowed at the knowledge this might be one of her final opportunities to talk with the woman who had comforted her so warmly after Mama's death. 'Isabella, find a good man to marry. Do not compromise. Your brother Burtenshaw is every inch his father's son—vain, shallow and mutton headed. She should never have married him.'

She is speaking of Mama, I think, although poor Prudence also has her trials to bear.

'I shall try my best, Aunt Morton,' Isabella replied, squeezing her hand gently.

Though I do not know what more I can do.

'See that you do!' the elderly lady retorted, with a flash of her old imperiousness. 'And, Max...' she turned to him '...remember what I told you. Speak to Freddy about a profession, for it is not good for any man to be idle. Even if you had the money, it would still be important to seek his blessing, for he is still head of the family, no matter how much we all might have wished otherwise.'

But he has spoken to Freddy and Freddy will not hear of it!

Sending a sympathetic glance Max's way, Isabella subtly glanced about her. The mention of money had reminded her once again of the sorry state of Great-Aunt Morton's house. From a life of ease and comfort while her husband was alive, Great-Aunt Morton's circumstances had slowly, gradually shifted to this—dingy bed curtains, only one servant, and frugality in everything from food to fuel.

If Max and Freddy argue, Freddy might cut him off. And if I refuse to marry, the same fate might claim me.

She shuddered. It was all very well Great-Aunt Morton adjuring them to be strong and assert themselves with Freddy. But their brother held the purse strings and made them all dance to his tune. The future looked grim and Isabella could see no way around the barriers before them.

Following their second dance lesson, Monsieur Dupont declared the Scots to be fully proficient and the delicious ordeal of dance lessons had to come to an end. Isabella knew not whether to be glad or sorry. It was a relief not to have to endure the sweet agony of having his hand in hers, of moving in harmony with him around the room, of being so close to him that she could inhale his scent, feel his warm breath… And despite the relief, she grieved that she might not ever dance with him again.

While the MacDonalds were enjoying an ever-wider circle of invitations, they had not yet been invited to a formal ball. It was as though everyone was waiting to invite them until someone else did it first. Freddy, thought Isabella glumly, would note such things, and use them to fuel his dislike of the MacDonalds—a dislike that was as unfair as it was irrational.

Each time she saw him, Isabella was coolly friendly towards Angus, but afterwards she would have a restless, disturbed night, awaking the next morning feeling as though she had not slept at all.

He is not for me, she told herself constantly, until even the words became an almost meaningless litany.

On April tenth, Lord Burtenshaw and his family attended the funeral of their Great-Aunt Morton. The ceremony was a quiet affair and it had to be said that Lord Burtenshaw conducted himself with great restraint, showing no unseemly emotion at the loss of his great-aunt. His younger siblings, on the other hand, were visibly sorrowful at the loss of the last of their mother's family.

Afterwards, as they stood in the churchyard quietly conversing, Isabella mentioned to Max that it was a shame Cooper had not been there, for he had always had time for the old lady when she had visited them in Sussex. Max's responding grimace had caused Isabella to frown.

'What? Does something ail Cooper? Tell me!' Her heart sank at the notion, for Cooper was one of the few friends she had in the world. Abruptly she recalled Prudence's cryptic words in the carriage, what seemed like an age ago.

Max spoke slowly, as if considering his words. 'I managed to speak privately to him, when Freddy called him to London that time.'

'Dear Cooper! I am so sorry to have missed him and I do hope nothing was wrong! I should have liked to see him, but I suppose he was needed back in Sussex immediately.'

Max grimaced. 'As to that, he is not apparently needed in Sussex at all!' He lowered his voice. 'Freddy has seen fit to give him notice to quit and will not tell me why, no matter how much I press him.'

Isabella's jaw dropped. *No!* 'But that is outrageous! Cooper has been loyal to the family since before we were born. How dare Freddy let him go!' She looked around the small gathering, lowering her voice. 'I shall speak to Freddy. This cannot be allowed to stand.'

Max was frowning. 'You can try. I wish you better success than me. He will not tell me why Cooper must go, just that, as Viscount, he is forced to make what he called "certain economies".'

She snorted in disgust. 'Economies should not include getting rid of as loyal a man as Cooper.' *Economies.* His words sank in. 'Are we…are there financial difficulties, Max?'

'That was my thought, too. There should not be, but I have recently begun to wonder…'

'Wonder what?'

'Papa always had a taste for gaming and I fear Freddy has inherited it—for cards in particular. He has not the brains for it, but cannot be told.'

'So are you saying he is getting rid of Cooper so that he can afford to play cards? Shocking!'

He shook his head. 'I have always worried a little about Freddy's gambling. It is a weakness that is entirely out of keeping with his otherwise *prudent* approach to life, but I understand such is often the case.' His brow furrowed. 'I cannot say for certain, but…something about his demeanour in recent weeks is concerning, and I wonder if he might have had a particularly bad run of luck at the tables.' He shrugged. 'Perhaps I am imagining it.'

'And perhaps not! I trust your judgement, Max.'

'We are promised to Barnstable's tomorrow, for a night of cards. I may know more after that.'

'And what of poor Cooper?'

'He has some money put aside, he tells me. I cannot imagine it will be much, given how poorly Freddy— yes, and Papa before him—given how poorly they pay the staff.'

'Can we do anything for him? Perhaps help him find another position?'

'I have only my allowance, as you know, but I have charged him to hire a crew at my expense and sail my yacht back up here. It will at least allow him to gather his belongings and bring them here, where he might have more opportunities for work.' He grimaced. 'The wharves will be a nightmare to navigate and normally not worth the trouble, but at least this way I can support Cooper and also perhaps get out to sea occasionally—even in the Season.'

'That is kind of you, Max. But how will Cooper find suitable work at his age, when he should be easing back and beginning to think of his pension?' The lump in Isabella's throat was becoming more painful by the minute. Losing Angus before she had ever won him was hard enough, then poor Great-Aunt Morton had died and now this. 'The world is full of trouble and pain,' she said quietly. 'And I can do nothing about any of it.'

'Chin up, Isabella,' her brother murmured. 'We still have each other.'

'But for how much longer? My time is almost up, for Freddy wants me to choose a husband in the next fortnight. He told me this morning.' Saying it aloud had a terrible finality about it. When Freddy had spoken to her earlier, just before they had left for the funeral, Isabella had been too shocked to take it in properly. *A fortnight!*

Attempting to make light of it, Max punched her arm playfully. 'Well? Who has caught your eye, Isabella?'

She snorted. 'You make it sound like choosing a bonnet at the milliners. It is very different, I assure you!' He held her gaze and she sighed. 'Lord Welford has retired to the country, declaring he will miss the remainder of this year's Season. That leaves only Mr Craven, Lord Embury, and the Dishonourable Geoffrey, and I do not like any of them!'

'So ladies really do call him the Dishonourable Geoffrey, then? Angus told me so, but I could hardly believe it.'

'Yes, well, one does not normally speak to one's brothers about the awful things ladies must endure.'

'I think that your brothers are exactly whom you should speak to!'

She raised a sceptical brow. 'You think Freddy would care?'

'I am not Freddy and I care!'

'But I do not wish you to make a fuss.'

'If more people made a fuss more often, perhaps the world would not be so full of trouble and pain.'

'Or more so,' she countered, 'for if you try and fail, the hurt cuts deeper.'

He eyed her sharply. 'What hurt? What do you mean?'

'I was speaking generally. I did not mean anything in particular,' she lied.

He is not for me.

'There you are, Isabella.' It was Freddy, interrupting their private speech without hesitation or subtlety. 'I meant to speak to you about Craven.'

Her eyes flashed fire. 'Never mind Mr Craven. Is it true you have dismissed Cooper?'

He puffed out his chest. 'My decisions as Lord Burtenshaw are naught to do with you.'

'So it is true. But *why*, Freddy? He has stood as our friend for so many years—'

'And that is the problem with the man!' There was a purplish tinge to Freddy's cheeks. 'There should be a clear delineation between the classes. *Never* should that sort of...of *intermingling*—' he shuddered '—be permitted. No, I shall not discuss this further—my decision is final. Now, as to the matter of your marriage, Isabella, your time is running out, as I told you earlier. I know you and Max think yourselves to be cleverer than me, but I am not so bacon brained as to fail to notice that Mr Craven has recently been spending all his time dancing attendance on Miss Bell.'

She shrugged. 'And what of it? He is too worthy, too self-righteous and altogether too...too *judgemental* for me.'

'And you are not being judgemental this very minute? You will have to act quickly to secure the man of your choice, Isabella, for if you do not choose, then I shall choose for you. You *will* be married soon and that is the end of it!' He spun on his heel and departed, leaving Isabella bereft of speech and close to tears.

Max, who had watched the entire exchange with a closed mouth and cynical air, placed a comforting hand on her shoulder. 'Freddy is just being Freddy. He cannot help it.'

'Yes, but would he really force me into marriage if I cannot find someone I like? Would he, Max?'

'You know how stubborn he is, and there is no denying young ladies are expected to be married off or be judged unmarriageable by the *ton*. You would not be the first young lady to accept a marriage based on convenience rather than felicity. Once you have the heir out of the way you might have freedom. Is there no one you like, Isabella?'

She looked at him mutely, all of her pain clearly revealed in her eyes. An exclamation erupted from him. 'Apart from Angus, that is. Oh, Isabella, how foolish to think that they might stay, or that people like us could go to Scotland! Do not allow a passing fancy to cloud your judgement.'

She shook her head. 'I would go to Scotland this instant if I could and never return. Now, please excuse me.' She hurried off before she said anything more to reveal her heart, or before embarrassing herself with tears.

Sitting in the carriage on the way back to the house, she pondered her own words. While they were uttered in the agitation of the moment, she stood by them. The thought of travelling to Scotland, of being Angus's wife and having Eilidh for a sister, would be a wish come true.

Yes, she would certainly miss Max and Cooper, and occasionally she might remember people like Mrs Edgecombe with fondness, but she honestly believed if Angus loved her and asked her to be his wife, she would say yes without hesitation. Despite Max's assertion, she knew this was no passing fancy, for she had never felt this way towards anyone before and her preoccupation with Angus showed no sign of wavering.

His words from that day came back to her, as they often did. If Island life was as harsh and uncomfortable as he had indicated, would she come to regret leaving behind a life of routs and ringlets, of days and nights when she had nothing to do but sit in parlours and ballrooms and make empty conversation? She could not imagine such regret. Oh, why had she not been able to convince him? If she had used different words perhaps… Around and around her thoughts went once again, like the ceaseless spinning of a busy water wheel, until finally they were home and she had to descend from the carriage and pretend all was well.

It is no use even dwelling on the matter, she thought as she passed her bonnet and cloak to a serving maid. *A lady cannot propose to a gentleman and he truly believes I might become dreadfully unhappy if he took me to Benbecula.*

No, she would be better putting the handsome Laird out of her mind and looking for another husband. But who?

Angus's habit of taking a walk at the same time as his neighbour, Mr Brummell, was now firmly fixed in his daily pattern. Initially his efforts to befriend the man had been with the cynical aim of getting to know another member of the *ton*, but over time he had come to enjoy the gentleman's company and conversation as they traversed the park. He seemed terribly well connected and even apparently knew the Prince Regent himself. While Angus naturally set no store by such things, he was fairly sure this was exactly the sort of person who would impress Lord Burtenshaw, yet frustratingly he had yet to encounter his neighbour at a social event.

After all this time in London he was also becoming decidedly impatient with what he felt was a clear lack of progress. He must speak to Lord Burtenshaw and soon. And then, one way or another, he and Eilidh could return home.

Burtenshaw remained frustratingly aloof, conversing with Angus in only a cursory way and occasionally making scathing, inaccurate statements about Scotland. Was there any sense in waiting much longer? Burtenshaw had surely formed an impression of himself and Eilidh by now and Angus had little hope of overturning the man's prejudice towards Scotland.

Eilidh still hoped they would be invited to a ball and they both knew this would matter to Burtenshaw, but Angus's instincts were telling him that matters must soon come to a head. He must make a direct offer to Burtenshaw to buy Lidistrome and he would succeed or fail as fate decreed.

From the things he said it was now clear to Angus that Burtenshaw had maintained an antipathy towards Scotland and her people because of a hatred of Jacobites inherited from his own father and grandfather. In an era when most enlightened English people thought Culloden to be ancient history, it was frustrating to know that the very man whom Angus needed to do business had the worst possible view of his country and its people in the circumstances. And to be fair, Culloden was anything but ancient history in Scotland itself. Nor was England's reputation a good one in his country.

On numerous occasions he had sought Burtenshaw out for conversation—sometimes aided by Max—but he still could not say there was any sort of connection or even conviviality between them. Indeed, in recent times he had probably been more often in conversation with Lord Burtenshaw than with Isabella, although Max, now a firm friend, was the family member he saw most.

Unfortunately Max and Eilidh seemed to have had some sort of falling out—probably relating to Eilidh's disapproval of what she saw as Max's empty, hedonistic life. Angus had not quizzed her on the matter, knowing it might provide an opportunity for Eilidh to quiz him in turn about his estrangement from Isabella.

For estrangement it was. Oh, he saw her everywhere, glittering and smiling as though she had not a care in the world, yet with him she was only polite. While he could be glad that she had decided to put her brief *tendre* for him to one side, he was ungenerous enough to be rather put out by it. Never one to hide from his flaws, he had told himself off for having such shabby notions. Isabella must marry. Everyone said so, even she herself. And she must marry an Englishman. The fact that Angus had yet to meet an Englishman who was worthy of her was irrelevant. It was up to Isabella whom she chose.

At least tonight he would be spared the pain of seeing her, for he and Max were promised to the Honourable Geoffrey for cards. He and Max had met early for dinner and a few drinks, for Max had stated he would need strength and fortitude to spend an entire evening with

Geoffrey and Freddy. Matched clodheads, he called them, and thanked Angus for agreeing to be there.

As they approached the man's front door, Max surprised Angus by declaring, 'I am determined that tonight I shall sign no vowels, for I find myself in somewhat straitened circumstances,' Angus sent him a quizzical look. 'An old family servant—Cooper, you will have heard me speak of him—has been let go, so I have commissioned him to do some work for me. It leaves my pocket light until quarter day, but is worth it.'

Knowing by now that 'vowels' referred to the IOUs that gentlemen signed at the gaming tables when they had run out of cash, Angus nodded in sympathy. 'That is well done of you. And it suits me to play for pennies anyway—not because I cannot afford it, but rather because I resent every shilling lost at the tables. But I think Barnstable intends for us to play deep tonight.'

Max sighed. 'I know it, which is why I have brought only the coin I am prepared to lose.'

The footman opened the door and both gentlemen braced themselves for the evening ahead.

Freddy was right, Isabella had to admit. Mr Craven, seemingly finally understanding that Isabella did not particularly like him, had turned his attentions to Miss Bell, who was much more receptive to his overtures. Oh, he politely danced with Isabella, but no longer was he asking pointed questions as if determining her suitability. She moved through the dance blessedly unencumbered by the notion that she was before a magistrate, yet acknowledging ruefully that, had she been as prudent as Prudence, he was the man she should have secured. Of her three suitors, Mr Craven was by far the least offensive. Lord Embury was positively ancient, while the Dishonourable Geoffrey…

Yes, perhaps I should have encouraged Mr Craven after all.

But then the dance ended and Mr Craven, in his solicitous way, offered to fetch her a drink and she had to suppress a shudder at the notion of spending her life as Mrs Craven.

He reminds me too much of Freddy.

Declining Mr Craven's polite offices, she watched as he made his way back to where Miss Bell was ready to welcome him. Stupidly, her overwhelming sense was one of relief.

After fetching her own lemonade, she made her way to where Mrs Edgecombe sat, embracing her mother's friend as if by doing so she could feel an echo of Mama.

'Now then, child—' Mrs Edgecombe's glance was piercing '—what ails you?'

'Oh, nothing that cannot be cured with a good dose of practicality, I should say,' she offered lightly. 'Mr Craven will offer for Miss Bell soon, if I am not mistaken.'

'But what is this? I thought he did not appeal to you?'

'He did not. He *does* not. But—'

Mrs Edgecombe patted her hand in a kindly manner. 'What of that dashing Highlander? He is much more the thing, is he not?'

She flushed, then dropped her gaze. 'Oh! He is not— that is to say, he is not on the hunt for a wife.'

'A pity, for he might have suited you very well.' She leaned forwards conspiratorially. 'Your mother had a fondness for Scotsmen, too!'

Isabella's eyes widened. 'She did? But of course, you were out in the same Season.'

'We were, though that was not exactly my meaning. But, Isabella, let me advise you.'

'Please do, for I am at a loss.'

'This may sound harsh, but I see few options before you. You are choosing a husband in a Season where there are not rich pickings, to say the least.' She took a breath, adding grimly, 'Do not refine too much upon your choice, but simply make the best of it. Once your husband—whoever he might be—has his heir, you will be left alone to enjoy yourself.'

'So I have heard it said, many times. But I have the oddest notion that I would wish to like or at least *respect* my husband. What I see around me—the marriages I see here—that is not what I wish for myself.'

Mrs Edgecombe gave her a kindly look. 'I know and I wish I could advise you to follow your heart or hold fast to your wishes.' She sighed. 'But we are raised to follow the strictures of duty and tradition. You, me, your mama, Miss Bell—all of us.'

'I know it.' She did. Duty was everywhere. It was her *duty* to marry according to her family's wishes. She had always known it, had been raised with a strong sense of the unwritten rules that governed society.

Oh, she could don old dresses and mess about in boats all she wished during family summers, but the *ton* expected her to marry. Freddy certainly expected it. Her parents would probably have expected it. It was, after all, the natural order of things, was it not? And truly, she had tried so hard to co-operate with Freddy's decision that she choose a husband this Season. Until she had met a certain chestnut-haired Scot.

'It is just—now that it comes to it, I feel like I am Anne Boleyn in the Tower.'

'I was exactly the same, you know, as was your mama.'

Her eyes flew to Mrs Edgecombe's face. 'Then— Papa was not her choice?'

Mrs Edgecombe shook her head. 'He was not and a bad business he made of it. Nothing she did was ever good enough for him.' She grimaced. 'Your dear mama was deeply unhappy in the early years of her marriage.'

'That I remember, even as a child. But she was happy in Sussex, I think.'

'She was, when he was not in residence.'

Isabella nodded thoughtfully. 'Yes, it was only when Papa came home that her smiles went away.' She bit her lip. 'Papa was a difficult person.'

They eyed one another wordlessly for a moment, before Mrs Edgecombe added, 'But your mother knew her duty and she adored you children. Afterwards—once her husband became more estranged from her—she was happy then. One must think not only of the immediate future, but of a span of years. Decades, even.'

Decades. The word echoed in Isabella's ears like the clang of a prison bell.

'Your mother earned her happiness eventually. So you see, all may yet work out well. We women are made of stern stuff and we can endure much.'

'But why must we endure? Why can we not *choose*?' The cry came from her heart, as Isabella sensed her fate closing in around her.

Mrs Edgecombe squeezed her hand. 'I too, wish the situation were different. Perhaps one day, all young ladies will freely choose their mate, but until then, most of us must endure matches made by our guardians. At least your brother is giving you the opportunity to choose from among the Season's bachelors.'

Isabella shuddered. 'And a sorry lot they are!'

Mrs Edgecombe frowned. 'It is time for a reckoning, Isabella. I cannot see how you can avoid this. Your brother is determined to see you married this Season and so you are running out of time.' She sent her a keen glance. 'My advice would be to take Embury. Why, he may not even survive the honeymoon and the life of a widow is a merry one, as I well know.'

Isabella glanced across to where Lord Embury sat with the other elders, his grey-white hair and lined face clear indications of his advanced years. 'Yes, and there are many gentlemen who live fourscore years and ten! Oh, it is all too difficult!'

She kept her tone light, but Mrs Edgecombe must have understood something of her desperation. 'Isabella, I know this is difficult and I cannot know what your mama would advise you, my dear. Sadly, we ladies move from being owned by our fathers or guardians to being owned by our husbands, and there is little we can do about it. One must simply hope for the felicity of widowhood.'

'The felicity of widowhood!' She sighed. 'I know you are right—I have been raised as you were, with the full knowledge I must someday marry to please my family. It is just that, now this fate is upon me, I find myself praying or wishing for…for something more.'

Mrs Edgecombe nodded sympathetically. 'I understand. There are some matters where we have a choice and others that are not in our ability to control. So choose well, child, when you choose your husband and be ready to endure what cannot be helped. Other ladies will stand your friend should you have any particular worries, you know.' She squeezed Isabella's hand. 'Now, think carefully about everything I have said. Will you promise me that?'

Isabella nodded. 'I shall.'

Inwardly though, her heart was screaming *No. I do not want any of them!*

Having tasted heaven with Angus's kiss, having felt that connection that she had not even known she yearned for, it was now a hundred times harder for her to accept a *ton* marriage, such as she saw all around her. Everything Mrs Edgecombe had said was true and sensible, and fitted with everything she knew about how marriages were made, but she still did not like it.

Would Freddy allow me to wait a year, if I faithfully promise to choose next Season?

Remaining unwed was her clear preference and, what was more, she had known it even before Freddy had set his impossible end date. But if she could not remain unwed forever, then at least next Season she might have new suitors to consider and Angus would be—*must* be long forgotten by then. There was nothing else for it. She must speak to Freddy and hope he would see sense.

'Freddy, we should go.'

Max's words were lightly uttered, but Angus shared the sentiment. It was late, his mind was filled with images of Isabella—who was apparently attending a ball tonight—and his head hurt. Max would no doubt have his own reasons for leaving and Angus understood exactly why Max wanted to get his older brother home.

Lord Burtenshaw had been losing steadily all evening and had now taken on board a considerable amount of wine. His decisions were becoming increasingly reckless, but it was clear to Angus the man's pride would not allow him to back down in front of Barnstable and his cronies. Were it not for a hint of anxiety in Max's tone, Angus would have been tempted to smile. Drunk men were the same everywhere, it seemed, and getting them home was ever a challenge. Now, how would this play out at a *ton* gentleman's party?

Yawning theatrically, Max continued, 'This has been a delightful evening, but I fear we must leave you. I have an appointment at a ridiculously early hour tomorrow. Freddy, shall we call for the carriage? Angus, may we offer you a ride home?'

'But I am not ready for home yet!' his brother declared sullenly. 'And why should you have any sort of appointment, when you are only a second son? What business could you possibly have?'

With remarkable restraint, Max did not rise to this, instead replying calmly, 'I am promised to my great-aunt's solicitor on the morrow.' He smiled ruefully. 'Lord knows what the old girl has left me, if anything, for she had hardly two farthings to rub together. I suspect I am named as executor, and will be required to settle her affairs. Still, there may be something among her personal possessions to remember her by.'

Lord Burtenshaw glared at his younger brother. 'And why should she leave you anything, when it is I who am head of the family? *I* am the one who must make ends meet and pay all the damned bills, not you!'

Angus's ears pricked up at this.

Bills? He has money worries? That would suit my purpose very well.

Logic decreed that selling an unimportant estate that Burtenshaw never intended to visit would be a sensible move, particularly if money was tight.

A hint of bitterness had now crept into Lord Burtenshaw's tone, as he continued with his self-pitying rant. 'Yes, you can play and drink to your heart's content, Max, while I cannot enjoy a few nights of cards without you acting like my nursemaid.'

'A few nights?' Max's tone was sharp. 'Have there been other card parties?'

Barnstable made haste to clarify. 'Perfectly unexceptional, I assure you. Plank and I—that is to say, Lord *Burtenshaw* and I have been indulging in a few practice rounds with a couple of other chaps, in preparation for this bigger party tonight.'

'I see.' Were the same alarms being sounded in Max's head that were currently ringing in Angus's mind?

Have they been fleecing Lord Burtenshaw?

'We shall play on, Max, for I have a feeling you are the cause of my ill fortune. You go. Yes, and you, too, MacDonald. Geoffrey and I shall do very nicely alone with these chaps. I have a feeling my luck will change without my brother and his Scottish crony glowering at me. You may send the carriage back for me when you are done.'

Crony? The urge to plant Freddy a facer was growing by the day. If he was not constrained by the need for diplomacy, Angus would relish the opportunity to tell Burtenshaw exactly what he thought of him.

There was little Max could do, in the face of such a direct order. His face set, he muttered polite farewells, as did Angus, and they each gathered their modest winnings and made their way silently to the hallway to await the Burtenshaw carriage. Max had too much pride to speak of it when they were alone, but Angus knew him well enough now to understand he was deeply concerned. Instead Max made inconsequential conversation, asking Angus what his plans were for the morrow.

'Eilidh and I have been invited to the Sandison ball tomorrow night, so no doubt I shall be subjected to knee breeches and lectures from my sister on her expectations of me. Our first *ton* ball and I cannot say I am anticipating it with any joy.'

Apart from the opportunity to see Isabella again.

Max gave a short laugh. 'Your sister is…formidable, Angus. I would there were more like her.' In the darkness of the carriage, Angus could not make out his expression, but there was some tone in his voice that made him wonder as to Max's meaning.

'Your own sister is fairly formidable, you know.'

'She is, but she will submit to Freddy's demands for all that. We men have our troubles, but women, too, must suffer in other ways.'

Angus swallowed. 'Has she—has she made her choice, do you know?'

'She has not. It is down to Embury or Barnstable, I think.'

'Barnstable! Surely your brother would not allow her to marry such a man!'

And Embury is not much better.

'You saw them tonight, Angus. Bosom bows, the pair of them.'

'I—yes, you are right. He does not seem to see Barnstable clearly.'

'He sees very little. It is one of his many limitations.'

'You would have been much more suited to be the elder son, Max.'

'I thank you for saying so, but what is, must be. In my own way I am as powerless as Isabella. The law demands and society upholds. It is ever so.'

They fell silent, and all around them an air of lowering pessimism grew and thickened.

Max is powerless against Freddy. As is Isabella. As am I. Their freedoms and choices all rested on the decisions of a limited, cloth-headed man-boy. *I might as well have stayed in Benbecula.*

While he still had hope that Burtenshaw would sell him Lidistrome, on a personal level all he had achieved was the pain of making a new friend he would never see again and meeting a formidable, enchanting lady he could never marry.

Chapter Thirteen

Morning dawned and Isabella sighed in relief as Sally opened the shutters. After the ball last night she had not slept well, tossing and turning for what had felt like hours. She had rehearsed her planned conversation with Freddy two dozen times, each time trying a different form of words, or upsetting herself by imagining the hundreds of different ways in which he could say no to her request to delay a year.

Her conversation with Mrs Edgecombe had been difficult, but it had cleared her mind. No longer could she wallow in dreaming of an unobtainable future with a man who would marry a Scottish girl and probably never leave his island again. Now was the time to be level headed and logical and to secure a stay of execution from Freddy.

'My brothers were not at the ball last night, Sally. Were they out late, do you know?' she asked in what she hoped was an innocent manner.

'Yes, Miss, they were at a card party together, I understand, but both are planning to attend Mrs Sandison's ball tonight, so you will have their company along with Lady Burtenshaw.'

'Two balls in a row! I declare I shall be yawning by suppertime!'

'That is why I left you a little later this morning, Miss.' Sally glanced at her anxiously. 'Would you like to rest longer, Miss?'

'No, for I am promised to Miss MacDonald today. It will be her first *ton* ball, you know.'

'Indeed, and a pretty picture the two of you will make!'

They were drifting from the matter at hand. 'Is Freddy yet up, Sally?'

'He is not yet downstairs, Miss.'

'Very well.'

By the time Isabella had dressed and breakfasted with Prudence, Freddy had still not emerged from his chamber. Biting down on her frustration, Isabella set off for Eilidh's house, Sally by her side. As she approached, her heart did its usual tattoo at the notion she might see Angus, but as ever she admonished herself not to indulge in thoughts of him. He must be set aside as a girlish fancy. She had womanly problems to grapple with: she must see to her duty and negotiate a palatable version of her own future.

And so she enjoyed her time with Eilidh, talking about tonight's ball and the significance of the invitation. 'There may be some high sticklers who would not have invited you, Eilidh. It seems they view any Scot with suspicion and a ball is considered the highest of events outside of Court. So even some who may have been agreeable towards you at less formal events may not be so courteous tonight.' She bit her lip. 'I should not like for you or your brother to feel insulted, or to think it is anything about you or him personally, for indeed it is not!'

'Never fear! In Scotland, too, the doings of our grandfathers and great-grandfathers still echo today and, to be fair, in some settings an Englishman might be looked on with the same suspicion.' She smiled. 'No, we can only hope that the invitation has a positive impression on Lord Burtenshaw, for my brother means to speak with him very soon.'

'I have the same notion myself. Oh, not about your estate. Freddy does not believe women have the minds for matters of business, so if I dared to mention such a thing it would only work against you, I am afraid.' Daringly, she decided to share her plan. 'I mean to speak with him about my marriage.'

Instantly, Eilidh seemed to become a little guarded, or was Isabella imagining it? 'Indeed? Does he still insist you marry this Season? For there are not many weeks left.'

'He does, but I mean to ask him if I can choose a husband next Season instead. My reasoning is that there are not very many eligible bachelors at present and I do not fancy Lord Embury or the Honourable Mr Barnstable.'

Eilidh appeared much struck by this. 'No indeed! But what of Mr Craven?'

'I expect him to offer for Miss Bell, if he has not already done so.'

'I had wondered about that. Is there an understanding between them, then?'

'Not that I know of. But Mr Craven grew tired of my disinterestedness, I think.'

'Ah.' Unspoken between them was the chestnut-haired reason for that disinterestedness. 'Surely your brother will see that neither Embury nor Barnstable would be a suitable husband for you? Next Season there may well be better choices for you.'

'Yes, and I mean to offer to promise faithfully to Freddy that I shall do my duty without complaint next year.'

'That seems more than fair.'

'I hope my brother agrees with you!'

The door opened, and instantly Isabella's heart leapt. 'Good day, Miss Wood!' There he was, in full Highland dress, his eyes meeting hers, and instantly she felt rather breathless. His smile, the handsomeness of him... Isabella knew she could not have him, but it did not stop her heart from yearning, or her body from longing for him.

'Good day, Mr MacDonald. Are you looking forward to your first ball in London?' Thankfully her voice sounded reasonably even.

He grimaced. 'I am and I amn't, I must confess. I am not sure it will make much difference to my business with your brother, for if he has not as yet formed an impression of my character, then why should one ball make a difference?'

His sister tutted. 'Yes, but as Isabella and I have just been discussing, being invited at all is significant.' She shrugged. 'Besides, we have come this far. We might as well go to the ball, on the possibility it might have some influence.' She grinned. 'As well as the possibility we might even enjoy it!'

'I fully intend to enjoy it, Eilidh, I assure you!' His blue-eyed gaze swung to Isabella. 'And may I speak up now for two dances with you, Isabella? Your choice of dance. I understand that I must not dance with any lady more than twice, is that correct?'

'Yes, for it might look as though...' She faltered, suddenly conscious of what she was about to say. It would draw comment if he did not dance with her, since they were known to be friends, but equally, dancing with any lady more than twice would be too particular.

He understood. 'As though I was singling her out for particular attention? I should not like to draw the attention of the gossips to any young lady.'

'Especially as the gossips will be watching your every move, Angus,' his sister responded tartly. 'Yes, and mine!'

'So tonight might be both ordeal and pleasure at once?'

'I hope,' Isabella offered, 'that it will not be an ordeal at all!'

'That remains to be seen,' said Eilidh, rather grimly. 'Still, our course is now set. We must see it through to its conclusion.'

Her words echoed with Isabella afterwards as she and Sally walked back home. Angus had not kissed her hand and, despite her own reaction to him, there had truly been nothing in his demeanour to suggest any particular friendship or connection between them. It was as though her own Angus had been taken away in exchange for a twin—a twin who was polite, friendly even, but who gave no hint of the passionate kisses they had shared, nor indeed of the special connection she had thought existed between them.

He cares nothing for me. The thought was lowering, and she walked on with her head down and a lump in her throat. *Was it even real, the connection that I thought had sparked between us?*

She had frequently heard it said that young men would sometimes develop a violent *tendre* for a lady, which would then pass like a storm, leaving no trace afterwards. It was perfectly clear to her that her dreams of happiness with him were doomed to failure and that she would be better to attend to the business ahead— persuading Freddy to wait a year.

'Are my brothers home?' she asked the footman on entering the house.

'Lord Burtenshaw is closeted in his library with a visitor,' came the reply, 'and Mr Wood has not yet returned from his morning appointment.'

'I see. Thank you, James. Please let Lord Burtenshaw know I wish to speak with him when he is free.'

Making her way to the parlour, she sat with Prudence for almost an hour—an hour of inanities and gossip, which she listened to with half an ear, making what she hoped were encouraging noises now and again. A pity Max was not here, to calm her and soothe her worries, but Great-Aunt Morton's solicitor had asked him to call. Max expected to be named as executor, which would give him the burden of helping to organise the old lady's affairs, including any debts.

She had no one else, I suppose, for only Max and I took any interest in her.

Finally the footman appeared to inform her that her eldest brother was free. Feeling decidedly nervous, she made her farewells to Prudence and went to the library. About to enter in her usual informal way, she hesitated and knocked. On his call she entered, to find him seated behind his desk looking particularly forbidding.

'Isabella! I wished to speak to you.'

'And I wished to speak to you.'

'Whatever it is, it can wait. I have today settled the matter of your marriage.'

'You…you have done *what*?' There was a roaring in Isabella's ears and the room seemed to sway about her. Reaching for the back of a nearby armchair, she clutched it to steady herself.

'I have been more than fair, Isabella. I gave you your pick of the Season's bachelors. Word is that Craven's betrothal will be announced tonight, and you know I would happily have agreed to him as a husband for you. But you could not bring him up to scratch and so, for the sake of the good name of our family, I must act swiftly.'

Isabella found her voice. 'Not bring him up to scratch? I did not want him! I do not want any of them!'

'You think me such a ninnyhammer that I did not know that? I have watched you, Isabella. Yes, and Prudence has, too! You have not as much as flirted with any of them. But I am your guardian and it is my duty to see you marry. You have declined to make a choice and so I have made it for you.'

'How dare you!' She was shouting now, but she did not care. Her temper was up and what he had done was unacceptable. 'This is outrageous! I knew you for a ninnyhammer, yes, but I did not think you capable of such utter folly! Yes, *folly*, and hubris and pure selfishness! I am ashamed to call you brother!'

He rose, his face flushed with anger. 'Isabella! How dare you speak to me in such a manner! You are the one who should be ashamed. If my father could see you now—'

'See *me*? Father was a pompous ass at times, but he

was never bacon-brained. And he would never have done something so heinous as this!'

His lip curled. 'Spare me the Cheltenham tragedy, Isabella. For years you have been allowed to run wild, but you are no longer a child and it is time you began acting like a lady, not a girl!'

'And you think forcing me into a marriage I do not want will suddenly make me older?'

'You need a firm, guiding hand. Your behaviour today simply confirms I have made the right decision.'

'But it is not your decision. It is mine.'

'No. The law upholds my right as your guardian to choose a husband for you.'

He is right, damn him.

'But you said nothing of this. Why should you suddenly do something so utterly foolish and unexpected?'

He swallowed, abruptly looking uncomfortable. 'I do not know what you mean. I have been considering this for a very long time.'

'Nonsense! Why, you have been baiting me about which suitor I would favour. Just a few days ago you told me I had another fortnight to decide, and now you are going back on that. What you are saying now is entirely unexpected and I wish to know what is behind it!'

'Nothing, save a desire to see you settled.'

He is lying. But why?

'Now, do you not wish to know who your husband is to be, Isabella? Perhaps that will reconcile you to my decision, for I believe him to be a man of sense and a good friend to me.'

Abruptly, her anger drained away, leaving a sort of hopelessness. 'No, I do not wish to know. I wish to have some manner of choice, as Mama did. As Prudence did.

Would you have taken Prudence if her father had forced her to marry you?'

'My marriage to Prudence is a good one and I trusted both our fathers when they agreed to it.'

Her jaw dropped. 'Then—you did not *choose* Prudence?'

'Not precisely, no. My father suggested her just before he died and I was content. And despite her limitations I have not lived to regret the match.'

Limitations. She closed her eyes briefly in horror at his manner of words. *She is his wife, for goodness sake! Can he not show some respect when he speaks of her?*

Of course he had had his marriage arranged, she thought bitterly, for he was always unlikely to have been able to find a mate any other way, despite the title. How could she make an argument in the face of such pompous, ill-conceived obstinacy? Sinking into the seat, she felt at an utter loss.

'You must see the advantages of entering the wedded state, Isabella. You will have your own household to run, with servants to command and plenty of blunt.'

'I care nothing for money and I never shall.'

He snorted. 'Such foolishness! You have always believed yourself to be cleverer than me, Isabella—no, do not deny it—but with those words you demonstrate that there is little between your ears. How will you live, or eat, or dress, without money? Tell me that!'

She shook her head. 'Naturally I know that a certain level of funds is necessary. But I have no desire for jewellery or finery, nor do I need three houses, only one. I should be more content with a gentleman of my choice, even if his income was modest.'

He laughed. 'And this is why I must be wise on your

behalf, for no doubt you would choose a hovel with a handsome soldier rather than opting for a man of sense and position!'

At least he did not say 'handsome Scot'.

Isabella's hopes were dwindling by the moment. All of her arguments were failing to impress him. Taking a breath, she tried her one last request. 'Can I wait until next Season, Freddy, if I faithfully promise to choose a husband then?'

He shook his head. 'It is too late. I have today signed the marriage settlements.' He indicated the papers on the desk before him and her eyes widened in horror.

'Signed? *Already signed?* Without even speaking to me?'

'You had your chances, Isabella. There is no turning back now.'

No turning back.

The prison bell knelled once more inside Isabella's head.

No way out. Trapped. Imprisoned. Given by my brother to some unknown man, as though I were a horse.

'How much is he paying you in marriage settlements?' Her tone was harsh.

'That is none of your concern. You will bring your dowry—a respectable sum—to the marriage, for it came from Mama and is fully protected in law. Whatever additional arrangements I have made with your future husband are between him and me.'

Isabella's mind was whirling and seemed unable to settle on any particular thought. While she knew she should pursue the issue of settlements, she already had too much to deal with. *I am to be married.* The inevitability of it washed over her. She had no choice. Nowhere to run to, no means to support herself, no one to rescue her. She was trapped on all sides like a cornered fox. A strange detachment washed over her briefly and in that instant she knew why the fox sometimes gave up at the very end.

'I am contented.' Prudence's words came back to Isabella now. *If this is inevitable, I must draw on Mama's strength and make the best of it.*

Taking a deep breath, she asked the key question, able to avoid it no longer. 'Who is the man, Freddy?'

Her brother began fiddling with a button on his waistcoat, a wheedling smile half-growing on his face. 'He is a member of an esteemed English family. Their ancestors go back to the Conqueror himself, you will be delighted to hear. He has a good income and has agreed a most generous settlement—but, of course, that is of no matter. He also greatly admires you, which has had an influence on my choice.'

As he was speaking, cold fingers of apprehension were pricking Isabella's spine. 'Who is it, Freddy? Just tell me!'

His reply made the room spin again, as her worst fears were realised. 'Barnstable.'

Chapter Fourteen

The Sandison ball promised to be the most glittering event of the Season so far. Everyone was there and delighted to be part of such a crush. Angus found his curiosity piqued and he was, despite himself, desperate to dance with Isabella.

Tonight he would be allowed to hold her hand as they danced and talk with her, and feel the now-familiar thrill as her eyes met his. Maintaining the act that they were simply friends was draining, yet he lived for moments he might store in his memory.

While he knew she could never be his wife, no matter how much he might wish it, he was conscious that he would soon be returning to Scotland and would never see her again. The thought sent pain arcing through him and he knew himself to be lost. Once more the voice of temptation began whispering impossible things. Should he ask Lord Burtenshaw for his permission to speak to her?

Instantly, he dismissed the thought. Lord Burtenshaw might or might not sell him the land, but the chance of his agreeing to Angus marrying his sister and taking her away to the Western Isles was nigh on impossible. No, tonight he must simply enjoy her company one more time and perhaps create more of those precious memories that would see him through the long, empty years ahead.

The ball itself, he soon realised, was nothing special. All of the usual people—and a few more—were crushed into the middle floor of a typical London mansion. There were copious drinks, flower displays, and dancing in a large room at the rear of the building. Downstairs was a cool outdoor terrace lit with flambeaux, as well as some card rooms and retiring rooms. Both floors—yes, and the hallways and staircase—were filled with ladies dripping with jewellery and wearing a rainbow of silk and satin gowns, and men in uniform knee breeches and coloured jackets. As Isabella had predicted, very few of them were fulsomely welcoming Angus and Eilidh, as if everyone was waiting for someone else to take the lead.

'Angus!' Thank goodness for Max, who by now cared not whether the *ton* liked his friends. He shook Angus's hand, bowed to Eilidh and expressed his admiration of her gown. Since this contained a great deal of MacDonald tartan and was a clear statement on her part, this was significant. 'Come and join us!' he added, leading the way through the crowds to where Isabella and Prudence stood with Lord Burtenshaw, near the fireplace in the Sandison drawing room.

Instantly, Angus detected that something was amiss. Burtenshaw was his usual taciturn self, barely acknowledging Angus and Eilidh's arrival, although he completed a shallow bow. Prudence was inscrutable as ever, but Isabella… He frowned.

Something ails her.

She was pale and her gaze held a deadness that he had never before seen in her. At the same time he became aware, as the conversation continued, that Max was exhibiting a sort of nervous energy, his eyes over-bright, and his speech fast and vacuous.

He and Eilidh exchanged a quick glance. She also had noted something amiss, it was clear, but her subtle shrug indicated that, like him, she knew not what. A footman appeared with a tray of drinks and they all selected one. Isabella drank hers quickly, which was most unlike her. She still had barely spoken. Angus and Eilidh along with Max and Prudence carried the conversation, which was punctuated by friends and acquaintances coming to speak to Burtenshaw and his family. Each time, they were no more than polite to Eilidh and Angus.

'Observe, Prudence!' Burtenshaw was suddenly alert. 'The Beau is here!'

He was looking at someone somewhere behind Angus, who naturally could not turn to look. Max undertook the explanations. 'The Beau is a close friend of the Prince Regent and an arbiter of fashion. His approval can be the makings of a man or lady and his disapproval a blow from which no one has ever recovered. His attendance tonight is something of a coup for the Sandisons.'

'And are you intimate with such an important man?'

There was a decided edge to Eilidh's tone and Max visibly bristled as he replied. 'No, although everyone here knows who he is. And I do not say he is important, though I am certain many here would think it.'

'Hush,' admonished Lord Burtenshaw, 'for he is

walking this way! Oh, my lord, what if he means to speak to us?'

'Stand up straight, Isabella!' Prudence hissed, as Lord Burtenshaw adjusted his waistcoat, an uncertain smile on his face.

'Good evening, ladies and gentlemen.' The man joined them and Angus turned, recognising him instantly. While Lord Burtenshaw stammered a few words about it being an honour and a pleasure to enjoy a moment of his time, Angus simply grinned, awaiting his moment.

'Mr MacDonald!' The Beau bowed deeply, a smile growing on his face. 'I thought it must be you.'

'Mr Brummell! I am glad to see you here, for I have missed our walks these past few days.'

'I, too. I have been out of town with Prinny. Perhaps tomorrow?'

'Perhaps.'

Depending on my interview with Burtenshaw.

The Beau stayed for almost ten minutes laughing and talking with Angus, and clapped a hand on his shoulder on making his farewell, clearly indicating to the gathered assembly that Angus was not simply to be tolerated, but embraced.

'Well!' Prudence was first to recover. 'Mr MacDonald, you have acquired some fine friends in London.'

Angus shrugged 'I did not know that he was a notable figure. I simply enjoy his company, for he has wit and humour. He might almost be a Scot!'

'I think not!' Burtenshaw retorted. 'The very notion!'

The effect of Beau Brummell's endorsement was not long in becoming clear. A train of people took turns to greet Angus and Eilidh, laughing at their every utterance and declaring them to be refreshingly different and entertaining.

As he concentrated on preventing his cynicism from showing on his face, Angus was conscious that Isabella remained detached from all conversation—as though she were there in body, but not in spirit.

Something is terribly wrong.

When Eilidh asked her to accompany her to the ladies' retiring room, he was relieved and hopeful that Eilidh might discover what ailed her.

Isabella welcomed the opportunity to get away from Angus, for the sight of him, along with knowing she would soon be wed to the last man on earth she would have chosen, was killing her. Her mind was incapable of sustained thought, she could barely string two words together and she was entirely consumed by fear, and sorrow, and heartbreak.

'Isabella!' Eilidh was eyeing her anxiously. They had just left the retiring room and were in the ground-floor hallway. 'Here, sit with me!' Eilidh indicated a nearby sofa which had just been vacated by two dowagers. 'Please, tell me what ails you. Are you unwell, my dear?'

'Unwell? Yes, I suppose I am. I shall never be well again.' Isabella forced the words out, knowing her speech was as slow as her brain and that she sounded odd.

Eilidh took both her hands. 'Tell me what has happened.'

'I am to marry Barnstable. It is all signed and agreed.' Her own words sounded far away and meant nothing.

Eilidh gasped. 'No! I never thought you would choose him.'

'I did not. Freddy chose him. I am not even to have a say.'

'But that is… I cannot understand it!'

'Nor I. But he is my guardian and so I must submit.' Isabella delivered her responses in the same flat tone. Her life was over and nothing mattered.

Eilidh quizzed her a little more and expressed her outrage in no uncertain terms, but eventually there was nothing more to say. 'Shall we return upstairs?' Isabella asked placidly.

'Are you well enough to be here, Isabella? Should you not go home?'

Isabella shrugged and they began making their way through the crowds towards the main staircase. 'It matters not whether I am here or at the house. I have no home.'

'There you are, Isabella!' It was Freddy, a jovial smile pasted on his face. 'Look who is here to see you.' He stepped aside to reveal the Honourable Geoffrey Barnstable, who instantly bowed and took Isabella's hand to kiss it. Shuddering, she snatched it away.

'Good evening, ladies, I hope you are well.' He bowed to Eilidh, who ensured both hands were busy with her fan as she curtsied in response.

'Yes, well,' declared Freddy, rubbing his hands together. 'Is this not delightful?'

Delightful?

Isabella eyed her brother in mild confusion. 'How so?'

'Step aside a moment,' he stammered, propelling Isabella to his right and jerking his head towards Barnstable. Addressing them both, in a lowered tone, he declared, 'My delight is because of certain recent events, that is to say, future events. No announcement yet, of course, for Isabella has only just—that is to say—'

'Now then, Burtenshaw,' the Honourable Geoffrey interjected. 'You promised me a special licence within the week.'

I must marry him within the week?

'He did?' Isabella turned to Freddy. 'You did?'

'No point in prolonging matters, is there?'

'Miss Wood! Isabella!' She turned to her betrothed, who was eyeing her in a decidedly lascivious way. 'Naturally I am desperate for our nuptials to take place as soon as possible. I am overjoyed at having won your hand and I—'

'I should sooner marry the stable hand!' Isabella declared, sweeping away back towards Eilidh, then on towards the staircase, Eilidh on her heels. Anger, the first discernible emotion Isabella had felt in quite a number of hours, was making itself felt. 'How dare Freddy do this to me!'

They reached the upper floor just as sets were forming for the first dance and both young ladies were taken off by their promised partners. Isabella saw little of Eilidh after that. Instead, she danced. Angus came to claim her for the first set and she managed to survive the ordeal. To see him so close by, to feel his warmth and take in his heady scent, when she knew of the horrors that lay ahead for her, was almost too much to bear.

'Are you well, Isabella?' he asked, as the steps brought them close together. 'You are never normally so quiet and you look pale.'

'I have a slight headache,' she admitted. It was perfectly true, although 'raging' might have been a more accurate description than 'slight'. The physical pain of her throbbing temples was demanding much of her attention and prevented her from looking over her shoulder at the thing that now stalked her. Her own future.

'Should you not go home? Perhaps Max, or Lady Burtenshaw—'

'No. I do not wish to go home.' Home, to her bedchamber, silence and solitude, and no distraction? No, she was better here, where she could manage to not think of it for a little longer.

He withdrew a little at her curt response. 'I meant only to help.'

He is cross with me. Or hurt. She reflected on this and her innards clenched. *Well, good. For if only he had proposed marriage, I would not be in this predicament.* Yes, and if he had not made her love him, marriage to anyone—never mind the appalling Geoffrey—might not have seemed impossible. *I might have taken Mr Craven.*

'I am to be married.'

She made the bald statement just as the dance took them apart, to turn with other partners in their set. By the time they came back together again, Isabella could read nothing of Angus's reaction. His gaze was shuttered, his expression frustratingly neutral.

'I see,' he offered, a hint of caution in his tone. 'I—I do not know what to say.'

Was that pity in his expression? A wave of anger shuddered through her.

This is your fault, if it is anyone's!

With vague notions of pride, and of Mama's steel rising within her, she tossed her head, pasting a smile on to her face.

'I dare say it will be a great adventure, to be out from under Freddy's thumb and mistress of my own establishment!'

His jaw slackened briefly, then tightened. His brow furrowed, he seemed incapable of further speech.

You do not wish me to marry, yet you would not offer for me yourself! Isabella seethed with frustration and pain, and somewhere deeper down, fear. *What is ahead of me?*

At the end of the dance she dipped a shallow curtsy without properly meeting Angus's eyes, then was immediately claimed by her next partner. After that she danced every dance, pausing only for supper which she spent with Mrs Edgecombe, who knew there was something amiss but, thankfully, did not press her.

Just two more dance sets, Isabella thought in desperation, *and then this ordeal will end.*

Checking her mental list, she realised she had no partner for the next set, while Angus had called the last dance of the evening. Each would last for almost half an hour, so she had only an hour more to endure, to not cry, to avoid Barnstable. She had lied when he had asked her for a dance, telling him that her card was entirely full. If he saw her now, he would likely make her dance with him and she could not bear it.

Glancing sharply about for any sign of him, Isabella swiftly made her way downstairs to the retiring room, concealing herself within for as long as she could. For the past couple of hours she had managed to avoid even speaking to him, although she had been aware of him a few times as she danced, watching her in a way that made her shudder. Angus, too, she had avoided after their dance, for being in his company was exquisite torture. Very soon he would be gone, and she would be left with Geoffrey for a husband and her dreams in tatters.

Emerging cautiously from the retiring room, Isabella made for the terrace in what she hoped was a calm convincing manner. Why should she not seek a little peace and fresh air, away from the heat and noise of the ball? Slipping out through the double doors, she made for the darkest corner, her gaze lifting to the starlit sky as if searching for a miracle.

Angus's patience had paid off. Having diligently searched the public rooms for Isabella, from top to bottom, he had hit on the notion that she had to be in the ladies' retiring room. Her news earlier had come as a severe shock to him, as he had not anticipated that he would be faced with the reality of her betrothal to another. In his imagination, that dreadful event would happen long after he had left London and he hoped to not hear of it for an age afterwards.

Something about it did not make sense. Why, earlier, Eilidh had told him that while Isabella was more accepting of the notion that she needed to choose a husband, her plan had been to ask Burtenshaw to delay until next Season.

Why had she changed her mind? Had she and the pompous Freddy argued, convincing her that marrying into freedom this year was preferable? 'Out from under Freddy's thumb,' she had said, 'and mistress of my own establishment.' Almost, he could understand this. Living with Freddy as guardian would be nigh on intolerable. For someone as quick-witted and spirited as Isabella, it would ultimately become impossible.

In a way it did made sense, particularly in light of the

coolness she had been showing towards him for weeks now. It hurt him every time they met, yet he matched her friendly distance with a similar coolness of his own. Perhaps, he had told himself, she had needed to protect her heart. Unfortunately for him, his heart was already lost and aching at the thought of leaving her for good. The news that she would soon marry was a hammer blow to his heart.

His thoughts went back to his other conversation with Eilidh, just now. His sister's hissed words had given him the shocking information that Isabella was to be married to Barnstable. *Barnstable, of all men!* What on earth had made her choose such a vain, self-serving blackguard?

Or had it even been her choice? The Isabella he thought he knew would never have consented to such a match. Yet earlier, it had seemed as though she wanted the marriage.

Perhaps I do not know her as well as I believed.

Or perhaps her pompous eldest brother had forced this on her, somehow. It seemed strange to even think of such an outrageous possibility, but London society was very, very different to the Islands. Nevertheless, he now meant to ask her directly, being a person who believed that plain speech was always better than obliqueness. That need for openness was partly why he was chafing so greatly at not having shown his hand to Burtenshaw about Lidistrome.

Well, at least I have put that right.

Earlier in the evening he had asked Burtenshaw if he might call with him on the morrow, to discuss a matter of business. Burtenshaw had looked first confused, then a little intrigued. Crucially, he had agreed to the meeting and they had fixed upon a time.

By this time tomorrow I shall know the outcome and one way or another Eilidh and I shall be packing for home.

Home. The word triggered a wave of longing for Broch Clachan and its people. Oh, how he missed his homeplace! And how wonderful it would be to return! As ever, an image of Isabella by his side formed in his mind. He would take pride in bringing her to the machair, to the top of Rueval, to his cousin's castle at Ardmore. In his mind's eye she was smiling, happy and contented. Ruthlessly he pushed the thoughts away. He could not risk her unhappiness.

But I know she will be dreadfully unhappy with Barnstable...

There she is!

He straightened as he spied her emerging from the retiring room and watched as she made her way to the terrace.

Now is my opportunity to speak with her.

With a swift glance about to ensure no one was watching, he followed her outside into the blessed coolness.

At first, the only people he could see were a couple of matrons, fanning themselves to his right. He paused, looking about, then spied her in the darkness to the far left. Silently he made his way across. Her head turned towards him and he knew the moment she recognised him, for she stiffened.

'Isabella.' Conscious that the ladies at the other end of the terrace might be observing, he kept his voice low so they could not hear.

'Mr MacDonald.' Her pointed use of his surname was a rebuke.

He ignored it. 'Isabella, tell me truly, do you wish this marriage? Eilidh has said—though I cannot believe it—'

'That I am to be married to B-Barnstable? It is true.'

'And you have agreed to this?'

'What choice do I have?' Her words shot back at him like arrows. 'He is the only man to have offered for me and, as you well know, my brother insists I marry this Season.'

Pain knifed through his chest. The pain of knowing that the most unworthy man in London had won her. Barnstable would share Isabella's life and her bed. He would be father to her children.

Because I did not offer for her.

Glad of the darkness, he squeezed his eyes shut for a moment, as a wave of agony went through him.

'Then your brother would not let you wait a year?'

Her face was tight with anger. 'No. But at least I shall be free of Freddy's control.'

There is nothing I can do.

Gathering his strength, he repeated the formulaic words, 'I wish you happy, Isabella.'

'Happy? *Happy?* What does happiness have to do with marriage, pray tell?' Her tone was clipped, brittle.

'I… Well, one would naturally hope—'

'I see it now. You are glad to be rid of me. Well, let me tell you, sir, that my happiness and my marriage is none of your concern.'

'Isabella, I only meant—'

'I care not what you meant! Haven't you done enough to harm me? Why should you come to me now?'

Her words knifed through him and he responded without thinking. 'Why? Because I am concerned about you! Because I cannot understand how you came to be betrothed to a man like that! Because I—' He stopped, barely managing to prevent declaring himself. What good would it do? He could never take her away from England and she was now betrothed to another. 'Because I wish things were different,' he offered finally, knowing that his words sounded flat. Flat and weak.

Her strangled sound of disgust indicated that she knew it, too. 'Do not bring me wishes, Angus. Wishes mean nothing. Just go back to Scotland, and do not ever return.'

'As you wish.' He could hear the pain in her voice, knew that he was the cause, yet he could not fix anything. Where was the fierce Laird of Broch Clachan, leader of men? For the first time he felt how London had emasculated him, had taken away his voice and his fists and his very Scottishness. 'I do not belong here. I never did. I hate the knowledge that I have brought you pain, Isabella. It was never my intention.'

'No? Intentions are meaningless, Angus. Intentions are not real. But this is real. You going back to Scotland. Me marrying Barnstable. We all must grow up eventually. Childish dreams are just as imaginary and just as false as fine intentions. Now, please let Prudence know that I have the headache and shall wait here for the ball to end. I am afraid I must decline to dance with you again.'

The finality in her tone was crystal clear. No last dance. This was as clear an adieu as he had ever heard. He half-reached out a hand towards her, then let it fall again.

'*Beannachd gu bràth, mo ghràdh.* Goodbye.' *My love*, he added silently.

Turning before he risked shedding unmanly tears, he strode across the terrace and into the house. Once inside he made his way upstairs to where Prudence had sat all evening. 'Lady Burtenshaw.' He made a bow and she turned to him, her expression inscrutable. 'Miss Wood is downstairs and has charged me to inform you that she has the headache. She intends to stay on the terrace until the ball has ended.'

'Does she?' Prudence nodded slowly. 'I shall take her home instantly. She has had a trying day.'

There was a pause, loaded with unspoken words.

What does she wish me to say?

'Ladies,' Prudence continued, looking him directly in the eye, 'are raised to know their duty.'

'Of course,' he agreed. 'But what if the thing they are asked to do is too much? Or simply wrong?'

She eyed him evenly. 'We only have the choices that are given us. We cannot make others do as we wish. Now, if you will excuse me, I must call for the carriage and inform my husband we are leaving early.'

While her words were a little obscure, it was clear Prudence knew it was because he had not offered for her that Isabella had ended up promised to Barnstable. The knowledge made him sick. His mind still awhirl from the revelations of the past hour, he considered the matter.

He had assumed that, once he had stepped away, Isabella would find a good husband from among the gentlemen of the *ton*. Instead she had somehow ended up paired with Barnstable, of all men. How could such a man ever make her happy? And would taking her away from her home and her family to live in the Western Isles really be worse?

* * *

Finding a corner in which to loiter, he had dealt with occasional conversations from fellow guests and made it through to the end of the ball. Once in the carriage, Eilidh was full of outrage at Isabella's fate. 'I mean, Barnstable, of all people! What was her brother thinking? And what has Max done for her? I'll tell you what: nothing! That man is such a disappointment!'

Angus felt every word like a kick in the gut. Burtenshaw was determined to see Isabella married and Max could not conjure up an alternative suitor from thin air, so Eilidh's words seemed harsh.

But not if applied to me. I am the disappointment. I have failed her.

The fact he could not have reasonably anticipated this outcome meant nothing. He loved her with all his heart. He suspected she loved him. As with Alasdair and his ill-fated bride, love might not be enough. But it was a damn sight better than condemning Isabella to a life of misery with the Dishonourable Geoffrey!

He sat up straighter, knowing that he needed to act. *I must ask Burtenshaw for her hand!*

His conversation with Burtenshaw now had double significance and he had to hope the man would see sense in relation to Isabella's nuptials. Allowing Eilidh to exclaim in frustrated anger all the way back to Chesterfield Street, he began to plan how he might broach the subject with her pompous, anti-Scottish guardian.

Chapter Fifteen

'Come now, Isabella, we must see to your packing. I shall ring for Sally and for a couple of footmen to bring some trunks.'

Prudence's tone was brisk, but her words sent fear shivering through Isabella. Her mind remained agitated, her spirits low. All her life she had chafed at the notion of duty, yet had co-operated as much as she could manage. The freedom of Sussex in summer had made her life tolerable so far, but who was to say what might happen once she was married. Even one day a year spent in *that man*'s company would be too much.

Like all young ladies who knew Barnstable, she could barely manage the twenty minutes of empty discourse expected in social settings. To have to take his name, to feel the pity of every lady in London, to endure his company at breakfast, at dinner, at social gatherings… She shuddered. And she dare not even *think* about what he might do to her or expect of her in the bedchamber. How could Freddy give her into the power of such a man?

Last night's ball had been the worst experience of her life. To have that loathsome man kiss her hand and then to find Angus so callous as to wish her happy… Truly, standing there on that terrace, the stars mocking her with their romantic beauty, she had never felt so low. If she could have chosen death last night she would have taken it.

She might never see Angus again and he had wished her happy. His coldness towards her could not have been clearer. Oh, he had tried to express concern afterwards, but it meant nothing. Angus should have been the one she was betrothed to. Not Geoffrey. But Angus did not want her. Or not enough, anyway.

She frowned. Angus certainly had *seemed* to want her—to care for her, even, until their conversation at Greenwich had put paid to her hopes. Vaguely she recalled his worries she might be unhappy in Benbecula. Her lip curled bitterly.

He cares nothing for my happiness. If he did, he would have offered for me rather than allow Freddy to give me to Geoffrey.

Sally arrived, along with a train of footmen bringing three large empty trunks.

Three trunks, to remove all trace of me from Freddy's house.

She stood helplessly by as the footmen deposited the trunks and left, and Prudence and Sally began emptying drawers and packing her things away.

'Why must I pack now? Surely I have plenty of time?' Even as she asked the question, Freddy's mention of a special licence came back to her.

Prudence sent her a sympathetic look. 'My husband and Mr Barnstable have fixed the wedding for tomorrow at noon in St George's. Lord Burtenshaw has got a special licence from the Archbishop.'

'What? *Tomorrow?* Are you saying I must marry that creature *tomorrow*?'

Her sister-in-law nodded grimly. 'Mr Barnstable has insisted upon it, I understand.'

'But *why*? And why should Freddy agree to it?'

Prudence shrugged. 'Isabella, what cannot be prevented must be endured.'

'Endure. That word again.' At Prudence's enquiring look, she explained, 'Someone told me recently that we women are made of stern stuff and we can endure much. But I do not *wish* to endure, Prudence!' The cry came from her heart.

Prudence laid a hand on her arm. 'I know, my dear. Now, let us get more of this done now and some can wait for later.' She opened the door to Isabella's garderobe—the same cupboard that had contained her gowns since she had graduated from the nursery as a little girl.

'I am to leave my home—the place where my mama kissed me goodnight and sang me to sleep when I was little. And I am to go who-knows-where with a *toad* who is known only for his unwanted attentions towards ladies! How am I to endure it, Prudence? How?'

She shook her head. 'Honestly, I do not know, Isabella. We suffer for men's actions.' She grimaced. 'And their inaction. 'Twas ever thus.'

Isabella could bear it no longer. The tears that had seemed frozen inside now erupted, and she cried long and bitterly. In vain did Prudence try to comfort her. She tried everything—stern words, warm words, but Isabella, lost in grief, heard nothing. Her distress lasted most of the day until, in desperation, Prudence sent for laudanum. Isabella, welcoming the oblivion the laudanum would bring, drank deeply and sank into blessed nothingness.

* * *

Angus's heart was pounding like thunder as the footman led him to Lord Burtenshaw's library and scratched at the door. On hearing the command from within, he opened the door, announced Angus, then left.

'Please sit, MacDonald,' Burtenshaw offered, after the initial pleasantries. Angus accepted the offer of tea, it being too early in the day for wine, and then, finally, Burtenshaw sat back, asking, 'What was it you wished to speak to me about?'

This is it.

In an instant, Angus saw in his mind's eye the faces of the farmers, weavers, and fishermen on the Lidistrome estate, the beautiful house falling to ruin, the young ones emigrating to Nova Scotia and the Carolinas because of the punitive rents imposed by Burtenshaw's factor and steward. All of their hopes and dreams now rested on him and on this conversation.

For this, he and Eilidh had left their home to travel all the way to London. For this, he had paid out considerable sums on everything from hiring a house and servants, to spending on tailors, dressmakers, wine and card games. All for this moment.

Taking a breath, he began, the carefully rehearsed words flowing from his tongue, while his focus never left Burtenshaw's face. 'My home, Lord Burtenshaw, is in Benbecula, in the Western Isles of Scotland. It is a beautiful place and the same people have farmed the land for many generations. Next to my lands is a neighbouring estate, Lidistrome, which used to belong to a branch of my family and which I understand is now in your possession. I am here to make you a generous offer for it.' He named a sum that was more than fair. Now, how would Burtenshaw respond?

The Viscount had been looking rather nonplussed, but at this, his brow cleared. 'Ah! And so it becomes clear. Tell me, MacDonald, was it you who raised this matter with my man of business a couple of months ago? He mentioned that a Scot had offered to purchase the estate.'

Angus inclined his head, smiling.

Not the worst of starts.

'I did. I know that your family does not have much use for the land and the house is falling to ruin. Besides, the rental income is low by English standards. Indeed, I doubt anyone would wish to purchase it, save someone like me.'

Burtenshaw, he realised, was only half-listening. 'Then my man Inglis has already given you my answer. The estate is not for sale and it will not ever be for sale.'

Angus's heart sank. Keeping his tone pleasant, he asked, 'Might I enquire as to your reasoning?'

If I understand his motivation, perhaps I can hit upon a means of persuasion.

Burtenshaw leaned back, bringing his hands together, the fingers joining theatrically as though he were a clergyman giving a sermon. He looked entirely at ease. 'For a Scot, you are not particularly objectionable and I know that my sister and brother have formed something of a friendship with you and your sister— which is hardly surprising, I suppose. But I digress. Let me tell you something of my grandfather.' He rose, bidding Angus accompany him to view a large portrait which hung over the fireplace.

Angus followed him, his gaze searching the portrait

for clues. There was nothing obvious, beyond the traditions of the aristocracy to ensure they looked good in commissioned portraits. The portrait showed a man against a landscaped backdrop, a sword by his side and a proud look in his eye. Judging by his clothing, he had been alive at the time of the Jacobite uprising.

'The third Viscount,' Burtenshaw intoned, 'was convinced of the evils of Catholicism and the need to keep the throne away from the Stuart line. He sent troops to support Cumberland in the defeat of the Pretender. That estate was his reward, gifted to him by the King himself. It is more than land to me, more than an asset on paper. Let me show you the deeds.'

How on earth am I to argue against this?

Burtenshaw's own words indicated that his rationale was emotional and that he would not be swayed by logic. This was more than money, more than the disposal of an estate that added little to the Burtenshaw coffers. This, to Lord Burtenshaw, was his family's history and pride. Angus's heart sank.

With a flourish, Burtenshaw removed some papers from his strongbox, laying them on the large, polished table. There, tantalisingly close, were the deeds of ownership, along with a frail-looking parchment gifting the Lidistrome lands and properties from Clan MacDonald to the third Viscount Burtenshaw.

'Wait.' Angus frowned as he thought it through. 'Was this the only gift made to your grandfather at that time?'

'It was and a precious asset it is.'

Angus could not help it. He laughed. 'This is no precious asset, my lord. You are entirely mistaken. This is an insult!'

Burtenshaw stiffened. 'An insult? How dare you, Sir!'

'Think about it. Have you any idea how many thousands of acres were confiscated by the Crown after the battle of Culloden? How many hundreds of rich estates within easy reach of Glasgow or Edinburgh, with fine arable land and sound castles and manor houses? I should also point out that some of them have since been returned to their Scottish owners.' Burtenshaw looked at him blankly.

'For your ancestor to be given only this poor estate, fit only for sheep and basic farming, in the wilds of the Western Isles, was a *rebuke*, not a compliment, my lord. Now why should the King do that?'

Burtenshaw looked flabbergasted. 'There was some talk that they had anticipated a larger company of troops from my grandfather, given his level of wealth, but I confess I have always discounted it.' He sank into his chair, a hand on his head. 'Have I been in error, all these years?' He paused for a moment, then shook his head. 'No. It cannot be so. You, Sir, are here to blarney me with falsehoods, trying by any means necessary to make me part with this land. Well, it shall not happen!'

'I assure you, Lord Burtenshaw, I am stating only my honest opinion.' Another notion occurred to him. 'Tell me, how old was your grandfather at the time of these events?'

'Not yet thirty, I believe.'

'Younger than you are now, then. Yet he was expected to navigate the politics and practicalities of providing support to Cumberland during the uprising. Inheriting at a young age can be a trial.'

Burtenshaw seemed slightly mollified by this. 'Well, I should know. I was just three and twenty myself when my own father died.'

Angus's eyes widened. 'You were twenty-three? As was I.' There was a moment's pause, a brief sense of affinity. 'I had no clue how to be Laird, beyond memories of my father and a reliance on the tenets I was raised with.' He shook his head. 'Lord knows I have made many bad judgements these past five years!'

'Others will never understand the burdens of leadership unless they have carried them themselves.'

Angus chose to ignore the implied criticism of Max. 'Indeed.'

'It matters not. The estate is not for sale!' Burtenshaw's fingers were now drumming on the table and Angus's gut was twisting.

I have failed. Failed them all. And so I am dismissed and the hopes of all the islanders die here, in this room.

'Is there nothing I can say that might change your mind?'

'Nothing at all,' Burtenshaw confirmed, 'which is a pity, for you are not the worst chap, despite...' He trailed off.

'Despite being Scottish?' Angus's tone was wry.

'Indeed. You are a decent card player, the Beau approves of you and all doors have been opened to you here in London. But this land has great symbolism for me and I cannot sell to you, or any man. Now,' he continued brusquely, 'was there anything else?'

Setting aside the heartbreak he was feeling over the precious lands, Angus paused for a moment.

I might as well ask, although I know well what his answer will be.

'Actually, there was.' He took a breath, then asked the question that had been echoing in his mind forever. 'Lord Burtenshaw, I should like your permission to pay my addresses to your sister.'

The Viscount's eyes grew so round that Angus thought they might pop from his head. After a moment when the world seemed to pause entirely, he threw his head back and laughed. 'Ah, the wily Scots! What you cannot win by one means must be sought by another, eh?'

Angus remained stony faced. 'You misunderstand me, my lord. The two matters are entirely separate. I have a sincere affection for your sister and would count it an honour if she became my wife.'

'An honour? For you, indeed it would be! I am certainly not going to agree to my sister marrying a Scot, least of all a Scot whose holdings are only a poor estate, fit only for sheep. Is that not how you described it?'

'That is how a Sassenach might view it, yes. To me, it is God's paradise on earth.'

Burtenshaw snorted. 'Well, you cannot have it both ways, man.' His look was almost gleeful.

He is enjoying this.

Old wise words came to Angus. *Those who love power are unsuited to it.* It described Burtenshaw perfectly.

He gritted his teeth. 'So the answer is no, then?'

'It is and shall always be.' Burtenshaw smiled cruelly. 'You should know that Isabella is soon to be married, to an Englishman of impeccable lineage.'

Angus rose, having heard enough. 'Do you mean the Dishonourable Geoffrey? Yes, that is how he is known by the ladies of the *ton*. Such a marriage brings shame on your house, sir.' He made a shallow bow. 'I shall bid you good day.'

He left before Burtenshaw could form a reply, his last image of the man looking remarkably like a fat salmon flapping on the shore. In the hall, awaiting his hat and cane, he glanced longingly at the drawing-room door and at the stairs. Was Isabella at home? How was she faring? Would she be told that he had called?

'Angus!' He turned, seeing his friend.

'Good day, Max.' The footman handed Angus his possessions, but he hesitated.

I should tell Max.

He sent his friend a meaningful look.

'Let us step in here for a moment.' Max indicated a reception parlour just off the hall. Closing the door, he asked bluntly, 'Now, what is amiss, Angus?'

'Your brother has refused to sell me the estate.' Saying the words aloud made Angus's gut twist anew.

Failure. Heartbreak. Disappointment for all my people back home.

'And he has declined to allow me pay my addresses to Isabella.' He closed his eyes briefly against a wave of what felt remarkably like grief.

A flash of surprise crossed Max's face. 'Then you would have married her?'

Forcing the words out past the painful lump in his throat, Angus nodded. 'Aye, I would and gladly. And I would have done all I could to ensure she was happy in Scotland.' He frowned. 'What is it, Max?'

Max's expression was inscrutable. 'With regard to the estate, do not despair, for I may yet have an ace to play. My situation has changed recently, but—' He shook his head. 'Best not give you false hopes. My ace may be as nothing in the face of my brother's intransigence.'

Angus laughed hollowly. 'I thought I had played an ace myself during our conversation.' Briefly, he explained his interpretation of the Benbecula estate being awarded to the Burtenshaw family.

'That makes perfect sense,' Max replied. 'The difficulty you have is that for a man like my brother, sense is secondary to pride and stubbornness, and slowness of thought.' He squared his shoulders. 'I shall try him, though I can make no promises.'

'Thank you, Max.' Angus sighed. 'Regardless, Eilidh and I shall leave here very soon—in two or three days, if we can make ready in time. You have been a good friend and I shall miss you.'

'Keep your farewells, my friend. We shall speak in the morning, when I have tried Freddy and when I have had time to *think*. Too much has been happening and I cannot—' He broke off. 'I shall send a message in the morning.'

The day of Isabella's wedding dawned and luckily, the effects of the laudanum, though fading, were enough to give Isabella a welcome sense of detachment. Her dreams had been strange, monstrous things and she felt more tired than she could ever remember.

Listlessly, she allowed Sally to dress her and put her hair up, ignoring the maid's tears, then descended to the breakfast room. Prudence was there looking, it had to be said, a little pale, but she admired Isabella's dress with some enthusiasm.

Isabella looked down, having not particularly noticed which gown Sally had put her in. It was the divine dress of cream silk trimmed with lace and when she and Eilidh had ordered it Isabella had dreamt of Angus admiring her in it. How long ago that seemed, and how far away!

The door opened and Freddy appeared briefly, full of bluster and nonsense. 'You shall feel much more the thing when you have breakfasted, Isabella!' was his eventual reply when she made no response to his sallies. When she remained listlessly absent he blanched, muttering, 'Prudence, I shall be in my library. Call me when it is time to go.'

Vaguely, Isabella was conscious of the tiniest flame of hope sputtering and dying. Freddy would not be turned. She knew him too well.

Once he had departed, Prudence gently tried to tempt Isabella with some food. Since the very notion made her feel sick, her sister-in-law instead bade her drink tea and not think too much.

Not think too much? She was not thinking at all.

If I am to get through this day I must remain hidden inside myself and not see or hear or feel what is happening.

The door opened and Max burst in. 'Is it true? Freddy tells me you are to be married *today*! Bella, is it true?'

For answer, Isabella nodded mutely, still incapable of speech.

'I had known him to be foolish, but I had not thought him capable of such cruelty!' With a muttered expletive, he departed abruptly.

'Oh, dear,' murmured Prudence. 'I do hope they will not come to blows.'

Isabella had no answer. What did any of it matter, when her life was to be over this day?

Prudence sighed, then rang for a footman. 'Tell the coachman to prepare the carriages,' she said flatly, 'and send my maid to Miss Wood's chamber, for we must depart within the hour.'

Angus and Eilidh had been up since early morning, allowing the servants access to their chambers to begin

packing. It would not take long, for they had hardly any
possessions of their own in London. Searlas was today
making arrangements to let the servants go, to relin-
quish the hired house and to reserve inns and changes
of horses for their long journey northwards.

Eilidh was clearly upset, drawn and pale.

*And why should she not be? All of our efforts here
have been for naught. I have failed my clan and my
homeplace. And I have failed Isabella.*

Wild thoughts of asking her to elope with him kept
crossing his mind, but could he really do such a thing
to her—even to save her from Geoffrey? If someone
ran away with Eilidh, taking her from her home and
her family, it would break his heart.

*But is Burtenshaw truly going to marry Isabella to
that monster?*

Hopefully his revelation yesterday about Barnstable's
reputation among the ladies would make her pompous
brother think twice. But Isabella must have agreed to
it, even if she would have preferred someone other than
Barnstable.

Out from under Freddy's thumb.

Sadly, he could not rely on Burtenshaw doing the
right thing and so drastic actions kept presenting themselves in his mind, until he thought his head might
explode. 'I am going out to walk in Green Park,' he
announced. If he was to act, it must be soon, for he and
Eilidh would leave London soon. And he might already
be too late. Isabella was rightfully angry with him and
might well have put him out of her mind and her heart.
Would that he could do the same!

The banns would be read for four consecutive Sun-
days, he knew. Perhaps in a month Isabella would be
entirely reconciled to her fate. Or perhaps not. He strode

through the park like the legendary giant Fingal, uncaring of the astounded looks and wariness of the Londoners out for a late morning stroll.

Should we delay our return to Scotland until I can speak to Isabella again? Might I try to see her today or tomorrow?

Lost in his own thoughts, he remained entirely unaware of anyone or anything around him, until a person caught his eye. A tall man, a stranger to him, standing stock still in the centre of the path. Greying hair, dark eyes and an air of someone who was comfortable in their skin was the impression Angus formed in one swift glance. The man was looking directly at him. Angus slowed, eyeing him warily.

'Angus Macdonald, Laird of Broch Clachan, in the Isle of Benbecula?' the man asked softly and Angus froze. He had spoken Gaelic!

'I am he. And who would you be?'

'My name is Cooper.'

Cooper! Isabella's friend, who had worked for her family for decades. He held out a hand. 'I am happy to make your acquaintance.'

Cooper's eyes widened briefly, but he clasped Angus's hand. 'Come with me,' he declared, indicating a path to his left. Unquestioningly—for somehow the man inspired trust—Angus turned, falling into step beside him. 'I had forgotten how the men of the clans behave towards those whom the English treat as servants,' Cooper murmured.

'Hard-working people earn as much respect as lairds and ladies. More, for honest work is to be applauded.'

'Aye.' Cooper shook his head pensively. 'I have been from Scotland too long.' He nodded. 'But today is a day for reckoning. A day for change.' He turned his head to fix Angus with an inscrutable gaze. 'A day for decisions. Tell me, what do you make of the Burtenshaw family?'

Without searching inwardly why he felt so at ease with Cooper, Angus answered from the heart. 'Lord Burtenshaw is a pompous nodcock with misguided notions of what constitutes duty. Max is a good man frustrated by his own idleness...'

'And Iseabail?' He used the Gaelic version of Isabella's name and Angus's heart turned over. How many times had he imagined telling her of his heart, speaking her Gaelic name, taking her in his arms and never letting her go?

'She is...she is moonrise on the darkest night, the quiet after a storm, the machair in bloom. She is my heart and my love.' His voice was quiet, but his own words flooded though him like a vast wave in a stormy sea.

Cooper nodded. 'As I thought. Ah, here they are!' He called to two familiar forms who were ahead of them on the path. 'Max! Miss MacDonald! I have found him!' To Angus he added, 'We split up, the better to search for you.'

'Thank the lord!' Max hurried towards them, Eilidh by his side. 'Quickly, to the carriage, for it is almost noon!'

Angus's stomach clenched in fear. 'Why, what is amiss?'

'Freddy means to marry Bella to Barnstable today. And she does not want him.'

Time stood still as the import of Max's words sank in. *She is being forced?*

Then the other shocking news. *Today?*

But they had only told Isabella of the betrothal two days ago. It would take four weeks for the banns to be read, surely? Abruptly, the answer came to him.

They have procured a special licence, the blaggards!

Everyone was looking at him and he was conscious of an eerie feeling, as though every action he had ever taken, every day he had spent on God's earth, had led him to this moment and this decision. He glanced at Eilidh and she gave the smallest of nods. Not that it changed anything, for his course was now set, but he was glad to have her approval.

'Not if I have anything to say about the matter!' Even he heard the anger in his own voice, thickening his accent and sending a rush of heat to his muscles.

Max hit him a brotherly slap on the shoulder. 'I knew it! We shall need to make haste though!'

His heart swelled. Finally, he could take action, could shake off the cloak of London manners and do this his way. The Hebridean way.

'Lead on, Max, for I have had my fill of English manners. It is time to show these fine gentlemen how we do business where I come from!'

Chapter Sixteen

Isabella had still not spoken. She felt as though she might never speak again. Her power of speech had vanished along with any sense of personhood, of self, of ability to act. She was simply Freddy's creature, to be ordered and manipulated at will. Soon he would pass her to Geoffrey and the death of the old Isabella would be complete. In her place was a changeling, an empty puppet, an automaton.

Prudence had given up trying to get a response from her, while Freddy had not even tried. There were only the three of them in the carriage, for Max had vanished.

He does not wish to witness my execution. I am to be a sacrifice on the altar of Freddy's pride.

Fleetingly, she thought of Anne Boleyn. She could not feel even sorrow that she would be entirely friendless as they married her to Geoffrey.

A second coach followed, filled with trunks containing her clothes and jewellery, her books and her precious miniature of Mama. She might need that in the days and weeks to come, if her body lived on. At this point, she cared not. How long could someone survive without food and water? She had often heard it said that someone had died of a broken heart, but today, she truly understood how it might come about.

St George's in Hanover Square was familiar to her, for she had been coming here since she was a little girl. The Vicar, Mr Hodgson, greeted them at the portico with smiles and felicitations, to which Isabella remained unresponsive. Freddy, however, had bluster and chatter enough for the three of them and Prudence tucked her hand into Isabella's elbow as they made their way up the aisle.

To support me, or to prevent me from leaving?

It mattered not. Isabella remained the cornered fox who had lost all hope, simply allowing the pack to tear at her.

There he was, waiting at the foot of the altar, an appalling grin on his face. Geoffrey's teeth were various shades of yellow and brown, his belly protruding over his unmentionables, and he had a nervous energy about him. There were a few people in the first row beside him—Geoffrey's family members, Isabella assumed. The church was otherwise deserted.

Mr Hodgson bade Freddy and Prudence sit, then without further ado, turned his attention to Isabella and Geoffrey, beginning the liturgy of matrimony.

'Dearly beloved,' he intoned, 'we are gathered together here in the sight of God, and in the face of this Congregation, to join together this Man and this Woman in holy Matrimony; which is an honourable estate, instituted of God in the time of man's innocence...'

Isabella focused her attention on the large painting behind the altar. The Last Supper.

How appropriate!

'...and is not by any to be enterprised, nor taken in hand unadvisedly, lightly, or wantonly, to satisfy men's carnal lusts and appetites, like brute beasts that have no understanding; but reverently, discreetly, advisedly, soberly, and in the fear of God.'

At this, her lip almost curled. Whatever reasons Freddy had for giving her to Geoffrey, her future husband had only one aim: to satisfy his carnal lusts and appetites. Why was that not clear to everyone present?

A brute beast without understanding was an excellent description of the Dishonourable Geoffrey.

'First,' the priest continued, 'it was ordained for the procreation of children...'

There will be no children, if I can help it!

She would never willingly submit to Geoffrey. Although she knew that to fight him would perhaps bring greater physical punishment, she could not imagine submitting to him willingly. If she went away in her mind, as she had done today, would he see that as submission? She shrugged inwardly. He would not care, either way, as long as he got what he wanted. It was perfectly legal for a husband to take his wife by force; the law would not interfere in such matters.

Perhaps I shall never be a mother.

If Geoffrey accepted her wish not to be intimate with him—an unlikely outcome—then she would die childless. Dreams of chestnut-haired Scottish children were simply that: dreams.

'Secondly,' the priest continued, 'it was ordained for a remedy against sin, and to avoid fornication...' Such sin and fornication was literally Geoffrey's reputation among gently-born ladies. Isabella shuddered to think what he might have done to servant girls and laundresses, for he had little self-restraint. Vaguely, she was aware that her mind was working again, albeit sluggishly, and that she was perhaps not, after all, going to die today. Perhaps she could fight him? Fight for the right to protect her body from him? If the marriage was not consummated, she might even live in hope of an annulment.

'Thirdly, it was ordained for the mutual society, help, and comfort, that the one ought to have of the other, both in prosperity and adversity...'

At this she almost shook her head, so nonsensical was it when applied to herself and Barnstable. She would seek no comfort from him, nor offer him any. Their marriage was doomed to hostility and contempt—from her side at least. How could any man want that from a wife? For the first time she wondered if Geoffrey truly understood the depth of her abhorrence for him, and the fact there could never be amity between them as husband and wife.

'Therefore if any man can show any just cause why they may not lawfully be joined together, let him now speak, or else hereafter forever hold his peace.'

Isabella held her breath. *Max! Angus! Someone, please rescue me!*

Nothing. No one appeared, no one shouted out, and the Vicar continued relentlessly.

Mr Hodgson was now eyeing them both, a stern expression on his face. 'I require and charge you both, as ye will answer at the dreadful day of judgement, when the secrets of all hearts shall be disclosed, that if either of you know any impediment, why ye may not be lawfully joined together in Matrimony, ye do now confess it. For be ye well assured, that so many as are coupled together otherwise than God's Word doth allow, are not joined together by God, neither is their Matrimony lawful.'

Isabella's ears pricked up.

Why have I never noticed this part of the ceremony before?

Any impediment? Would her reluctance be enough of an impediment? No, the Vicar had said 'lawfully'. That probably meant that they had to declare if one of the parties was already married, or underage—

It was too late. After the briefest of pauses, Mr Hodgson turned to Geoffrey. 'Geoffrey Algernon Barnstable,' he intoned, 'wilt thou have this woman to thy wedded wife, to live together after God's ordinance in the holy estate of Matrimony? Wilt thou love her, comfort her, honour, and keep her in sickness and in health; and, forsaking all other, keep thee only unto her, so long as ye both shall live?'

Geoffrey replied without hesitation, 'I will.'

Isabella's trembling, which had until now been contained inside, now finally erupted into her body. She began to shiver uncontrollably, her teeth chattering as though she were outside on a freezing winter's day.

'Isabella Jane Margaret Wood,' the Vicar said, and as he intoned her full name Isabella was reminded again of Anne Boleyn and the swordsman of Calais, 'wilt thou have this Man to thy wedded husband, to live together after God's ordinance in the holy estate of Matrimony? Wilt thou obey him, serve him, love, honour, and keep him in sickness and in health; and, forsaking all other, keep thee only unto him, so long as ye both shall live?'

Isabella locked eyes with the Vicar, unable to move, or speak. As the silence grew and stretched, she was conscious of the desire of everyone in the church that she say the words they expected. *I will.* Two simple words, yet if she uttered them, all would be lost.

Was she failing in her duty by not complying? Was she disgracing her family? Would Mama be disappointed in her?

'*Duty. Endure your duty.*' Prudence.

Then Mrs Edgecombe. '*It is time for a reckoning, Isabella. Choose well, child.*'

She could recall every detail of Mrs Edgecombe's expression and tone of voice, but strangely, the image faded again, to be replaced this time by Great-Aunt Morton. '*Do not compromise.*'

'You say, *I will,*' the Vicar prompted, as though she did not understand what was expected of her.

Still she said nothing. How could she possibly promise to love such a man? To serve him and honour him and obey him? If she made this promise before God it would be a lie. She dared not think of Angus, for he was already lost to her. No, if a rescue was to be made, she must do it herself.

A lifetime of compliance in public was urging her to speak, to say the required words as though it were a performance in a drawing room. 'Did you *feel* the Mozart piece as you were playing it?' Angus had asked that night, so long ago. 'No,' she had replied then. Hiding one's feelings, doing what was expected, following the rules and expectations placed on her by society…

A frown grew slowly on Mr Hodgson's face, then a thought seemed to occur to him.

'Many young ladies have an attack of nerves on their wedding day. Perfectly understandable.' He gave a reassuring smile. 'I ask again, Miss Wood, will you have this man as your wedded husband?'

Do not compromise. Do not compromise.

'No.'

Isabella's reply was little more than a whisper, but, judging from his raised eyebrows, the Vicar had heard it. So, apparently, had Geoffrey.

'Miss Wood! Isabella!' She turned to look at him and the sight of his shocked face made her insides churn. 'This was all agreed!'

'Not by me.' Suddenly the pent-up words flowed out of her, as though a dam had broken. 'I do not want this marriage. I loathe you. I cannot stand here in church and lie. Whatever agreement you have made with my brother means nothing to me. I know he is my guardian and therefore he can probably force me to wed you, but no one can force me to speak an untruth while taking a solemn oath in the house of God!'

Geoffrey's jaw dropped and he looked aghast. Freddy, meanwhile, had left his seat and was now bustling towards them. 'Isabella! How dare you disgrace me in this way?'

Isabella eyed him directly, all sense of caution gone. 'You have disgraced yourself, Freddy. You always do.'

Her brother's face was now an interesting shade of purple. 'Outrageous, headstrong girl!' He appealed to the priest. 'As my sister has already admitted, as her guardian I have the legal power to choose her husband. Now, please proceed.'

'Stop!' A loud bellow came from the back of the church. 'Stop this wedding!'

Chapter Seventeen

They all turned to look. There, striding up the aisle in full Highland dress, was the chestnut-haired Scot she had been praying for. Someone followed behind him, but Isabella had eyes only for Angus.

My beautiful, handsome, daring Angus! He has come!

He spoke directly to the priest. 'This woman is being forced against her will to marry an unsuitable man. Surely the church should not condone such a thing? This wedding must be stopped instantly, or annulled if needs be!'

'You!' Freddy's voice contained clear loathing. 'How dare you interrupt a private family event!' His brow creased. 'And how did you even know—?' His face twisted in anger as he saw who was with Angus. 'Max! You did this? You would work against your own family?'

Max's expression was severe, his tone sober. 'I have done what I believe to be right. Our sister's welfare matters more than your pride.'

'This is an absolute outrage!' Geoffrey was clearly incensed. 'Plank! Burtenshaw, I mean—we have signed a legal agreement for this marriage—an agreement that also entails the settling of your gaming debts!'

Now it was Freddy's turn to pale. 'Barnstable! We agreed to keep such matters confidential!'

'Only if I got the girl! Our agreement is now void and I expect full settlement of your debts *today*!'

Freddy, aghast, managed to stutter, 'But—you know I cannot—that is to say, my c-current circumstances do not allow... Perhaps we might come to some arrangement?'

Isabella found her voice again as their words sank in. 'Debts? You agreed to this marriage in exchange for the settling of your gaming debts, Freddy? And you *dared* to speak to me of honour and duty? You have *sold* me—or tried to. There is no other word for it.'

'That is a very ugly word, Isabella.' Puffing out his chest, he elaborated. 'As Head of the Family my responsibility is to address all matters, including financial matters. Wedding settlements are normal.' He turned back to the priest. 'Please proceed with the ceremony. All else can be addressed later.'

Mr Hodgson, who had taken a step back and had been watching proceedings with great attention, now stepped forward again. 'Most of you seem to be aware of the law of the land, which does indeed allow a guardian to choose a husband for a young woman.'

Isabella gasped at this. *He will allow this?*

'However,' he continued, 'I should like to educate you a little. Are any of you familiar with the *Decretum Gratiani*?'

Everyone looked at him in expectant silence. Isabella's shivering was continuing, though his use of 'however' had infused her with the tiniest flame of hope, rather than despair. Would the Vicar suffocate that hope and insist they continue?

'It is a twelfth-century textbook of Canon Law that stands to this day,' he continued, 'and it has much to say with regard to marriage. Under civil law, it is enough for the couple to simply be present.'

Isabella gasped. *No!*

'Under *church* law, however, both parties must consent and consent freely. So you see, I *cannot* continue with the ceremony and nor would I wish to. Now,' he added briskly, 'I must ask all of you to leave this place. Any further discussion between you should take place outside the church. There will be no wedding this day.'

His words caused Isabella's heart to lighten, as though she had been released from prison. She met Angus's gaze and they shared a perfect smile. *Angus!* He nodded at her and she understood that he was both filled with rage on her behalf and, at the same time, perfectly calm. He had no intention of allowing any harm to come to her. Quite how she knew this, she could not say. It was something about the perfect *ease* with which he stood there, a head taller than Freddy and every inch the Laird. It was as though she was seeing him fully for the first time. He exuded confidence, and authority, and...*Laird-ness*.

'Outside, where *he* may contrive to carry her off to Gretna and ensure my humiliation is complete?' Freddy jerked his head towards Angus and Isabella's heart skipped with joy. Running away to Gretna with Angus sounded like the most *delightful* humiliation she had ever faced.

Oh, might all her dreams come true today? Was Angus here simply because he wanted to prevent her from being forced to marry Geoffrey, or because he wanted to marry her himself? While she suspected she knew the answer, she could not be certain until he revealed his hand. Her stomach still sick from how daringly she had rebelled against a lifetime of compliance, her pulse was also racing with hope and relief, and joy.

I did not marry Geoffrey!

'Outside,' Mr Hodgson repeated implacably, and slowly they complied. Isabella managed to mouth a silent 'thank you' to him, which he acknowledged with a nod and a softening of the eyes.

Freddy took her arm and would have propelled her down the aisle, but she stopped, waiting until he removed his hand with a muttered expletive. 'Shocking language, Freddy,' she murmured. 'Father would be most displeased.'

'Father? *Father?* But he is not—' Clamping his mouth shut, he stomped off, leaving her to follow. And follow she did. But she walked on her own terms and with no one's hands on her.

I am Isabella again.

Freddy and Prudence were in front, Angus and Max behind. She felt as though she were an Army general, lieutenants at her rear, routing the enemy. And maybe, just maybe, she would prevail this day and be able to follow her chosen path after all.

Outside, the two Burtenshaw carriages and the Barnstable one had been joined by a fourth—the hired carriage Angus and Eilidh had been using during their time in London. Eilidh, who had been waiting outside, first looked to Max and Angus for some signal as to whether the wedding had been prevented, then, with a strong sigh of relief, wrapped Isabella in a fierce hug, whispering. 'Be strong! All will be well!'

Isabella did not need to be told, for she was already strong. She was a mountain, a metal rod, a stormy sea. From being nothing, she was now *everything*, fully herself. She had taken her power back and, while Freddy still held some of the cards, she now knew that under Canon Law she could never be compelled into marriage. And Freddy knew it, too.

Her eye fell on the carriages. Someone was currently moving her trunks from Freddy's carriage to Angus's and, whoever he was, she felt she could kiss him! He turned, and—'Cooper!' Her delight was complete. Stepping forward, she hugged him—this man who had been her friend and protector all her life. That he was here today made everything perfect.

'I might have known he had a hand in this debacle,' commented Freddy bitterly, as Isabella, smiling, stepped back to the edge of the portico.

'This "debacle" is entirely of your making, Freddy.' Max's tone was terse. 'You did not need to do it.'

'You have no idea, Max. No idea of the burdens I must bear.'

'Like gaming debts to Barnstable?' Max shot back.

Freddy recoiled, but managed to mutter, 'Any man might have a run of bad luck at the tables. I must pay my debts.'

'You have no head for gambling, Freddy. Just like Papa. And why did you not speak to me of the debts? Why, eh?'

Freddy shrugged. 'There is no one who can help me. This is my riddle to solve.'

As they conversed, Angus made his way to Isabella.

Bowing, he held out both hands and she placed her hands in his. For a moment they simply gazed at each other, then, reverently he lifted both her hands, kissing each one in turn. Her heart was ready to burst from happiness at the warmth in his eye. *He loves me! I knew it!*

'How do you, Miss Wood?'

'Very well, Mr MacDonald. I was not so well before, but all is right now.'

'Yes,' he said simply. 'Yes, it is.'

Max and Freddy were still arguing, Max now continuing in a calmer tone. 'Freddy, yesterday I offered to buy from you a certain estate in Benbecula. You declined my offer. If you had accepted it, you would not have needed to bring Isabella here today.'

At this, Isabella and Angus's heads both whipped around.

Max offered to buy it? But how?

Freddy gave a short laugh. 'You forget, Max, I know your income almost to the penny. No doubt you had good reason for making such a foolish offer, but as you now know, my situation has an added urgency.'

'Indeed it does.' Geoffrey, who had been consulting with his family members, marched up to them. 'I am decided. If your debts are not settled by midnight, then I shall declare you to be a scoundrel lacking in honour and I shall ensure the *ton* knows of it!'

'But—but—be reasonable, man!'

'You think me unreasonable, after the insults delivered to me today by you and your family? No, it is clear who is lacking in honour here and all of society shall soon know it. Good day!'

With this, he departed with his family and without looking back. Isabella had the strangest feeling she would never see him again—a notion which filled her with delight. She watched the carriage leave, keeping her eyes on it until it turned the corner.

I should have been with him, in that carriage today. My trunks strapped to the back and all hope gone.

Instead her trunks were on Angus's carriage and here she was, standing in the sunshine, having somehow avoided her doom.

Perhaps I am not Anne Boleyn after all.

'Oh, Lord!' Freddy was wringing his hands, now genuinely agitated. 'Oh, Lord. Oh, Lord. Oh, Lord.' He turned to Isabella, his face twisting. 'Now see what you have done! We are ruined, ruined!'

Before Isabella could retort, Prudence, who had remained in the background the entire time, stepped forward. Placing a hand on her husband's arm, she declared calmly, 'All will be well, Husband. If you will permit, I should like to play a part in this situation.'

He looked at her directly and her gaze seemed to have a somewhat calming effect. 'Yes, do, Prudence, for I am at my wits' end. How am I to possibly find such a sum by midnight?'

She nodded and turned to Max. 'Does this have to do with your Great-Aunt Morton?'

A gleam of admiration lit Max's eye. 'Well deduced, Prudence. Yes, the old lady's penury was apparently self-imposed, for she had a fortune in the Funds which she never touched.'

'And she left it to you?'

'Every penny,' he confirmed.

To Isabella's left, she heard Eilidh gasp. 'Then—'

Max nodded to her, his expression solemn. 'Here

is my chance to see what sort of man I may be. That should please you, Miss MacDonald.'

'And your first act was to offer to buy the Benbecula land?' Eilidh shook her head slowly. 'This surprises me, I admit.'

Angus sent him a keen glance. 'The ace you had to play, Max?'

'Indeed. Freddy turned me down, which is hardly surprising since I did not have the opportunity to disclose to him that I was my great-aunt's heir—a fact I have only recently discovered myself.'

'Wait.' Freddy was frowning. 'She left you a fortune? *You*, the useless second son? But—'

'I should be careful who you insult today, Freddy.' Max's tone was mild, but he was speaking with a surety Isabella had not heard from him before. 'You have already made some gaffes today,' he continued softly. 'I should not like to see you miss your last opportunity to avoid social ruin. Now tell me, what is the sum of your debt to Barnstable?'

Freddy looked uncomfortable. 'I shall whisper it in your ear, Max, for such matters should never be discussed unless strictly necessary.' Stepping closely together, the brothers engaged in a brief private conversation.

'Isabella.' Prudence's voice was soft. 'I am heartily sorry and I know I should have acted sooner. But I have been raised to obey without questioning. Of course, I may be questioning on the *inside*, but I am never to show it, for it would be a breach of my...' She paused.

'Your duty?' At Prudence's nod, Isabella continued. 'That word again! Surely we have a *duty* to challenge when challenge is required, to use the brain we are given and to be brave when we must?'

'You have taught me that,' her sister-in-law replied simply. 'I shall endeavour not to forget it.'

'Now, Freddy,' Max increased his voice again, glancing toward them. 'You know that I have the means to mend this. Sell me the Benbecula land—or sell it to Angus—and use the money to pay Barnstable.'

Everyone froze, awaiting Freddy's response. Isabella watched, fascinated, as he looked from Angus to Max and back again. He closed his eyes, groaning. 'I—I cannot. No, not even to avert Barnstable's threat. Our family name is everything to me and I cannot bear the thought that our prize for service to the Crown will leave the family and go back to the Scots from whom it was confiscated! No, not even to save my own reputation will I do it!'

Despite herself, Isabella felt the glimmerings of respect for Freddy. He did have a true, if misguided, devotion to his own code of moral duty, even in the face of Geoffrey's threat.

'If I sell it to you,' he continued, his tone that of a man tortured, 'then you will simply pass it to *him*. And that cannot be.'

Isabella's left hand was still in Angus's. She squeezed gently and he replied in kind.

This is so important to Angus, yet he must bite his tongue and allow Max to lead, for he will surely rouse Freddy's ire if he intervenes.

Her heart swelled at the thought of the islanders, who did not know this was the hour their fate would be decided.

My fate, their fate...it is all of a piece.

With remarkable patience, Isabella thought, Max tried to reason with him. 'But our family name will be more directly destroyed by Barnstable's tattle than by your selling a small estate in Scotland, even if it *was* given to the family by the King.'

Freddy stuck his lower lip out mutinously. 'Perhaps people will not take Barnstable seriously. Perhaps…'

Max sighed, then nodded. 'Very well. There is only one option left.' He straightened. 'Sell it to me and I shall promise not to sell it to Angus—or, indeed, to any Scot. I vow to keep it in my ownership all my life.' Max's expression was grave and there was a nobility to him Isabella had never seen before.

Isabella sensed Angus stiffen beside her. She understood his consternation, for how would that help the families dependent on the estate? Angus had planned to bring it to life again, but he could not do so unless he had possession of it…

Freddy, after a moment's thought, nodded. 'Very well. I am selling it to my own brother, with his word he will not sell it on. I think my grandfather would be content with that.' He stuck out a hand and Max clasped it.

While they agreed the practicalities of deeds and agreements and quickly accessing some of Max's new wealth in the Funds, Isabella was conscious of Angus's disappointment. 'Angus?' she asked softly and he turned his head to look at her. 'I know this is not what you wanted. I am sorry. But at least with Max as the owner something may be done with the estate?'

He shook his head. 'It could never work. There is so much to be done and London is so far away. There would be myriad decisions to be made—decisions that should not be in the hands of an agent or steward.'

He shrugged. 'Still, I know Max will not wish to actively harm the families there, which is better than I might have hoped for. Earlier today I had thought all was lost, but now...' His eyes bored into hers, making her breath catch in her throat. 'At this moment there are more important matters than the Benbecula land to address. Matters more important to me as a man.'

'Eh? What's that?' Freddy, abruptly, seemed to notice for the first time that Angus was holding Isabella's hand. 'Unhand my sister, Sir!'

Angus opened his mouth to reply, but Isabella forestalled him. 'It is for *me* to decide who will hold my hand, Freddy. Not you. As the Vicar made clear, consent is necessary for a marriage to take place. I shall choose my own husband and I hope you will support my choice.' Without as much as glancing sideways, she added, 'I hope that he does, too.'

Freddy shook his head. 'As your guardian, I must also have a say. Church law may be on your side, but the law of the land is on mine.'

'English law,' Angus asserted coolly. 'In Scotland a woman of your sister's age may marry without the consent of her guardian.'

Isabella gasped and turned to him. 'Then—?'

He took her other hand again. 'Isabella, would you do me the very great honour of becoming my wife?'

About to give him an enthusiastic response, she caught her breath. 'Are you asking because you believe you must rescue me from Geoffrey? For that threat is gone and I believe I rescued myself!'

'You did that, but if it is not Geoffrey today, it will be some other man in the future. And I strongly believe that no one must marry you but me.'

'Why, Angus?'

'Because I love you, *mo leannan bhoidheach*. And I have some hope that you might love me, too.'

'Well of course I do!' She twinkled at him, her heart full. 'What do those Gaelic words mean?'

'They mean "my beautiful sweetheart". Now kiss me and say that you will.'

'Oh, I will, I will!' She kissed him with enthusiasm, ignoring Freddy's disapproving noises. *I will.* The very words she could not bring herself to say a short time ago.

They surfaced soon after, knowing they could not give way to kisses with such an audience. It mattered not.

I shall be kissing him my whole life.

Isabella's heart was singing. Never in her life had she felt so happy.

'Isabella! Have some decorum, please!'

'I am sorry, Freddy.' She thought about this for a second. 'Actually, I am not in the least sorry for kissing Angus and I warn you I intend to do it again shortly, but I am sorry that you do not approve of my choice.'

'I most certainly do not! In fact, I cannot permit my sister to marry a Scot!' he declared with loathing. 'I have only just averted the threat of some of our family lands going to them!'

'Angus is my choice,' she declared firmly and he squeezed her hand. She glanced up at him and his eyes were blazing with love for her. Love and happiness, and—was that pride? She stood a little straighter, strengthened by his admiration.

'You cannot expect me to stand in a church and condone it, Isabella, for it goes against everything I was raised to hold dear.'

'Then give us your blessing and we shall wed in Scotland.' Angus's voice and demeanour remained entirely calm, in contrast to Freddy's purpling outrage. 'You need not be there.'

'Never! I—' He broke off, as Prudence once again laid a hand on his arm.

'Let them go, Freddy,' she said softly. 'It is for the best.'

She called him Freddy!

In the midst of the most important moment in her life, Isabella could not help but notice her sister-in-law's use of her husband's given name. It seemed to shock him, too, for he paused and they gazed at one another, some silent communication passing between them. Prudence remained still, eyeing him steadily, and after a moment he exhaled slowly, all the fight seeming to go out of him.

'Very well, but, Max, our agreement stands. You are not to sell the land to MacDonald, even if he is Isabella's husband.' He glowered at Angus. 'Come see me in the morning and we shall go through the wedding agreements.'

Angus bowed. 'With pleasure!'

Stomping off towards the carriage, Freddy paused to say something to Cooper, who remained impassive. Prudence, meantime, wrapped Isabella in a tight hug. 'Never fear,' she declared in a low tone, 'for I mean to take my husband in hand. No more gambling, no more biting my tongue when he says or does something outrageous. I mean to manage him—and I shall do it, I assure you!'

'I do not doubt it!' Isabella, moved, returned the hug, then Prudence left to join her husband.

Isabella, holding her breath, waited until the carriage was moving away before announcing, 'I declare he has forgotten about me!' She smiled, elated. 'I am as yet unwed and have nowhere to live!'

'Well, that is easily remedied,' Angus responded, 'for I shall repair to a hotel for a few days and you can move in with Eilidh while we prepare to go to Scotland.'

'An excellent plan!' Eilidh hugged Isabella for a second time. 'And we are to be sisters! I could not be happier!'

As Max then Cooper added their felicitations, Isabella kept her hand in Angus's, where it belonged.

'We have begun to pack anyway,' said Eilidh, 'and although I dread the weeks on the road, it will be wonderful to be back in Benbecula again.'

Max coughed and they all looked his way. 'As to that, I have a suggestion. Cooper, would you mind?'

Cooper grinned. 'I understand you, Max, and I think it an excellent notion. But—are you certain you wish to do this?' Isabella looked from one to the other, mystified.

Max nodded. 'This is my opportunity and I intend to take it!' Turning back to Isabella, Angus and Eilidh, he declared, 'We shall sail my yacht to Benbecula and I shall accompany you!'

After taking part in the ensuing melee of exclamations and questions, Angus gently drew Isabella aside. 'I wish to echo Cooper's question to Max. Isabella, are you certain you wish to leave your London life behind and live in the Outer Hebrides, far away from your friends and family? To go to a place where you are not known by anyone, where the winters are long but the hearths are warm? To marry me and live there forever, with only rare trips back to England?'

Isabella looked up at him, allowing all the love she had for him to shine in her eyes. 'I should like nothing better. I know it will not always be easy, but it will always be worth it. I love you, you see.'

'And I love you.' Time seemed to stand still as their words fell like pebbles in a pool, rippling through their hearts with the realisation neither would ever feel loneliness again. Then with a muffled exclamation, he pulled her close in a warm embrace and she closed her eyes as the warmth of his body enveloped her. They stood like that for a moment, her head resting on his shoulder and his arms wrapped tightly around her.

'Now,' he said, releasing her a little so they could look at one another, 'what was it you were saying about kissing me again?'

Epilogue

Dawn was breaking over Benbecula and the newly-wedded Laird and Lady were still awake. After a long night of love, they had moved their blankets to the window embrasure of their chamber in Broch Clachan and were now dreamily watching the sunrise, which was painting the sky with golden-orange light.

'It is so beautiful here,' Isabella murmured.

'Not so beautiful as you, *mo ghràdh*,' he replied, shifting slightly so she could curl against him more comfortably.

'More Gaelic words! I shall have to study very hard so I can be fluent. Wait!' She thought for a moment. 'Are those not the words you said to me at the ball? When you left me?'

He laughed. 'You are altogether too good a student! Yes, I said it back then. I also said them at Greenwich. And do you want to know what those words mean?'

She nodded, holding her breath.

'They mean "my love".'

She sat up a little. 'So back then you *knew*? And still you left me?'

'I did, but I truly believed you could not be happy in the Hebrides. Foolishly, I wondered if you had openly agreed to marry Barnstable, if you would become reconciled to your fate.'

She snorted. 'Whereas I was under the worst of compulsion and could see no way out of it. But the whole thing has caused me to wonder how many other ladies have been forced to wed, never knowing they could appeal to the priest? We are all held under the unspoken rules of society. What we do not know cannot save us.'

They fell silent for a moment, reflecting on how near to disaster they had been. 'We must be grateful and never forget how close we came to losing one another. And I shall never fail to remember how much you have sacrificed to be here.'

She shook her head at the notion it was a sacrifice. 'Do you still believe I cannot be happy here?'

'I still have worries, but two things have changed. First, the alternative for you was life with Geoffrey or some other equally unsuitable gentleman—a fate I should not wish on my worst enemy!'

'And second?'

'Second, I vow to make it my life's work to ensure your happiness, Isabella. Whatever it takes, you shall have it. We can order comforts from London or Glasgow—books from Hatchard's, lemons, fancy gowns—'

She stopped his lips with a kiss. 'I need none of those things. I need—' she kissed him again '—only—' and again '—you!'

There was a pause as their kisses became deeper, more passionate. 'Again?' he asked her and she nodded.

'Yes, if you please.'

'Oh, I please!' he declared, picking her up and carrying her to the bed, blankets and all. 'And I intend to please you, again and again, tonight and all of my life. I shall do so every time you wish it, until we are old and grey and cannot roll around this bed the way we have done this night.'

She giggled, then caught her breath as his hands began sweeping over her. 'Then stop talking and just do it, Angus!'

His reply was almost a growl. 'With pleasure, my lady!'

* * * * *

*If you enjoyed this story, make sure to pick up
the first book in Catherine Tinley's
Lairds of the Isles miniseries*

A Laird for the Governess

And look out for the last book

A Laird for the Highland Lady

*In the meantime,
why not check out her other miniseries
The Ladies of Ledbury House?*

The Earl's Runaway Governess
Rags-to-Riches Wife
Captivating the Cynical Earl
'A Midnight Mistletoe Kiss' in *Christmas Cinderellas*

COMING NEXT MONTH FROM

HARLEQUIN
HISTORICAL

All available in print and ebook via Reader Service and online

HIS INHERITED DUCHESS (Victorian)
Daring Rogues • by Bronwyn Scott

With his promotion to duke, carefree Logan must bear the responsibility of a new household...and its widowed duchess, Olivia. Unraveling Olivia is a challenge Logan never anticipated...but cannot resist!

A SEASON OF FLIRTATION (1830s)
by Julia Justiss

When Laura offers to tutor her friend in flirtation, she doesn't expect that she'll have to put her own lessons to use—on one Miles Rochdale no less!

MARRIAGE DEAL WITH THE EARL (Regency)
by Liz Tyner

A convenient marriage to long-term friend Quinton seems the only solution to her late husband's debt, but Susanna's not prepared when buried feelings start to resurface!

THE MAKING OF HIS MARCHIONESS (Victorian)
by Lauri Robinson

After Clara finds refuge in the Marquess of Clairmount's estate, her attraction to the marquess is bittersweet, as this Cinderella knows she doesn't belong in his aristocratic world...

BEGUILING HER ENEMY WARRIOR (Viking)
Shieldmaiden Sisters • by Lucy Morris

Captured by a Welsh prince intent on revenge against her family, Helga must keep her wits about her. Easier said than done when she desires him rather than fears him!

CONVENIENTLY WED TO THE LAIRD (Georgian)
by Jeanine Englert

Ewan and Catriona have one rule in their arrangement—they mustn't fall in love. Yet faced with Catriona's bravery, can Ewan resist the one rule he must not break?

YOU CAN FIND MORE INFORMATION ON UPCOMING HARLEQUIN TITLES, FREE EXCERPTS AND MORE AT HARLEQUIN.COM.

HHCNM1222

Get 4 FREE REWARDS!

We'll send you 2 FREE Books plus 2 FREE Mystery Gifts.

FREE Value Over **$20**

Both the **Harlequin® Historical** and **Harlequin® Romance** series feature compelling novels filled with emotion and simmering romance.

YES! Please send me 2 FREE novels from the Harlequin Historical or Harlequin Romance series and my 2 FREE gifts (gifts are worth about $10 retail). After receiving them, if I don't wish to receive any more books, I can return the shipping statement marked "cancel." If I don't cancel, I will receive 6 brand-new Harlequin Historical books every month and be billed just $6.19 each in the U.S. or $6.74 each in Canada, a savings of at least 11% off the cover price, or 4 brand-new Harlequin Romance Larger-Print books every month and be billed just $6.09 each in the U.S. or $6.24 each in Canada, a savings of at least 13% off the cover price. It's quite a bargain! Shipping and handling is just 50¢ per book in the U.S. and $1.25 per book in Canada.* I understand that accepting the 2 free books and gifts places me under no obligation to buy anything. I can always return a shipment and cancel at any time by calling the number below. The free books and gifts are mine to keep no matter what I decide.

Choose one: ☐ **Harlequin Historical**
(246/349 HDN GRH7)
☐ **Harlequin Romance Larger-Print**
(119/319 HDN GRH7)

Name (please print)

Address _____ Apt. #

City _____ State/Province _____ Zip/Postal Code

Email: Please check this box ☐ if you would like to receive newsletters and promotional emails from Harlequin Enterprises ULC and its affiliates. You can unsubscribe anytime.

Mail to the **Harlequin Reader Service:**
IN U.S.A.: P.O. Box 1341, Buffalo, NY 14240-8531
IN CANADA: P.O. Box 603, Fort Erie, Ontario L2A 5X3

Want to try 2 free books from another series! Call 1-800-873-8635 or visit www.ReaderService.com.

*Terms and prices subject to change without notice. Prices do not include sales taxes, which will be charged (if applicable) based on your state or country of residence. Canadian residents will be charged applicable taxes. Offer not valid in Quebec. This offer is limited to one order per household. Books received may not be as shown. Not valid for current subscribers to the Harlequin Historical or Harlequin Romance series. All orders subject to approval. Credit or debit balances in a customer's account(s) may be offset by any other outstanding balance owed by or to the customer. Please allow 4 to 6 weeks for delivery. Offer available while quantities last.

Your Privacy—Your information is being collected by Harlequin Enterprises ULC, operating as Harlequin Reader Service. For a complete summary of the information we collect, how we use this information and to whom it is disclosed, please visit our privacy notice located at corporate.harlequin.com/privacy-notice. From time to time we may also exchange your personal information with reputable third parties. If you wish to opt out of this sharing of your personal information, please visit readerservice.com/consumerschoice or call 1-800-873-8635. **Notice to California Residents**—Under California law, you have specific rights to control and access your data. For more information on these rights and how to exercise them, visit corporate.harlequin.com/california-privacy.

HHHRLP22R3

Get 4 FREE REWARDS!

We'll send you 2 FREE Books <u>plus</u> 2 FREE Mystery Gifts.

FREE
Value Over
$20

Both the **Harlequin® Desire** and **Harlequin Presents®** series feature compelling novels filled with passion, sensuality and intriguing scandals.

YES! Please send me 2 FREE novels from the Harlequin Desire or Harlequin Presents series and my 2 FREE gifts (gifts are worth about $10 retail). After receiving them, if I don't wish to receive any more books, I can return the shipping statement marked "cancel." If I don't cancel, I will receive 6 brand-new Harlequin Presents Larger-Print books every month and be billed just $6.30 each in the U.S. or $6.49 each in Canada, a savings of at least 10% off the cover price, or 6 Harlequin Desire books every month and be billed just $5.05 each in the U.S. or $5.74 each in Canada, a savings of at least 12% off the cover price. It's quite a bargain! Shipping and handling is just 50¢ per book in the U.S. and $1.25 per book in Canada.* I understand that accepting the 2 free books and gifts places me under no obligation to buy anything. I can always return a shipment and cancel at any time by calling the number below. The free books and gifts are mine to keep no matter what I decide.

Choose one: ☐ **Harlequin Desire**　　☐ **Harlequin Presents Larger-Print**
　　　　　　　(225/326 HDN GRJ7)　　　　(176/376 HDN GRJ7)

Name (please print)

Address　　　　　　　　　　　　　　　　　　　　　　　　　　Apt. #

City　　　　　　　　　　　State/Province　　　　　　　　　Zip/Postal Code

Email: Check this box ☐ if you would like to receive newsletters and promotional emails from Harlequin Enterprises ULC and its affiliates. You can unsubscribe anytime.

Mail to the **Harlequin Reader Service:**
IN U.S.A.: P.O. Box 1341, Buffalo, NY 14240-8531
IN CANADA: P.O. Box 603, Fort Erie, Ontario L2A 5X3

Want to try 2 free books from another series? Call 1-800-873-8635 or visit www.ReaderService.com.

*Terms and prices subject to change without notice. Prices do not include sales taxes, which will be charged (if applicable) based on your state or country of residence. Canadian residents will be charged applicable taxes. Offer not valid in Quebec. This offer is limited to one order per household. Books received may not be as shown. Not valid for current subscribers to the Harlequin Presents or Harlequin Desire series. All orders subject to approval. Credit or debit balances in a customer's account(s) may be offset by any other outstanding balance owed by or to the customer. Please allow 4 to 6 weeks for delivery. Offer available while quantities last.

Your Privacy—Your information is being collected by Harlequin Enterprises ULC, operating as Harlequin Reader Service. For a complete summary of the information we collect, how we use this information and to whom it is disclosed, please visit our privacy notice located at corporate.harlequin.com/privacy-notice. From time to time we may also exchange your personal information with reputable third parties. If you wish to opt out of this sharing of your personal information, please visit readerservice.com/consumerschoice or call 1-800-873-8635. **Notice to California Residents**—Under California law, you have specific rights to control and access your data. For more information on these rights and how to exercise them, visit corporate.harlequin.com/california-privacy.

HDHP22R3

HARLEQUIN
PLUS

Try the best multimedia subscription service for romance readers like you!

Read, Watch and Play.

Experience the easiest way to get the romance content you crave.

Start your **FREE TRIAL** at
www.harlequinplus.com/freetrial.

Get 4 FREE REWARDS!

We'll send you 2 FREE Books plus 2 FREE Mystery Gifts.

FREE Value Over **$20**

Both the **Romance** and **Suspense** collections feature compelling novels written by many of today's bestselling authors.

YES! Please send me 2 FREE novels from the Essential Romance or Essential Suspense Collection and my 2 FREE gifts (gifts are worth about $10 retail). After receiving them, if I don't wish to receive any more books, I can return the shipping statement marked "cancel." If I don't cancel, I will receive 4 brand-new novels every month and be billed just $7.49 each in the U.S. or $7.74 each in Canada. That's a savings of at least 17% off the cover price. It's quite a bargain! Shipping and handling is just 50¢ per book in the U.S. and $1.25 per book in Canada.* I understand that accepting the 2 free books and gifts places me under no obligation to buy anything. I can always return a shipment and cancel at any time by calling the number below. The free books and gifts are mine to keep no matter what I decide.

Choose one: ☐ **Essential Romance**
(194/394 MDN GRHV) ☐ **Essential Suspense**
(191/391 MDN GRHV)

Name (please print)

Address   Apt. #

City   State/Province   Zip/Postal Code

Email: Please check this box ☐ if you would like to receive newsletters and promotional emails from Harlequin Enterprises ULC and its affiliates. You can unsubscribe anytime.

Mail to the **Harlequin Reader Service:**
IN U.S.A.: P.O. Box 1341, Buffalo, NY 14240-8531
IN CANADA: P.O. Box 603, Fort Erie, Ontario L2A 5X3

Want to try 2 free books from another series! Call 1-800-873-8635 or visit www.ReaderService.com.

STRS22R3